The River Takes It's Own

The Cedar Valley Files

R. Davenport

Marigold Lake Press

For my Midwest roots—

the fields, the water, and the small towns

that remember more than they ever tell.

Contents

Prologue

The river was louder at night.

It thumped and shushed against the pilings as if speaking a language the town had decided not to learn. Crickets stitched their steady metronome across the fields. From the mill came the long exhale of machinery winding down, the last shift spilling out with lunch pails and tired jokes that would dissolve by morning.

Emily Carter ran.

Bare feet slapped the packed dirt of the levee path. She had left one sandal in the weeds by the boardwalk and the other on the last plank where it split and bit her heel. The cut had stopped stinging. Small mercies did that—hurt hard, then vanish, leaving only the pounding drum of her heart.

"Emily," a voice called, careful and coaxing. "You're scared. I understand."

The sound came from the shadow of the cottonwoods where the levee dipped. A truck idled there, hood warm, lights off. She had known that truck all her life. There were only so many trucks in Cedar Valley and only so many men who spoke like that—oil-slick kind, gentle on the surface, stone underneath.

"Please," she said, and her voice snagged on the air like a thread on a nail.

He stepped closer without closing the distance, a good man's posture he'd practiced in church basements and boardrooms. "You're making a mistake," he said. "You'll ruin your family. Folks will talk. They'll say things no girl should have to hear. You don't want that for your mother."

She thought of her mother's hands dusted with flour, wrists sturdy, the way she laughed at the radio as if it were a friend who had finally told a decent joke. She thought of her father on the porch at dusk, boots unlaced, gaze fixed on the place where the river bent like a question. And she thought: if I go with this man, none of that will stay as it is.

"It wasn't supposed to be me," she whispered, because the truth had grown heavy, and there was nowhere left to put it but in air.

"Then don't make it you," he said. "Let this go."

From the north, a pair of headlights swam through fog, turned off the road, and eased down. A second truck, familiar in a different way—more dust than shine, a sheriff's star dull on the door. The engine cut; a door creaked; a flashlight carved the reeds into silver bones.

"Evening," Sheriff Robert Hayes said to the dark, voice level. He hadn't seen them yet. Or he had, and the level was work.

Emily moved first. She stepped out where the river light made everything animal—wide-eyed, breathing hard—and raised a hand.

"Sheriff," she called. "I—"

The other voice snapped taut. "Emily."

His hand was on her wrist. Not rough. Final.

The flashlight found them then, hard and unblinking. It washed the scene clean and left nothing clean at all: a girl, a man, a sheriff, the river.

"Let her go," Robert Hayes said.

A pause, long enough for a lifetime to learn how to wait. The grip loosened, just a little.

"You don't understand," the man said. "This will burn the town to the ground. Everyone will lose. We're so close to making it better and you—you two—want to set it alight over rumors."

"It isn't rumors," Emily said, and felt the tremble leave her voice. "It happened."

Hayes kept the light still. "We'll talk at the station," he said. "Now."

Footsteps behind him, quicker, younger—the deputy, Frank Wallace, breath visible in the damp. "Sheriff?" he asked, and took in the tableau like a man memorizing where to put his feet.

"Take her to the truck," Hayes said without looking back. "Careful."

Frank reached for her with both hands open, as if she were something that might spook. Emily took one step toward safety—and heard the other one move.

"What if we don't?" the man said, and she felt his breath at her shoulder. "What if we file this under mercy?"

"Don't," Hayes said.

The river rose around the noise, a sudden slap of current against the levee stones as wind shouldered down from the cottonwoods. Far off, a screen door banged the way screen doors had always banged in this town, as if to mark the hour.

"Please," Emily said, to the sheriff, to the river, to whatever counted time in Cedar Valley.

For a second—the kind you can fit a life into if you must—everyone stood in a geometry that could still be solved. Then the geometry broke. The man's hand flashed; Emily twisted; Frank lunged; Hayes moved too fast for his age and not fast enough for physics. She felt the world tilt, felt air change temperature, felt water.

The river took her name the way it took everything: without favor, without malice, without noise.

A splash, muffled in cattails. A cry, strangled on a breath that wasn't there. The flashlight swung. Hayes threw himself to the bank, knees into mud, hands where hands could reach only water. Frank was there with rope, with angles, with curse words he would not repeat on Sunday. The river went flat and honest and said nothing.

"Emily!" Hayes shouted, and the echo came back empty.

By the truck, the man spoke, voice almost gentle. "We can make this right," he said. "For the town."

Hayes stood, mud slick up to mid-thigh, chest heaving, a look on his face Emily would never see and the town would never ask him about. He holstered the light and stared at the man until the man lowered his eyes.

"You'll file it," the man said. "You'll do what you always do. Keep us afloat."

Hayes wiped his hands on his trousers and spoke as if to the reeds. "The river takes its own."

Frank swallowed. "Sheriff?"

"Get back in the truck," Hayes said. His voice sounded old and young at the same time. "We'll do the paperwork."

Behind them, the mill exhaled one last tired breath. The town's lights blinked in the fog, warm and far. The river slid on, shouldering the weight of what it had been given, keeping its counsel as always, patient as winter.

Up the bank, a white ribbon had snagged on a stem—Emily's hair tie, the cheap kind sold six to a card at the drugstore. It fluttered exactly once and then lay still.

Hayes looked at it and then at his hands and then at the man. He would sign something in the days to come and write a refusal at the bottom. He would carry the sentence he'd spoken like a coin that burned his pocket.

On the levee path, a dog barked out of sight. A porch light snapped on, then off. A bullfrog called and was answered. The river told no one what it knew.

And Cedar Valley slept—some of it, anyway—believing morning would arrive politely, as it always had. It would. It always did. Morning forgives. Water does not.

Chapter 1

Corn and Concrete

The air above Cedar Valley rippled with heat and the smell of fried batter. August clung to the town like humidity on glass—seeping through shirts, settling behind knees, making everyone just a little more irritable. The courthouse square pulsed with summer noise: guitar chords from the main stage, the whir of the Ferris wheel, and the sticky-sweet laughter of people pretending they weren't sweating through their festival clothes.

Banners for the Cedar Valley Summer Festival hung from lampposts, faded from years of reuse. Plastic sunflowers framed the courthouse steps, where Mayor Daniel Pike had declared this year's theme *Our River, Our Roots*. Rowan thought it sounded like a slogan printed on a mug no one actually used. Anything involving "the river" or "heritage" usually meant someone was preparing to run for re-election.

She moved through the crowd in her uniform, badge catching the amber wash of string lights. Parents waved, teenagers pretended they didn't see her, and vendors tried to bribe her with free pie samples in exchange for "a little extra patrol" near their stalls. Rowan declined each offer with the same polite shake of her head. Light duty didn't mean she wasn't working.

"Evening, Detective!" a man at the ring-toss stand called. "You ever take a night off?"

"Sure," Rowan said. "Just not during the annual record-breaking streak of petty theft and sunstroke."

He laughed. "You sound like your dad."

Rowan froze for a heartbeat, though she managed not to show it. He meant it as a compliment—she knew that. But the words slid into her chest like a stone. Her father had been gone fifteen years, yet Cedar Valley still tossed his name into conversations as though invoking a superstition. Sometimes it felt like the whole town remembered him better than she did.

The festival dimmed around her for a moment—the calliope notes blurring into heat-haze—and Rowan was a kid again, standing on this same courthouse lawn with Sheriff

Robert Hayes beside her. His hand had been warm and steady on her shoulder as the parade drifted by.

See, Ro? he'd murmured, eyes on the river-themed banners flapping along Main. *That's what we protect. The good parts.*

The memory loosened, replaced by cicadas buzzing in the trees and a faint metallic tang rising on the breeze. Rowan tipped her head slightly, catching the scent of the river beyond the square—mud, algae, and something older. Familiar, yes. But tonight it carried a quiet edge she couldn't ignore.

Returning to Cedar Valley had always meant wrestling with ghosts. The river simply knew how to choose which ones surfaced.

A voice broke through her thoughts. "Big turnout this year?"

Deputy CJ Jenkins jogged up, cheeks flushed and grinning like he'd just discovered good news. Young, eager, and still naive enough to think the badge could fix the world.

"It's the free beer tent," Rowan said. "Always pulls a crowd."

"Oh come on, Hayes—can't you pretend you like people for one night?"

"I like people fine," she said. "Just not in groups exceeding five."

CJ laughed, and they walked together past food stalls and game booths. Kids darted past waving glow sticks. The smell of kettle corn mixed with the exhaust from a generator. Somewhere, a cover band was valiantly butchering Fleetwood Mac.

Rowan's gaze swept the festival automatically—habit, not suspicion. Calm surfaces rarely told the whole story. Two teenagers loitering near the lemonade stand stiffened when she looked their way; guilt rearranged their posture. They'd abandon whatever mischief they'd schemed the second she walked past. Some things didn't require a badge—just presence.

They paused at the edge of the courthouse lawn. The building stood like a brick sentinel, its clock tower permanently stuck four minutes slow. Below it, a plaque gleamed faintly:

Sheriff Robert Hayes, 1978–2010.

"Doesn't seem right," CJ murmured. "They should fix the clock."

"They tried," Rowan said lightly. "Never stayed on time."

CJ flinched, catching the unintended meaning. "Sorry."

"Don't be." She took a sip from her water bottle—already warm. "Just keep an eye out. Last thing we need is a brawl over funnel cakes."

From the far end of Main came the honk of a golf cart and a string of impressive curses. A vendor truck had stalled across the parade route.

"I'll handle it," CJ sighed.

"Please do," Rowan said. "Before someone declares martial law."

Once he jogged off, Rowan leaned against the courthouse railing. The metal was hot beneath her palm. Around her, life unfolded in stubborn, familiar rhythms—church ladies gossiping beside the lemonade stand, teenagers posing with the corn-on-the-cob mascot, the mayor shaking hands with anyone who held still long enough. It should have felt comforting. Instead, it felt like watching a movie she'd seen too many times, unsure why she kept hoping the ending would change.

A low rumble threaded through the noise. Not thunder. Not machinery.

The river—steady, unhurried, indifferent.

The same sound she'd grown up with... yet different. Or maybe she was.

A distorted announcement boomed over the loudspeakers:

"Fireworks test in ten minutes! Funnel cakes half off near the beer tent!"

Cedar Valley's idea of civic pride remained unshakably on brand.

"Detective Hayes? There you are."

Mayor Daniel Pike approached with the confidence of a man allergic to self-doubt. Crisp sleeves, starched collar, and enough hairspray to survive a windstorm.

"Glad to see you keeping the peace," he said. "Optics are everything tonight."

"Safety's nice too," Rowan replied.

He laughed, missing the edge in her tone. "Biggest festival in years! Think we might hit record attendance."

"Because nothing unites a community like deep-fried Oreos."

Pike grinned. "Mind posing for a quick photo? The *Gazette* is covering it."

"Ask CJ. He smiles better."

"Ah, but you carry your father's legacy. People love that."

There it was—her father's ghost, dragged into a conversation that didn't deserve him. Rowan exhaled slowly.

"Legacy's heavy, Mayor. You might pull something."

He blinked, then recovered with a laugh half a beat too late. "Well, don't work too hard. Optics!"

After he left, the crowd's noise thinned again, replaced by the river's steady hum—like it was circling the edges of the festival.

"The man could talk a scarecrow into voting," came a gravelly voice.

Rowan turned to find Lydia Bass stepping into the lamplight—retired reporter, menthol-gum enthusiast, and Cedar Valley's self-appointed truth guardian.

"Retirement didn't stick?" Rowan asked.

"Retirement's for people who don't need a new water heater," Lydia said. "Besides, someone's gotta keep this town honest."

"Good luck."

Lydia smirked. "You hear the rumor? They're renaming the bridge after Pike's uncle. Symbolic clean slate, they say."

"Of course they are."

"Speaking of symbolism—Emily Carter's parents are still asking questions."

Rowan stiffened before she could stop herself. Emily Carter. A name that lived in the town's bones. A case with too many gaps and too few answers. Her father's files from that time had been... curated. Purposefully so.

"Enjoy your funnel cake, Lydia," Rowan said.

"Enjoy pretending you don't care," Lydia replied, drifting back into the crowd.

Lanterns flickered on overhead, casting warm gold over the square. For a moment, Rowan let the festival move around her—the people she'd grown up with, the town that never changed and never stayed the same.

CJ returned balancing a corn dog and two water bottles. "Peace offering," he said.

"Appreciated." She took a long drink. "Parking situation?"

"Settled. I bribed them with dunk-tank coupons."

"Bribery suits you."

He grinned. "You ever miss the fun part of this? Before the badge? Before you knew the river had teeth?"

Rowan's gaze shifted toward the darkened waterline. "I grew up here," she said softly. "Back then I thought the river was endless, and nothing bad ever really happened in Cedar Valley."

She paused. "Turns out the river's just better at hiding things."

CJ glanced at her, uneasy. "You really think your dad's Carter case was dirty?"

"I think people did what they had to do to keep this town looking clean," she said. "And dirt settles fast when no one stirs it."

The band struck a new chord—bright, cheerful, out of tune.

For a fleeting second, Rowan felt almost at home.

Then a woman's scream cut through the music.

"Sarah? Has anyone seen Sarah?!"

The crowd stilled. Even the cicadas seemed to stop.

Rowan's pulse snapped tight. She pushed through bodies toward the panicked voice.

A woman stood near the food stalls, face blotchy with fear.

And beneath the murmurs rising around her, Rowan heard the river's low shift—its voice curling through the night like something that recognized her.

Something that had been waiting to speak to her again.

Chapter 2

The River Knows

The Cedar River, usually a sluggish vein bisecting Cedar Valley, had transformed into a restless beast.

Flashlight beams skated over its surface, slicing the humid dark as search parties fanned out along the levee. The festival's laughter and music had bled away hours ago, leaving the drone of generators, the bark of radios, and the soft, relentless slap of current against the bank. Paper banners that had promised *Our River, Our Roots* shivered on their strings like damp laundry.

Detective Rowan Hayes stood at the edge of the boardwalk, the scent of wet cedar and river muck thick in the air. August humidity clung to her skin like a second uniform. The string lights still strung above the booths swayed in the breeze, bulbs winking out one by one until the fairground felt like it was exhaling—reluctant, tired, done pretending.

The river churned below, louder than she remembered. As Rowan stepped closer, her boot paused midair—an involuntary hesitation she didn't like. Her body remembered something her mind wasn't ready to name. The shape of a night years ago. Her father's voice on this same bank, telling her quietly, *Some things the river won't give back, Ro.*

She forced herself forward.

The river moved like it had something to say and no intention of saying it to her.

Some days she wondered why she'd ever come back to Cedar Valley at all. There were places in the world where rivers stayed politely in their beds, where the past didn't cling like humidity, where a person wasn't known before she walked into the room. But this town held her in ways she couldn't fully shake—its unresolved promises, its ghosts, its stubborn, familiar pull. And every time she told herself she should've left sooner, something in her steadied, as if turning away would mean turning her back on a truth she owed.

"Anything?" CJ Jenkins called, jogging toward her. Sweat shone on his forehead, reflecting the jittery glare of lights. He carried a coil of rope and two industrial flashlights—the kind that turned fog to silver haze.

"Just mud and whispers," Rowan said, scanning the bank. "Prints are worthless—half the town stomped through here before we taped it off."

CJ handed her a light. "Fire's got the north levee covered. Volunteers are grid-searching east. Lucas is organizing boats to check the islands. Says he knows the river better than anyone."

Lucas. The name snagged like a fishhook behind her ribs. Coffee steam at dawn, porch arguments, the last door slam before silence. Memory pressed in under her armor before she shoved it back out.

"Good," she said. "Tell him the current's high and the eddies are pulling like anchors. We don't need a rescue on top of a search."

CJ huffed a laugh. "Already told him. You know Lucas—pretends not to hear, does what he wants anyway."

"Yeah," Rowan said, a corner of her mouth moving. "I know."

They walked, lights casting long cones over slick boards. The planks groaned under their boots, giving up the resin-sweet smell of wet wood. Ahead, volunteers in reflective vests moved in a line, combing the bank inch by careful inch.

Their calls—"Sarah! Sarah Miller!"—broke against the water and slid away downstream.

The booths that had been bright with laughter earlier were hollow now. A half-eaten funnel cake sagged in its paper boat. A loose sign banged the post with a stubborn, metallic clack. Streamers tangled in the reeds like riverweed, bright colors going dull in the damp.

"Anything?" a voice called from the rail.

Dale Lister, a volunteer firefighter, knelt with his beam steady on the boards.

Rowan and CJ hurried over. Dale didn't look up. "Here," he said quietly.

A stain no bigger than a coin, but the metallic tang lifted through the damp. Rowan pulled on gloves, scraped a sample into an evidence pouch, sealed and labeled it, then made herself breathe.

"Tag and mark," she said. "CJ, get forensics rolling."

Dale swallowed. "Jesus. How bad you think this is?"

Rowan didn't answer. Around them, the noise of the search dimmed without anyone saying a word. Radios lowered. Boots slowed. The river didn't slow—never did—but it sounded heavier, older. Like it knew.

As she turned toward the water again, her beam skimmed over a swirl of debris—driftwood, corn husks, and something pale caught for a moment on a submerged root. A scrap of fabric? A child's toy? It turned once in the current before slipping under. The sudden disappearance raised every hair on Rowan's arms.

The river was rising. Not from tonight's storm alone. It had been building, pulling, collecting. A quiet threat gathering shape.

"Thirty minutes," CJ said when he came back from the call. "They were already en route for the braid. They'll hit this first."

"We don't have thirty minutes," Rowan murmured, eyes on the black water. Every ripple looked like movement. Every shadow like something rising.

A half hour later, she stood under the sagging banner near the deflated bounce house, questioning a cluster of teenagers. Glitter clung to their cheeks. Fear made them look younger than their ages.

"We saw her," said a girl with bright pink hair, voice thin and determined. "Sarah. She was with... someone."

"Who?" Rowan kept her tone even. Open palm. No edge.

"Tall guy. Hoodie up. Couldn't see his face. They were...
kinda arguing? He grabbed her wrist. She pulled away."

"How long ago?"

"Nine-thirty? Nine-forty?" The girl's lip trembled. "I
didn't—I didn't check the time."

CJ jotted, neutral, professional. "You sure it was an argument?"

"Yeah." The girl stared at the mud. "We thought it was
just... like, boyfriend stuff."

"Did she look scared?" Rowan asked.

A hesitating nod. "A little. Not screaming. Just... tight."

"Thank you," Rowan said. "Go home with your parents. If you remember anything else—anything—call me."
She handed over a card printed with her cell.

When they'd been led away, CJ stepped close. "That's
three witnesses. Tall, hoodie, near the boardwalk. Argument."

Rowan's jaw ached from clenching. "We'll pull every
camera between the Ferris wheel and the levee. Vendor tents,
food trucks, traffic cams on Main. If it points at the river, I
want it."

"That's two blocks of grainy night footage," CJ said.
"This weekend's canceled."

"Cancel it twice," Rowan said.

He smiled despite himself. "Didn't have plans anyway."

Wind came up from the water, cool against sweat. Somewhere downriver a siren rose and fell, lost and found in the trees.

It was close to two when a flashlight beam shook through the mist and found them. Lucas Hale climbed the slope from the dock, jeans plastered to his shins, river mud splashed to the knee. He smelled like wet reeds and gasoline. The years had added lines to his face but not to his eyes; those were the same: steady, skeptical, brave enough to admit fear when it mattered.

"Nothing," he said. "We swept the islands, the north fork, the dead water behind the old barge slip. Not a damn thing."

"Thanks for helping," Rowan said, the softness in her voice arriving uninvited.

"Wouldn't feel right staying home," he said. "This river's taken too much already."

Their eyes met for a beat. Something old and safe and complicated tugged. Rowan dropped her gaze first.

"Get your men home," she said. "Rotating shifts at sunup. I'll call if that changes."

"Be careful, Rowan," he said. Quiet. Not for show.

She turned before warmth could crack the cold that kept her upright. CJ trotted up, phone to his ear, face set.

"Dispatch just pinged Sarah's phone," he said.

"Where?"

"Three pings. Then dead. The old mill." He swallowed. "Edge of the Bottoms."

Of course it was. Everyone in Cedar Valley knew the mill—half sunk into the bank, rust-boned, tired of standing. Teenagers told ghost stories about it. Rowdy men told quieter ones. Rowan's father had investigated there once, his voice rough when he came home, saying only, *Don't go down there alone.*

"Gear," Rowan said. "Now."

The road east was a black ribbon edged in corn and ditch water. Gravel clattered under the cruiser as they dropped off the paved shoulder and followed the line that hugged the river. Cicadas screamed. Rain ticked and then hammered. The wipers dragged arcs across the windshield that didn't feel fast enough for anything.

"I don't like this," CJ said, squinting into the rain.

"Nobody does," Rowan said.

The mill rose as they turned the last bend, a jagged silhouette against the faint, bruised sky. The roof sagged in the middle. Windows gaped like pulled teeth. The whole structure leaned, as if bored with its own ruin.

The river licked at the eroded foundation. The air held the iron taste of wet metal and old oil. Rowan cut the engine. The sudden quiet made the rain sound louder.

"Stay sharp," she said, stepping out. Weapon holstered, light low. "Flashlight waist-high. Don't silhouette yourself."

They slipped inside. The threshold complained under their weight. Drips plinked somewhere deep in the belly of the place. Machinery hunched in the dark like sleeping animals. Spray paint ghosts—names, crude hearts, a smiley face with X's for eyes—floated on the walls in the thin reach of their lights.

CJ moved left along a scarred workbench. Rowan took the main corridor, beam skimming low. Dust motes spun in the cone like minnows.

Something clicked under her boot. She crouched and angled the light.

A smartphone. Mud-caked. Screen spidered.

"CJ," she said. "Phone."

He was beside her in two heartbeats.

"Time stamp?" he asked.

She pressed the side button. The cracked display flared, struggling. "9:47 p.m. Passcode screen. Battery at three percent—was." She bagged it, marked the location in a whisper: "Main corridor, ten feet from east entry, south side."

"She was here," CJ said. "Tonight."

"Yeah."

The silence stretched. It wasn't silence, not really—the rain whispered through seams in the roof, something creaked slow and arthritic, the river ground against stone—but the space between those sounds felt deliberate, like a held breath. Rowan's neck prickled.

A noise rose out of the dark. A stifled sob. Not a ghost. Small and human and terrified.

Rowan's heart kicked once, hard enough to make her breath catch. She drew her weapon and made a hand signal. CJ nodded and peeled toward the left.

They followed the sound. The hallway widened into a chamber, floor strewn with broken pallets and rusted bolts. Her light slid across a cinderblock wall and landed on a shape trying to turn into a corner.

Rowan raised her off-hand, palm out. "Sarah?" she said. "Sarah, it's Rowan. Police."

The shape flinched. The girl's face lifted into the beam: swollen eye, split lip, hair hacked and ragged. The shredded green of a tank top stuck to her, dark with damp.

"You're safe," Rowan said, lowering the muzzle an inch. "We've got you."

Sarah's voice was a split reed. "He's still here."

CJ dropped to a knee beside her, moving like a man trying not to startle a bird. "Who's still here, Sarah?" His voice was warm. "You're okay. You made it."

She shook her head hard. "He said— He said he'd—" Her breath hitched; she swallowed it like a fishbone. "He said he'd kill me if I told."

The scrape came from behind them. Sharp. Metal on concrete. Not imagination.

Rowan turned. A figure stepped out of the draft of shadow by the column. Tall. Hoodie. Knife shining like a tongue.

"Drop it!" Rowan barked. Her voice hit the walls and came back bigger.

He lunged.

Everything fractured: boots on grit, the flash of steel, the concussive crack of Rowan's service weapon. The body jerked and hit a machine with a factory-dead thud, slid, and settled. The knife spun, clanged once, and lay still.

For half a second there was only the ringing in Rowan's ears and the slam of her heartbeat. Then CJ's voice threaded in, low and steady. "She's breathing. She's okay."

Rowan moved in slow, muzzle fixed, light on the hand near the knife. She kicked the blade out of reach and crouched, gloves squeaking against the slick hoodie as she took the edge and pulled it back.

Her blood went cold, then hot enough to hurt.

Deputy Frank Wallace.

Her father's old partner. Older now, heavier at the jowls, hair gone white at the temples—but the face was the same. The man who used to fill their kitchen with coffee steam and stories. The man who'd promised to look after them when the flag folded over the coffin.

Behind her, CJ's voice trembled. "You... you know him?"

Rowan kept her eyes on the face that hadn't changed enough. "Yeah," she said, the word like iron. "I know him."

Rain raced along the roof and plunged through a rusted seam, tapping the concrete in a clean rhythm. Dawn began to push a thin gray through the shattered panes.

"Get her out," Rowan said without looking away from Frank. "Ambulance. State police. Crime scene. Call Rourke.

Tell Dispatch we have an officer-involved shooting at the old mill—suspect down."

CJ's footsteps moved, a murmur to Sarah, the slow rise of her sobs, the careful lift. Rowan's radio crackled alive with voices that sounded like they were a mile away, underwater.

She holstered, breath returning in slices. "Why, Frank?" she asked the quiet room. "What did you bury with my father?"

The mill didn't answer. Wind whistled through the ribs of the place. The river outside kept whispering the one song it knew.

Outside, the horizon bled pale orange across the flat, waterlogged fields. Paramedic lights pulsed against the rusted siding, blue and red strobes painting the old bolts like ornaments. They loaded Sarah, her mother climbing in behind, clutching her daughter's hand and saying her name over and over like a prayer.

CJ stood apart, phone pressed to his ear, bartering for resources with a voice that carried the shaky brightness of a man who'd survived his first nightmare and hadn't decided if he should fall apart yet. He nodded. "Copy. Copy. Understood." He wiped rain off his face with the heel of his palm and tried again.

Rowan found the river with her eyes. It churned around the mill's footing, hauling driftwood and beer cans and whole shrubs downstream—evidence, maybe, or just more ghosts. Her father's voice rose, unhelpful and familiar: *Some truths aren't meant to surface, Rowan.* He'd said it about the river once. He'd meant people.

Boots scuffed the gravel near her. Lucas came up out of the wet, mud drying to river-gray on his jeans. He stopped beside her without touching, looking where she was looking.

"Heard you found her," he said.

"Alive," Rowan said.

He let out a breath like he'd been holding it too long. "That's something."

"It is," she said. The word had weight. "It's not everything."

Lucas watched the current grind its way past the mill. "The river gives back what it takes," he said softly, not quite asking.

"Eventually," she said.

"You don't sound convinced."

"I'm not." She thought of a badge in a lockbox, of the braid on the bank like a calling card. "Because it never gives it back the same."

The rain backed off to a steady tick. The new light picked out the gouges in the concrete and the places where kids had once struck sparks with rocks just to see them. CJ ended his call and looked at her across the mud, waiting for a signal she didn't have yet.

Rowan turned toward the open doorway and the body waiting inside, to the paperwork and the statements and the calls that would carry this story into the houses where people slept, trusting the river to mind its own business. She felt the case twisting open inside her—the missing girl, the man she'd known since childhood, the long shadow of her father reaching from the past as if to steer her away.

"Get some rest," she told Lucas.

"You won't," he said.

"Probably not."

He touched the brim of an imaginary hat—a habit from his grandfather he hadn't been able to quit—and stepped back. "Call if you need me."

She nodded. "I will."

He left her alone with the river. It murmured, patient and unhurried, as though it already knew how this would end.

Rowan squared her shoulders and went back into the mill.

Chapter 3

Paper Ghosts

The first tendrils of dawn clawed at the eastern sky, painting the underside of the clouds a bruised purple. Detective Rowan Hayes stood beside the Cedar River, the beam of her flashlight cutting a futile swath through the murk. The air, thick with humidity and the metallic scent she'd come to associate with endings, clung to her skin.

The river whispered steadily, swallowing any sound foolish enough to come close. What had been a sluggish ribbon through town days ago now moved with purpose, swollen from the storm. Floodwater had smeared the banks into slick, matted grass and knots of dead weeds. The mill's silhouette hunched over the current like a thing that knew too many secrets.

Behind her, yellow tape snapped in the breeze, sectioning off a wedge of shoreline downstream from the mill. They had state divers now. Searchlights flared and died in the gray light. Radios murmured, hushed for once, as if even static knew when to stay quiet.

"Detective?" CJ Jenkins called across the levee. He approached with two uniformed officers in tow, his voice smaller than the river. "They're bringing something up."

Rowan nodded, throat tight. Not a sixteen-year-old girl—Sarah was alive, sedated at County, wrapped in a blanket and a mother's shaking arms—but something else the river had kept until now. She'd seen the current cough up half a town's history over the years: tires, deer bones, a rusted bike that made a grown man cry. Sometimes it offered up people. Sometimes just what they left behind.

She thought of Emily Carter's parents sitting on a sagging couch two decades ago, her mother twisting a dish towel that never dried, her father staring past the sheriff's badge on the coffee table like it was a verdict. The river hadn't given them anything back, not then. Just silence and search parties and a grave with no body. If this was her, if these bones finally had a name, it wouldn't be closure. It would be a wound learning a new shape.

The dive team emerged slow, synchronized by practice and gravity. Water sheeted off their suits. They carried a shape between them—a bundled mass, dark with mud and silt, lashed by a length of chain that left flecks of orange on the diver's gloves. Not heavy enough for a body. Heavy enough for a bundle.

"Easy," Rowan said, more to the water than the men. The river didn't care, but it made her feel like someone did.

They set the bundle on a tarp. The chain clinked as a deputy freed a corroded padlock with bolt cutters. A ripped canvas tarp peeled back in layers. Denim appeared, darkened with age to a dull blue. Beneath the denim, bones.

The world narrowed to breath and rain and the clean click of evidence markers. A small radius of time opened in which no one looked away and no one said the thing they were thinking. Rowan had lived in those radiuses her entire career. She still hated them.

CJ stood very still. "Christ."

"Stay with it," Rowan said. "Camera on. Mark coordinates. Record everything."

The divers worked with the reverence of surgeons. What lay inside was partial—a torso and legs, skeletal, tattered denim fused to bone at the hip by silt and time. The skull was missing. The river wasn't always generous with symmetry. Debris eddied at the edges of the scene—sticks, a shredded plastic bag, a length of frayed rope caught on a half-submerged root, tugging against the current like it was trying to remember being useful. The river was changing this bank, pulling at it harder than usual. Rowan filed that away. Rising water didn't just uncover things; it shifted what was buried.

"Bag the denim separate," Rowan said, crouching. A knot of fabric cinched near where a wrist would have been—rotted thread, a faded scrap still looped in place. Her light made the weave bloom into clarity: a half-hitch, practiced and neat. It itched in her memory as if she'd learned to tie it from a ghost.

CJ knelt beside her. "Same knot as the strip Rourke pulled off Sarah's wrist?"

Rowan didn't answer. She couldn't get her voice up and over the shape of the thought forming. The knot wasn't a match because of Sarah. It was a match because of twenty years ago—because of the sealed photos in a thin file and a girl whose parents had never stopped asking.

She stood. "Get Rourke on site. Tell her we've got bones and textile. And call State—this location stays locked until she clears it."

CJ was already moving, radio up, voice concise, steady. He was good in the tight places; it's why she'd chosen him when she could have chosen safer. Still, she caught the way his jaw flexed when he said "skeletal remains." Good. It meant he wasn't numb to it yet.

Rowan took three steps down to the waterline. Dawn put a sickle of pale light on the river. It looked flat from here, docile even, but her calves remembered the pull when she stepped wrong in mud, the way the current found your ankles and pretended to be a friend. The mill complained with a metal groan that had no source but the wind.

Her father's voice—low, rasped from nicotine and years of callouts—rose uninvited. *Don't get too close, Ro. The river doesn't give back what it takes.* He'd said it kindly. She'd grown up thinking he meant driftwood and bikes. Adult language for "stay on the grass." Only later had she learned there were other things a river could mean.

What if he'd known more than he'd ever written in his reports? More than he'd ever said at the dinner table, even when the news showed Emily's school photo on repeat? The question cut across her thoughts like cold water. She pushed it aside—for now. The job first. Doubt later.

"Rourke's on her way," CJ said behind her. "Fifteen minutes. State wants a live feed when she arrives."

Rowan nodded without turning. "Get me a drone over the downstream snags. Anything wrapped, anything caught. If the river's giving up one piece, there might be others."

"Copy." A beat. "Hospital called. Sarah's stable. They'll keep her sedated for a while. Wallace is... they're calling it."

Rowan breathed slow through the word that wasn't spoken. It rose anyway: *dead.* Deputy Frank Wallace—her father's old partner—under fluorescent morgue lights where Rourke would don a different pair of gloves and exhume a different truth. The night had ripped open, and morning wasn't interested in stitching it shut.

"Call Lydia," Rowan said.

CJ blinked. "You want Bass here?"

"I want Bass corralled," Rowan said. "She'll get wind of this inside an hour. If she's going to scavenge, I'd rather choose the bone."

He grimaced. "Copy."

They worked in the slow, clean way you work when you can't afford to make a mistake. Evidence bags labeled from left to right. Coordinates repeated to eliminate error. The denim peeled free in sections, weighted by silt. The bones were small—teenage, maybe. Female, likely. Rourke would say for sure. If this was Emily Carter, if the river had held her at the edge of town all this time, her family would finally have a place to stand and grieve that wasn't just a framed photo and a question.

Sirens rose low and near, not the festival kind—the kind that meant the county woke up early for grief.

Rourke arrived in a rush of purposeful motion—hair knotted tight, eyes sharpened by the kind of sleep you only pretend. She bent to the bones with gloved hands, her breath appearing in the cool morning air.

"Adolescent," she said without preamble. "Female pelvis. Growth plates suggest mid-to-late teens. Time in water—long." She angled for light. "This binding... don't cut. Photograph, then I'll remove."

Rowan crouched opposite her. "Half-hitch."

Rourke glanced up. "You see it too."

"Carter," Rowan said.

Rourke's mouth made a line. She didn't add *Emily*. She didn't have to. Rowan pictured Emily's mother again, the way the woman's hope had thinned over the years into something brittle and dangerous. If this was her daughter, the truth would hurt, but so had the not-knowing. There was no version that didn't break something.

They worked in tandem, two halves of a thing that didn't require speech. The fabric around the delicate bones lifted, string by string, until the knot sat whole in Rourke's palm. She set it on a clean tray as if it could breathe.

"Denim," she said. "Older weave. Faded by water, not sun." She rotated the fabric under a loupe. "Check this edge."

Rowan leaned in. Along the hem, barely there, a wavering line of thread caught light like mica. Letters, clumsy but careful. *E C.*

CJ made a sound that wasn't quite a word. "Jesus."

"It wasn't public," Rourke said softly. "Not the knot, not the letters. The Carter file mentions a fabric binding, yes. But the photos and notes were sealed. Only a handful of people ever saw them."

"My father," Rowan said. The words clinked down like coins in a jar. "Frank. Rourke—" She stopped. She didn't want to say Wallace's name beside the bones. "The old guard."

Rourke set the fabric in a specimen bag. "We need lab time. DNA from compact bone if we're lucky. Thread analysis. But the age and the knot and the initials—Rowan..."

"I know," Rowan said.

CJ looked between them. "We're saying—what, the mill's been sitting next to a grave for twenty years?"

Rowan looked at the river. "The river's been sitting next to one. And it doesn't bury things by accident. Currents pushed this here, held it here. Either it got snagged, or someone knew this bank would chew away slow and keep its mouth shut."

Rourke taped the bag. "I want the chain, the lock, everything that touched this. If I find residue under those threads that matches a storage compound from twenty years ago, I'll scream into a pillow and then I'll put names on a report."

"State's on standby for custody," CJ said. "They'll move the bundle to lab as soon as we clear."

"No," Rowan said. "We'll move it. I don't want a chain-of-custody gap bigger than a breath."

She didn't add that she didn't trust the distance. Not yet. Not with old names in play and the river finally spitting out what it had been asked to keep.

Back at the station, the day pulled itself together and pretended to be ordinary. The fluorescent lights buzzed as if they'd been practicing. The whiteboard bore two case headings now: MILL / MILLER and RIVER / CARTER. Under both, arrows converged toward a knot that had never been untied.

CJ set two coffees on Rowan's desk and nodded at the open file. "You really want to go through all that again?"

"No," Rowan said. "But we don't get to choose what the river drags back."

He leaned against the doorjamb, tablet balanced in one hand. "Witness re-interviews are a wash. 'Tall hoodie' could be half the county. Security footage from vendor row is grainy, but I've got timestamps on Sarah near the boardwalk and again cutting toward the levee at 9:38. The ping at the mill was 9:47."

"She was moved fast," Rowan said. "Or lured. The boardwalk to the levee is what, four minutes at a walk? Less if you know the path."

CJ hesitated. "Eve texted. Wallace is confirmed. Fatal on scene. State wants a joint presser by afternoon—your call."

"Mayor Pike wants to look like a life preserver," Rowan said. "He'll announce 'ongoing cooperation' and smile like a wax museum. We'll say less. We always say less."

CJ's mouth twitched. "Lydia's left you six messages."

"Tell her I'll give her one quote if she stops calling me on the hour. And make sure Pike hears I said that."

He snorted. "You play nice with everyone."

Rowan gathered the Carter file to the center of the desk. Her father's handwriting threaded through the margins—impatient loops, abbreviations no one had taught her, notes to himself that assumed he'd be around later to read them. On one page, in a moment too honest for a report, he'd scribbled: *River patterns unpredictable. Evidence may resurface.*

She pressed her thumb hard against the paper until the pad went white. Had he written that to warn himself—or to justify letting something slip away? The doubt pressed behind her ribs again, sharp and insistent.

"Carter family's mostly moved," CJ said, scanning his notes. "Her brother's still here—runs the bait shop by the reservoir. Name's Wade."

"Set it," Rowan said. "Quiet. Off the books. If this breaks early, it breaks on facts, not fear."

"You worried about your dad?" CJ asked gently.

Rowan stared at the file until the letters blurred. "I'm worried about this town's memory," she said. "And how far people will go to keep it friendly."

CJ nodded, eyes averted. "I'll make the call."

Mayor Pike chose the courthouse steps for his late-day performance. He was crisp in shirtsleeves with the cuffs staged just right, hair sprayed into civic submission. "We will not rest," he said to cameras that blinked like bugs. "We are working closely with county and state authorities."

Rowan stood at the edge of the semicircle of press, arms crossed, watching Lydia Bass scribble without looking down. Lydia lifted her chin when the mayor said "cooperate" and made a sound that could have been a laugh or a cough.

Afterward, Lydia found Rowan on the periphery by the chipped statue that claimed a Union soldier had stood there and thought brave thoughts.

"Quote me something true," Lydia said, recorder already up, menthol on her breath.

Rowan looked past her to where the river flashed through trees. "We found something old," she said. "Old things tell on people who forget they exist."

Lydia's eyes sharpened. "Emily Carter."

"Off the record," Rowan said.

Lydia lowered the recorder half an inch. "You don't owe this town a lie just because your father tried to keep it from breaking."

Rowan didn't flinch. "I owe this town the truth in the order I can prove it."

Lydia studied her for a long beat. "I liked your father," she said, softer than Rowan expected. "I also think he let this river keep a few secrets because it was easier."

"Maybe," Rowan said.

"Call me when you're ready to stop letting it," Lydia said, and left.

Night fell the way it always did here—quick enough to make you check the time. Main Street blinked out one storefront at a time until the water kept its own counsel. Fog crept low from the east, easing around Rowan's boots. Crickets filled the silence at a polite distance.

She crouched at the bank, flashlight off. Let her eyes and memory adjust. The courthouse clock reflected a smear on the current—four minutes slow, same as the day it had given up matching time. The river took the smear, stretched it, and let it go.

Her father's voice surfaced: *The river remembers, Ro. Even when the people don't.*

She sighed, low. "Show me what I'm supposed to remember."

The water did the only thing it ever did: moved, owning everything it touched.

Gravel crunched behind her. CJ's stride, careful, respectful. "You still here?"

"Couldn't sleep," she said.

"Rourke's in the lab," he said. "She'll work all night. She thinks the denim's older than the binding. Said she's seen that half-hitch before—years ago. You probably did too."

Rowan nodded. "Wade Carter?"

"I tracked him down. Bait shop opens at six. He'll talk, he says, if you promise not to bring cameras."

"No cameras," Rowan said. "No promises either."

CJ shoved his hands in his jacket pockets, gazing at the dark sheet of water. "Everyone's asking the same question: how did Wallace end up at the mill with a girl the same age as the one who disappeared when your dad wore the badge?"

"Because nothing that happens here happens by accident," Rowan said. Her voice came out level. "And because someone learned a long time ago that the river takes what you give it."

CJ's swallow sounded loud in the quiet. "You think your dad knew?"

Rowan let the question sit with the fog until it beaded on her skin. "I think he knew enough to break him," she said. "And not enough to fix it."

Far downstream, thunder rolled—more promise than threat. A section of the far bank had slumped in the last storm, roots exposed like ribs, the soil still raw and unsettled. It looked less like erosion and more like something uprooted from beneath. Rowan couldn't shake the sense that the river was working at the land on purpose, chewing its way toward some buried truth.

She stood, brushing grit from her knees.

"What if Rourke proves it," CJ said. "What if it's the same person who tied that knot twenty years ago?"

"Then we finish what my father couldn't," Rowan said. "And we do it in daylight."

They walked back toward the cruiser, flashlights bouncing off mist. Behind them, the river whispered the only language it had, tugging at its banks like it wanted to speak—as if something about this riverbank remembered the things people tried to forget and was finally, slowly, letting them go.

Chapter 4

The Station

The fluorescent lights of the Cedar Valley Sheriff's Department hummed—a thin, needling sound that made Rowan feel like she was standing inside a beehive. Outside, the last scraps of festival bunting still clung to streetlamps; in here the air was stale, paper-dry, and haunted. Somewhere beyond the concrete walls, she knew the river kept moving, grinding past the town like a slow, patient saw. She sat hunched over her father's old desk, the wood scarred and worn like a roadmap of his career.

The Emily Carter files—what was left of them—lay fanned across the blotter: crime-scene photos glazed with age, witness statements in carbon-smudged triplicate, yellowed *Gazette* clippings whose headlines promised answers they never delivered.

Each page felt like a whisper from the past, a past she thought she knew—now mocking her with its inconsistencies and omissions.

She picked up a photo. Emily at seventeen, half-smile pinned to her face like it hurt to hold. Thrifted dress. Cheap corsage. The Cedar Valley gym bleachers a soft blur behind her. The edges had curled, but the expression hadn't—the same unease Rowan had seen in a hundred families who'd stood in this office asking for miracles.

The statements, when the handwriting was even readable, were a mess. Contradictions bloomed like mold: times that didn't match, clothing colors that changed, an argument that might have happened or might have been gossip growing to fill a silence. It was as if the town had chosen to forget the moment the ground shifted under it—pretending hard enough to make it untrue.

Her gaze tracked down the inventory lists, looking for details that meant more now than they had when she was a teenager eavesdropping on adult conversations. Fabric binding, recovered near riverbank. No description of the knot. No mention of initials stitched into denim. Those details had lived only in sealed photos and her father's memory—and now in the bundle they'd pulled from the river. The official file had been trimmed until it barely held a spine.

Sometimes she wondered if this desk remembered more than she did.

Her father's pen strokes, the late-night calls, the cases he carried home in the set of his shoulders—this room had witnessed it all. Rowan wasn't sure whether she'd come back to honor what he'd started or to finally confront the pieces of him the town had quietly buried. Either way, the past felt closer here, breathing just behind her ear.

One name recurred, over and over, in her father's scrawl and in the clippings: Harold Sterling. Owner of Sterling Mill when the mill still ran, a man with money and friends and the permanent squint of someone who assumed the world was in his pocket. Several witnesses placed Emily near the mill the day she vanished. One claimed she'd argued with Sterling. Blurred dates. Hazy details. Nothing that would hold a charge.

Rowan rubbed her eyes. The ache behind them throbbed in time with the building's hum. She slid the stale official reports aside and pulled her father's working notes closer—the real diary of a case, not made for court but for the ugly work of doubt. Scrawls and arrows. Phone numbers with first names only. Asterisks where something had snagged his mind.

Harold Sterling's name wore a question mark in three different places.

She flipped a page and found a note tucked into the back, nearly translucent with handling. Her father's hand again, looser here. Three lines, written two days before he died:

Sterling — River Bend Land Deal — FOLLOW THE MONEY.
Check Wexler ledger? Who signs?
Call Pike Sr. re: "development agreement."

Rowan stared until the words floated. River Bend. The Bottoms renamed—again—so people could stomach it: River Bend, Riverview, Cedar Shores. This round had promised a resort and a golf course and a "lifestyle center," whatever that meant. Land where families had lived for generations, deeds mixed with handshakes and bad memory. Sterling had pushed. Some sold. Some didn't.

Emily Carter's parents had not.

The chair springs groaned as Rowan leaned back. Could it be that simple—land, power, and a girl who made the wrong person angry? If her father had seen the outline, why hadn't he followed it to the end? Had he run out of time, or had someone leaned hard enough to make him turn his head?

Because the file was incomplete. Whole sections of original reports were gone. Interview sheets referenced in later memos had vanished. One evidence inventory had been replaced by a clean copy with fewer lines and no signature. Someone had scrubbed the record like a countertop, and her father had died with the rag still in his hand.

For a moment she was a kid at this same desk—legs swinging while her father's pen skated across a yellow pad and the radio murmured weather reports. Back then she believed work solved things. The lesson that the river took and didn't always return had come later, with a funeral, a folded flag, and a case that quietly stopped being mentioned.

The clock read 2:17 a.m. Rowan closed the file. The town slept; the river gnawed. The hum of the building and the faint vibration of trucks on the highway braided with a deeper, almost imagined sound—the low, constant drag of water against its banks. She needed someone who remembered the first story before it had been rewritten. Someone whose bias was straightforward and well-earned.

Lydia Bass.

Rowan texted CJ—stepping out; phone on—grabbed her keys, and left the hum behind. As she walked down the corridor, she had the sudden, irrational sense of being watched—not by eyes behind doors, but by her father's name on the office wall, by the cases that lined the shelves. By the fact that she was about to pull on threads he'd never gotten to tie off.

Lydia's house sat at the end of a gravel lane where the town began to forget itself. The porch light burned like a small lighthouse through a tangle of lilac bushes months past their prime. When Lydia opened the door, the smell of old books and cold coffee rolled out.

"Rowan?" Lydia rasped, glancing at the darkness over Rowan's shoulder. "This hour means good news or trouble. Your face says not good news."

"I need your help," Rowan said. "Sterling. River Bend. Whatever you didn't print in '93."

Lydia's eyebrows climbed, then knit. "You're in it now."

"It's connected," Rowan said, stepping into the entry where stacked newspapers rose like stalagmites. "Emily. And maybe Sarah."

Lydia held her gaze for a long beat, then nodded once. "Kitchen. I'll make coffee. The truth goes down better warm."

They sat at a small table nearly buried in maps, envelopes, and a drift of paperclips. Lydia moved with the economy of someone who'd done this ritual for decades—kettle, mugs, a scoop of grounds thrown by instinct.

"Harold Sterling was king," she said while the kettle groaned. "Owned the mill, the softball team, and the judge's fundraiser. He could charm a church committee and bleed a contractor dry before lunch."

"River Bend," Rowan said.

"Sterling wanted it," Lydia replied. "Talked like Moses about to lead Cedar Valley into prosperity. Resort, golf course, shopping village with fountains. Pike's father was ready to lay out the carpet. But a handful of families wouldn't sign. The Carters were bedrock stubborn."

Rowan wrapped her hands around the mug Lydia slid over. The heat felt medicinal. "Sterling pushed."

"He applied pressure with a smile," Lydia said. "Tax re-assessments. Code-enforcement gnats. Then his men—contractors, he called them—started showing up with clipboards at odd hours. Measurements, they said. I called it trespass.

Your father kept a lid on what he could, but Pike Sr. wanted a ribbon-cutting. There was a meeting—a 'development agreement.' I never got the notes."

"My father was there?" Rowan asked, throat tight.

"Ro, he was sheriff," Lydia said, voice gentler. "He was always there. That's not the same as agreeing."

Rowan set the mug down, ceramic clicking lightly on wood. "Who did agree?"

"Wexler's people handled the numbers," Lydia said. "Sterling handled the squeeze. Pike Sr. handled the smiles. After Emily vanished, nobody handled the truth."

Rowan felt the old desk return under her palms—the scars, the grooves where pens had dug in. "There's a knot we just found—same as the Carter file. And initials stitched no one made public. Whoever tied it either had access to sealed evidence—"

"—or was there," Lydia finished softly. "And you're asking how far the old guard would go to keep Cedar Valley pretty on paper."

Rowan didn't answer. The kettle ticked as it cooled. Somewhere beyond the lilacs, the river turned over in the dark, working at its banks the way it always had.

Lydia slid a manila envelope across the table. "Old clippings I couldn't print then," she said. "And one note a city clerk slipped me after she retired. Not proof. A map." She tapped the flap. "You follow the money, you'll find the men who thought the river would keep their secrets."

Rowan drew the envelope close. "Then we make the river talk."

Lydia's smile didn't reach her eyes. "Rivers don't talk, Detective. They just stop letting you lie."

"Emily disappeared a week after," Rowan said.

A beat of quiet. "Yes."

"And you think Sterling—"

"I think the timing stunk and no one wanted to admit it," Lydia said. "After Emily, the town became two towns. People stopped saying Sterling's name out loud. When your father pushed too hard, pressure came from above. Donations threatened. Budgets squeezed. Then the storm that took him came, and everyone said it was a heart that gave out. It's tidy to call it that."

Rowan swallowed. The coffee was bitter enough to bite. "He kept notes," she said. "Sterling, River Bend, follow the money. He wrote that two days before he died."

Lydia's fingers stilled on the mug. "Then he was closer than anyone knew."

"Who else was at those meetings?"

"Pike Sr. The county board chair. A lawyer out of Cedar Falls—Hennessey, maybe. And Harold, of course. Maybe Wexler. The lines blur. They always do."

"Can I see your archives?" Rowan asked. "Not the printed stuff—the margin notes. The letters people sent you and asked you to burn."

Lydia huffed a laugh. "I don't burn things. I hoard them for the day someone asks the right question."

She levered up two battered boxes. "Here. The Carter years. And Sterling's grand project. There's a map in there—pretty picture of fountains and glass storefronts. Look close at the parcel numbers. You'll see which lots never agreed to sell."

Rowan slid the boxes closer. "Thank you," she said, meaning it.

"Be careful," Lydia said, voice low. "Sterling had friends who kept their hands clean by letting others do the dirty work. And Harold's not the type to leave his bones where anyone can find them."

"I know," Rowan said. "I met one of those others last night."

The image of Frank Wallace—the hood, the shock of a familiar face—flashed sharp. The memory hit her with a dull, delayed ache. She'd shot a man who'd once sat at her kitchen table and told her bad jokes while her father made coffee. Whatever he'd become at the mill, he had been part of the circle that knew more than she did. "He's not a ghost anymore."

Lydia's eyes sharpened. "Wallace? My God."

Rowan stood. "I'll call you tomorrow. Or later today. It's later today, isn't it?"

"It's always later today," Lydia said, squeezing her arm once—both blessing and warning.

Rain began in earnest on the drive back—a steady hiss that turned the road into a silver ribbon and blurred the horizon. By the time Rowan pushed through the station door, her jeans were clammy and grit stuck to her heels. The red message light on her desk phone blinked like an irritated eye.

She hit play.

"Detective Hayes," Mayor Pike's voice flowed, smooth as always. "I trust you're making progress on the Miller case. The town is counting on you to bring this to a swift resolution. And, ah, a word of advice—don't stir up old ghosts. We all know some things are best left buried. For the good of Cedar Valley."

The message ended with a soft click that sounded to Rowan like a lock turning.

Her hand hovered over the receiver. For a second she pictured pounding on his door until the whole block heard his careful voice crack. She let the picture pass. There were better ways to wage war than shouting on a stoop.

She hauled Lydia's boxes onto her desk. The cardboard was soft with age. She pried open the River Bend file first. On top lay a glossy development plan—trees drawn in perfect circles, couples frozen mid-stride with shopping bags in hand. She turned it over.

On the back, parcel numbers were hand-inked in a different pen. Some were neatly ticked off.

Three—clustered tight against the bend where the river slowed—were circled in red and left unticked. The Carters' lot was one. Two neighboring tracts were the others. In the margin, a name repeated beside all three: H. Sterling.

Another hand—her father's—had written NO in sharp black ink and underlined it three times.

Rowan took a breath that trembled on the way out. Her father had seen the same pattern she was tracing now. For reasons she didn't yet understand, he'd stopped at the edge and written a warning instead of a report.

CJ appeared in the doorway, tablet in hand, hair spiked damp from the rain. "Report from Eve," he said. "Preliminary tox is clean. Ligature marks ante-mortem. She's running DNA from under Sarah's nails, rush order."

Rowan nodded. "We're going to the old mill."

He blinked. "Now?"

"Now."

The county had condemned the mill two years ago, which meant someone had hung a sign and left. The gate sagged; the chain looped through it was more theater than lock. The place no longer smelled like work. It smelled like rot, iron, and the sour breath of the river sending up mist through broken boards.

Rowan's flashlight skimmed the familiar shapes: conveyors frozen mid-arc, ladders leading nowhere, graffiti layered like sediment. Wind prowled through broken windows and set a chime of loose metal whispering overhead. Somewhere beneath it, she could hear the low rush of the current battering the pilings, eroding the bank a grain at a time. She and

CJ moved in practiced rhythm—her path forward, his to the flank, radio checks like a pulse.

The office sat in back, a prefab rectangle grafted to brick. The door stuck, then gave with a soft cough of plaster dust.

Inside, the desk was half-collapsed. Rodent droppings dotted the floor like obscene punctuation. But the thing about offices—no matter how stripped—is that paper breeds in them and tends to hide.

Rowan crouched, sweeping her beam beneath a rusted file cabinet. Something thin and water-buckled lay jammed under the lowest drawer. She worked it free—a ledger book, canvas-bound, edges swollen. The cover read *WEXLER GRAIN – ACCOUNTS* in faded gold script.

"Bingo," CJ said softly. His voice carried a thread of excitement under the fatigue, the way it always did when the case shifted from guesswork to something he could put his hands on.

The pages cracked when she opened them. Rows of numbers neat enough to be printed marched down columns: dates, amounts, recipients. Many entries were mundane—diesel, parts, payroll. Then a different rhythm began. CASH DISBURSED – Carter Family – $400. Next month the same. And the next. A second column—the approvals—alternated between initials: HS in tight, stern strokes and GP in a wider, more theatrical hand.

"HS," Rowan murmured. "Harold Sterling."

"GP?" CJ asked.

"Gideon Pike," she said. "The mayor's father."

A notch of silence opened. Wind hissed through the window frame as if to fill it. Water slapped the foundation below, persistent and steady.

"This isn't wages," CJ said. "It's hush money."

"It's leverage," Rowan said. "Payments that stop when Emily disappears." She flipped forward. The entries ended abruptly in September 1993. "And then silence."

CJ swallowed. "You think your dad saw this?"

Rowan's thumb grazed the inside back cover. A slip of paper lay tucked into the binding, folded twice, edges soft with years. She eased it out. A photocopy of a check—Sterling Development LLC to County Clerk for fees—was stapled to a property schedule. Parcel numbers lined up, including the Carters' lot and its neighbors. Beside the Carters' parcel someone had handwritten *contingent.* In the margin, a note in the same pen: FIND "ASSIGNMENT" DOC.

"Someone did," Rowan said. "And they left a breadcrumb trail because they couldn't do a damn thing with it."

Bootsteps scuffed behind them.

"Detective," Mayor Daniel Pike said from the doorway, "I thought we had discussed your... fascination with ruins."

He looked freshly pressed, as if he ironed himself before stepping into any room. Behind him, rain beaded on his overcoat like he was immune to damp.

"We locked this property up months ago," he went on smoothly. "Condemned. Unsafe."

"Then you shouldn't be here," Rowan said without turning the ledger away. "Liability and all that."

He smiled a politician's smile. "County business. Prospective redevelopment draws interest, even now."

"From who? Sterling's ghost?" She lifted the ledger. "How about from the folks who signed checks to a family whose daughter went missing?"

Pike's gaze flicked down, cool and quick, then rose to her face. "Old charity entries," he said. "Mr. Sterling had a habit of generosity."

"Generosity that stopped the month Emily vanished," Rowan said. "Interesting habit."

CJ shifted, angling himself nearer, eyes steady and not friendly. His fingers tightened on the tablet, knuckles pale. He didn't interrupt, but every line of his posture said he was braced to step between her and whatever the mayor thought he could do.

Pike clasped his hands like a man closing a prayer. "Rowan. You're tired. This case is already tearing the town up. I need you focused on the present. That's where leadership lives—here, now."

"And here, now," Rowan said, "I'm holding evidence that points your father and Harold Sterling straight at the center of an obstruction twenty years old." She kept her voice level. "Tell me about the development agreement. Tell me why my father wrote *follow the money* and then died before daylight hit it."

For a heartbeat the mask slid. Gideon Pike's son, not the mayor, stood in front of her—a man raised in rooms where truth bent like tin in hot hands.

"You're looking for villains," he said. "But Cedar Valley survives because good men make hard choices. Your father knew that."

"My father died with a pen in his hand and a storm in his chest," Rowan said. "Don't you use him as a shield."

Pike's mouth thinned. "Be careful."

"Am I being threatened, Mr. Mayor?" she asked, and the way she shaped the title made it sound cheap.

He let the question hang, turned, and walked out—rain swallowing him whole at the threshold.

CJ blew out a breath. "I'd call that a hit."

Chapter 5

The Lockbox

The Cedar Valley Sheriff's Department sounded busier than it looked. Phones rang, printers spat paper, and the faint buzz of fluorescent lights hung like a migraine waiting to bloom. Outside, rain beaded on the windows and turned the parking lot into a gray mirror. Inside, the coffee had burned itself into bitterness hours ago.

Detective Rowan Hayes stood at the incident board, marker in hand, watching the red lines between names multiply. The air smelled of paper, ink, and exhaustion. Somewhere beneath the building's hum, she could have sworn she heard the river—muted, steady, an undercurrent pressing against her ribs.

CJ Jenkins perched at the next desk, tapping through reports, half a donut slowly petrifying beside his keyboard.

"You know it's bad," he said, "when the donut gives up before we do."

"Quit eulogizing breakfast and tell me what you've got," Rowan said.

CJ's grin flickered, but he sobered quickly. "Three viable leads from last night's interviews. None of them clean."

"Figures."

He scrolled on his tablet. "Mark Olsen—ex-boyfriend. Witnesses say there was an argument near the Ferris wheel. He swears it was nothing."

"The ex-always swears that." Rowan wrote his name on the board.

"Next up, Dale Krantz. Lives down by the river. Locals call him the River Rat."

Rowan raised a brow. "Every town's got one."

"Yeah, well, ours keeps showing up in the background of half the festival photos." CJ swiped to the next image. "No record except trespassing."

"Doesn't mean harmless," she said.

CJ flipped the screen again. "And number three—Mr. Peterson. English teacher. Fifteen years at the high school. Solid rep, zero complaints."

Rowan capped the marker. "And yet he's the one who makes your voice go tight."

CJ rubbed the back of his neck. "Because when I talked to him, he looked like a man grading his own alibi. Fidgety. Too careful."

Rowan leaned against the desk, arms crossed. "So—a jilted kid, a hermit, and a nervous teacher. Hell of a triangle."

"Want me to start with Olsen?"

"Bring him in. I'll handle Peterson."

CJ nodded and headed for the bullpen. "Rourke said she's coming up from the morgue—wants five minutes with you first."

"Good," Rowan said. "Maybe something finally talks back."

Rourke's Update

Dr. Eve Rourke arrived like she always did—crisp coat, damp hair, thermos of coffee in hand, and the demeanor of a woman who'd already been awake far too long. She set a folder on Rowan's desk and peeled off her gloves.

"Morning, Detective. You look marginally less dead than your suspects."

"Flattery before caffeine, Rourke? Dangerous move."

Eve smirked. "I bring data, not charm. Preliminary on Sarah Miller."

Rowan motioned for her to continue.

"Time of death between nine-thirty and midnight. Cause: strangulation. No water in the lungs—she was gone before she hit the river. Same thumb-pressure pattern I mentioned last night." She tapped the photo. "And here's the kicker—ligature fibers. Pre-2000 nylon cord. Manufactured by a plant that doesn't exist anymore."

"Carter case used the same stock."

Eve's eyes lifted. "You remember your father's notes."

"He didn't forget much," Rowan said quietly.

"I ran the sample through the archive. Same polymer signature, same fray pattern." Rourke's expression tightened. "Whoever tied Sarah Miller's knot learned it from history."

CJ appeared with two coffees and froze at the image on the desk. "I'll—uh—pretend I didn't look."

"Do that," Rourke said dryly. She repacked the folder. "Full report this afternoon. DNA under Sarah's nails is cooking."

Rowan met her gaze. "Anything else I should brace for?"

"Only politics," Rourke said, slinging her bag over one shoulder. "And I don't do autopsies on those."

Rowan almost smiled. Almost.

When Rourke left, Rowan turned the blinds half-open and spread her father's files across the desk. The paper carried that faint metallic smell of decades and dust. Rain drummed lightly on the window, a soft percussion synced to her pulse.

She compared old handwriting to new printouts—Emily Carter, 1993, and Sarah Miller, 2024. Same missing hour. Same witness phrase: *"She went to meet someone by the river."*

The symmetry tightened her chest. Two girls, two summers, same stretch of shoreline. Same lie wrapped in two decades of silence.

Her father's scrawl filled the margins: **FOLLOW THE MONEY. Sterling / Pike / Wexler = Circle.**

She traced the words with her fingertip, as if contact could translate memory. The wall clock ticked four minutes slow—exactly as it had the night he died. Time hadn't moved forward in this office; it had only deepened.

CJ drifted back in, balancing his phone on his shoulder. "Olsen's on his way. Says he's innocent and misunderstood. Also wants his lawyer."

"Good. Let him wait."

CJ ended the call and leaned against the doorway. "You ever sleep?"

"Sometimes I blink slow enough that it counts."

He grinned, then sobered when he saw the open file. "You still think this ties back to Carter?"

"I think the river's coughing up everything my father tried to bury with decency."

CJ let out a low whistle. "That's poetic. You sure you don't want to teach English instead?"

"Only if I can grade on honesty."

The knock on her door was too polite. Mayor Daniel Pike stepped in without waiting for permission—his suit immaculate, smile pre-polished.

"Detective Hayes," he said warmly, "thought I'd drop by. How's *our* investigation?"

Our. Rowan hated that word. "Progressing."

"Good, good." He clasped his hands like a man holding a prayer hostage. "The town's nervous, understandably. Rumors breed faster than facts. I'm hoping you'll keep this contained—avoid stirring up, ah, old ghosts."

Rowan closed her father's folder slowly. "You mean avoid the Carter parallels."

"I mean," Pike said, "focus on the present. Cedar Valley needs confidence, not conspiracies. The past can stay respectfully buried."

She rose, closing the distance between them until the scent of his cologne—something expensive that tried too hard—cut through the stale office air.

"'Respectfully buried' is what we called Emily Carter until her body wasn't," Rowan said. "I don't plan to repeat that."

His smile flickered. "Detective, a little discretion keeps this department funded."

CJ appeared in the hall, sensing the tone. Pike noticed him and dialed his charm back up. "Officer Jenkins, always a pleasure."

CJ nodded stiffly. "Sir."

When the mayor left, CJ exhaled. "He always smell like politics?"

"Like fear and citrus," Rowan said, sitting again. "Next time he drops by, remind me to light a candle."

The day dragged. Olsen's interview added nothing but teenage grief and too many swear words. Peterson's answers were smooth to the point of script. Krantz refused to come in, so they'd have to go to him.

By afternoon, the rain eased into mist. Rowan stood by the evidence board again, connecting threads that refused to stay straight. Behind her, CJ typed a report that would read calmer than either of them felt.

Rourke called. "DNA update. Partial match pending—male profile. Not Wallace, not Olsen. Something new."

Rowan thanked her and hung up, staring at the red-yarn web that looked more like a trap than a map. The river outside hissed against the gutters, rising again with the storm runoff—as if urging her forward.

CJ spun in his chair. "So, what now?"

"Now," she said, "we follow the ghosts everyone wants forgotten."

Before he could answer, Dispatch crackled:

"Hayes, Jenkins—possible lead. Farmer near the old factory in The Bottoms found something suspicious. Might connect to Miller."

Rowan's pulse steadied instantly. "What kind of suspicious?"

"Didn't say. Just that you'll want to see it yourself."

She met CJ's eyes. The Bottoms again—land that wouldn't stop whispering.

"Grab your gear," she said. "Looks like the river's ready for round two."

They walked out into the cooling afternoon. Puddles mirrored a bruised sky; thunder muttered far off, promising another storm.

CJ unlocked the cruiser. "You think this is it—the break?"

Rowan slid into the passenger seat, watching the courthouse clock through the rain-streaked windshield. Still four minutes slow.

"Break or warning," she said. "Either way, the river's talking again."

The engine turned over, and they drove toward The Bottoms—toward the bend in the river that never forgot a secret.

Chapter 6

The Bottoms

The drive to the Carter farm felt longer than it should. Maybe it was the weight of the request Rowan was about to make, or maybe it was the humidity that clung to the cruiser like guilt. The air conditioning worked overtime, but sweat still traced a line down her spine. The cornfields flanking the county road seemed to close in, their stalks whispering to each other in the wind—too quiet, too knowing.

The Carter place hadn't aged so much as surrendered. The white paint peeled off the farmhouse in long, curling strips, and the front porch sagged like a tired sigh. A rusted swing set leaned in the corner of the yard, half-swallowed by weeds. Rowan parked at the end of the gravel drive and killed the engine. Cicadas buzzed in the heat, loud and relentless, like static from an old confession.

As she walked up the cracked sidewalk, a curtain twitched in the front window. They were expecting her, or at least expecting someone. She mounted the porch steps—each one groaning under her weight—and knocked.

The door opened a cautious few inches. Martha Carter stood behind it, face lined and pale, eyes ringed with the kind of grief that had become habit.

"Detective Hayes," she said softly. "We were expecting you."

"Mrs. Carter. Thank you for seeing me."

"Come in, please."

The air inside was thick with dust and potpourri, a cloying sweetness that couldn't mask the smell of things too long remembered. Plastic slipcovers crackled under her as she sat on the faded floral couch. The walls were lined with photographs—Emily smiling from high school portraits, childhood Christmases, a girl forever caught between laughter and loss.

George Carter sat opposite, skeletal and silent, his eyes milky with years and distance. He nodded once but said nothing.

Rowan kept her tone gentle. "I know this is difficult, but I need to ask you some questions about Emily."

Martha sighed. "We've answered questions for twenty years, Detective. It never brings her back."

"I understand," Rowan said. "But this time, we found something. A connection between Emily's case and the death of Sarah Miller."

Martha's eyes widened. "Sarah Miller... the festival girl?"

Rowan nodded. "There are similarities. A piece of fabric, a knot. It suggests a link."

George stirred, voice rough as gravel. "You think the same man did it?"

"It's possible," Rowan said. "That's why I need your help. Anything you can remember—anything that didn't make sense back then."

Silence thickened between them, punctuated by the steady tick of a grandfather clock in the hallway. Through the thin walls, she could hear the river's distant rush, as if it had followed her here, listening.

"There was a man," Martha said finally, her voice trembling. "A businessman. He used to come around before Emily disappeared."

Rowan leaned forward. "Who?"

Martha's eyes flicked toward her husband. "I don't want to say."

"Mrs. Carter," Rowan said gently but firmly. "If you know something, you need to tell me. It could help us bring justice for Emily—and Sarah."

Martha swallowed. "His name was Pike. Daniel Pike's father."

The words hit like a blow. Rowan blinked once, steadying herself. Pike. The mayor's father. The same man who had funded half the town's early developments—and, apparently, something darker.

"What do you remember about him?" Rowan asked.

"He was always too interested in Emily," Martha whispered. "Brought her gifts. Said he wanted to help her get a job at his office."

"Did Emily like him?"

"She hated him," Martha said flatly. "Told me he made her skin crawl."

Rowan felt her pulse quicken. "Did you tell my father?"

Martha's expression hardened. "Yes. We told him everything. But he said Mr. Pike was a respected man and we shouldn't jump to conclusions."

"Did he investigate?" Rowan asked. The question came out thinner than she intended.

"We don't know," George murmured. "He never told us. Just said he was 'looking into all possibilities.'"

The air seemed to constrict. Her father—had he looked away because it was easier, or because someone told him to? The thought scraped against everything she'd built around his memory.

"Was there anything else?" Rowan asked.

Martha hesitated. "A few weeks before Emily vanished, she came home crying. Said Mr. Pike tried to kiss her. When she pushed him off, he got angry. Told her she'd regret it."

Rowan's hand tightened into a fist against her knee. "Did she tell anyone else?"

"Just us. We wanted to go to the police, but she begged us not to. She was scared of what he might do."

Rowan felt the cold weight of understanding settle over her. Power, land, a girl who said no. It fit too well.

"And Sheriff Hayes?" she asked quietly.

Martha nodded. "We told him. He said we had to be careful accusing a man like that. That it would only bring pain."

Rowan looked away, unable to mask the hurt tightening her jaw. She could see him saying it—gentle, tired, trying to balance a town on one hand and justice on the other.

Martha's voice cracked. "After she disappeared, he came here. Said it was best to let things go. That stirring up trouble wouldn't bring her back."

Rowan's heart stopped at the next words.

"He said," Martha whispered, "the river takes its own, and sometimes, it's best not to ask too many questions."

The phrase hollowed her out. Her father's voice echoed in it—the same cadence, the same quiet authority. It had been a warning to these people, and a confession he'd never meant her to hear.

She could almost feel the river's pull through the floorboards.

Rowan thanked them, promised to return, but her voice sounded far away even to herself. Martha's fingers clutched the edge of her skirt like a lifeline. George stared past her at the door, as if watching Emily leave all over again.

Outside, she stepped into a wall of late-summer heat that felt like suffocation. The air wrapped sticky around her lungs. Cicadas screamed. Somewhere beyond the corn, the river moved, indifferent.

The drive back blurred. Cornfields swayed, whispering secrets, and every bend in the road seemed to lead her deeper into a past she'd tried to revere but never fully knew. Her father's face on the mantle. His badge. The neat scrawl in the Carter file: FOLLOW THE MONEY. Had he written it as a promise, or an apology?

The House on Cedar Lane

The Hayes family house sat where the town began to fade into fields—a squat, weather-beaten structure with its windows shuttered and its porch sagging toward the river. Rowan hadn't been back since the funeral. She'd driven past a hundred times without turning in, as if proximity alone might count as grief.

She unlocked the front door. The hinges groaned, releasing a smell that hit her all at once: old oil, pine cleaner, and a hint of the tobacco her father had favored. The floorboards creaked in complaint beneath her boots.

Dust swam in the beam of her flashlight, catching on framed photos and forgotten trophies. The kitchen clock still ticked four minutes slow, same as the courthouse. Time here had never bothered to catch up.

She set her bag down, breathing shallowly.

The living room hadn't changed. His hat hung by the door. His chair still faced the river window, a coffee ring frozen on the end table beside it. She could almost see him there—broad shoulders, uniform half-unbuttoned, muttering about reports and rain. The phantom of his presence pressed at the back of her eyes.

The silence pressed close, like the house was listening.

She crossed to the study. Her father's desk sat under the window, drawers mostly empty except for a few pens and the faint smell of varnish. Beneath it, a floorboard looked wrong—edges uneven, slightly lifted.

Rowan crouched and pried it loose with her pocketknife. Dust spilled upward, dancing in her light. Something metallic glinted beneath. She reached in and pulled out a small lockbox—canvas-wrapped, edges rusted, weight heavier than it should have been.

Her breath caught.

She carried it to the desk, hands trembling slightly. The box was secured with a simple latch. No key. She considered forcing it open, but something in her resisted. She sat there instead, staring at it while her flashlight beam quivered against the wall.

The smell of old paper and iron filled the air.

And then memory rose up, uninvited.

Flashback

She was nine, sitting on the stairs in pajamas, listening to her father's voice through the cracked study door. Another voice answered—angrier, lower. Frank Wallace, his longtime deputy.

"It wasn't supposed to be her," Frank hissed.

"Keep your voice down," her father said.

"She was just a kid, Bob. You think the town'll forgive this if it gets out?"

A long silence. Then her father, weary: "We do what we can to protect what's left."

Something crashed—maybe a chair. Then the slam of the back door.

She had sat frozen, heart pounding, knowing somehow that the river outside was listening too.

The Box

Now, decades later, Rowan stared at the same spot on the floor where she had crouched as a child, trying to piece meaning from sound. She wiped her palms on her jeans, then flipped open the latch. It gave with a dry snap.

Inside: a tarnished badge. Her father's. The edges were worn smooth, the metal dull.

Beneath it, a folded photograph—her father and Frank standing by the old mill, smiles too tight, eyes turned toward the unseen photographer. Behind them, the Cedar River curved like a secret.

And under that, a note on yellowed paper, ink faded but legible:

Let the river keep it.

Her throat constricted. She traced the handwriting with her thumb—it was unmistakably his. Not a sheriff's report. Not an official line. Just a sentence that sounded like surrender.

A whisper of air moved through the cracked window, stirring the dust. Outside, the river's low hum answered, steady and ancient, like it had been waiting for her to read those words.

Rowan folded the note carefully and slipped it into her pocket.

She stood, box in hand, feeling the full weight of her father's silence pressing through the years. He hadn't buried evidence, not where anyone else would find it. But he'd buried his conscience—and maybe, the truth he couldn't bring himself to drag into daylight.

Wallace's face flashed in her mind, pale under the mill lights, the knife spinning across concrete. "It wasn't supposed to be her." Had he been talking about Emily then? Sarah now? Or someone else the river still hadn't given back?

Her phone buzzed. CJ's name lit the screen.

"You still at the station?" he asked.

"No," she said quietly. "I'm somewhere I should've come a long time ago."

"You okay?"

"Not yet."

He hesitated. "Rourke's pushing the lab on the Carter bones. She thinks we're close to confirmation."

Rowan looked out the window toward the dark line of trees hiding the water. "So are we," she said. "Tell her to keep going. We're done letting the river do our work for us."

She ended the call, pocketed her father's badge, and turned off the flashlight. The house sighed around her, settling back into its stillness.

As she stepped onto the porch, the boards creaked a farewell. The air smelled of pine, oil, and coming rain.

The river waited beyond the trees, whispering the same words it always had. For years, people had heard them as a warning to look away.

She looked toward its dark shape and said softly, "Not this time."

Then she walked down the path toward her car, the lock-box under her arm, the note warm against her heart, and the wind rising behind her like breath.

Chapter 7

The Reporter

The Millstone Café sat on the corner of Main and Hemlock like it had been poured into the foundation when Cedar Valley was new and then forgotten about. A bell above the door gave a tired jingle when Rowan entered—one of those sounds that belonged to simpler times, or at least the version of them people liked to remember.

The air smelled of fried batter and old lemon polish. The ceiling fan hummed lazily overhead, stirring the scent of coffee and grease. Gus, the café's owner and unofficial town historian, poured coffee into mismatched mugs with the slow precision of someone who'd been doing it since before she was born.

Lydia Bass was already there, tucked into the corner booth beneath a fading photo of the '78 softball team. She wore confidence like armor—hair pinned up haphazardly, glasses perched low, notebook open. When she saw Rowan, she raised a hand without getting up.

"Detective Hayes. You look like hell."

"Good morning to you too," Rowan said, sliding into the opposite seat.

Lydia gestured toward the counter. "Coffee's decent today. The pie's worse, which means it's safer. I ordered lemon. For luck."

"Luck's not the word I'd use for this town."

"Then call it superstition," Lydia said. "Same thing."

Gus arrived with two steaming mugs and a plate of lemon pie. "Don't say I didn't warn you," he said.

Lydia stabbed a bite anyway. "Journalistic best practice," she said dryly. "Citrus wards off small-town spin."

"Does it?"

"Only in theory." Lydia leaned in. "You didn't call me here to talk about pie."

Rowan wrapped her fingers around her mug. "I found something last night. In The Bottoms."

Lydia's fork stopped mid-air. "Go on."

"A badge. Old. Initials J.B." Rowan kept her tone even, though the discovery still pressed against her ribs like an ache.

"Not anyone in my father's department. Maybe pre–Vietnam era."

Lydia tilted her head. "And you brought this to me because...?"

"You're the one who keeps files on ghosts."

A faint, humorless smile touched Lydia's mouth. "I keep stories. Ghosts just make them easier to sell."

The ceiling fan creaked overhead, filling the pause.

"You shouldn't have been in The Bottoms," Lydia said after a beat. "That land's condemned—unofficially. Half of it's still tangled in Sterling's old River Bend deeds. The kind of parcels that were supposed to turn Cedar Valley into the next Branson."

"Sterling's dream."

"Sterling's con," Lydia corrected. "Harold Sterling wanted a resort. Gideon Pike funded it. I covered the ribbon-cutting. Wrote about prosperity and progress." Her smile thinned. "Didn't realize I was drafting the first chapter of a cover-up."

Rowan studied her expression. "You were working the Emily Carter case then."

Lydia's gaze dropped to her coffee. "Working it, yes. Reporting it... not well."

Rowan said nothing.

"I wrote a glowing feature on Sterling's 'charitable contributions' the same week Emily vanished," Lydia murmured. "My editor called it human interest. I call it my biggest mistake."

"So this is redemption?"

"This is penance with caffeine."

A gust of cool morning air fluttered the napkins on the counter as the door opened and shut again. Rowan waited until the sound settled.

"Did you ever hear of a deputy named Ibermeyer?" she asked.

Lydia frowned. "Frank Ibermeyer? Your father's partner. Quit suddenly after the Carter case. Last I heard, he moved north. Why?"

Rowan hesitated. "I remembered hearing them argue—my father and Ibermeyer. About the mill."

Lydia's pen moved without her looking. "Memory or fact?"

"Both." Rowan took a slow sip of coffee. "But the mill keeps turning up. Wallace, Emily, Sarah... they all circle the same place."

"You're not chasing this just for Sarah Miller anymore," Lydia said quietly.

Rowan didn't respond.

"That's not a criticism," Lydia added. "Old cases don't stay buried just because we want them to. Your father's shadow weighs heavy. Happens to the best of us."

"Maybe I just want the truth."

"Truth's expensive," Lydia said. "And everyone thinks they can afford it until the bill comes due."

Rowan's jaw tightened. "I've already paid."

Outside, the sky bruised with gathering clouds. Thunder murmured somewhere far off—low, patient, inevitable.

They finished their coffee, left enough cash for Gus to pretend he hadn't been listening, and stepped outside. Main Street stretched ahead, mostly quiet except for the whine of a delivery truck and the hum of flickering neon signs. Shuttered storefronts lined the sidewalks like teeth dulled by time.

Kids on bikes splashed through puddles, their laughter bouncing off brick facades. The smell of fryer oil, wet pavement, and something faintly metallic hung in the air—Cedar Valley in a single inhale.

"You ever think this town's haunted?" Rowan asked.

"By economics or conscience?"

"Either."

They passed the barber shop—closed again, pole frozen mid-spin—and the old Gazette office where Lydia once wrote stories that made or broke local politics.

"I used to write from that window," Lydia said, nodding toward a second-floor room. "Back when news smelled like ink and guilt."

"You still write."

"Obituaries and council blurbs." Lydia shrugged. "Half the town reads them. The other half pretends they don't. Balance."

A kid veered too close and drenched both of them with muddy water.

"Sorry, Detective!" he called.

"You should be," Lydia muttered. "That was my last clean pair of jeans."

"Happens when you walk with the police," Rowan said.

At the next corner, a black sedan idled near the post office. Too new. Too dark. Windows tinted enough to reflect their own shapes back at them.

"You know him?" Lydia murmured.

"No."

"Think you're being watched?"

"I always think that."

The sedan didn't move. Rowan forced herself to look away, though prickling tension crawled up her spine.

"You ever eat something without analyzing it?" Lydia asked, trying to cut the air.

"Not lately."

"You're missing out. Fear burns calories."

"Then I should be a runway model."

Lydia barked a laugh. "Headline writes itself: 'Local Detective Loses Weight, Gains Ghosts.'"

They turned down a quieter street, hydrangeas sagging under rain-heavy blooms. The world felt briefly softened—cooler air, muted noise, the hush before another storm.

"You think your father chose peace over truth," Lydia said softly.

Rowan didn't answer for a moment. "I think he forgot which side of the badge he was supposed to stand on."

Lydia's expression gentled. "Redemption's not a headline. It's a retraction no one reads."

"Then let's make it front page."

"Careful, Detective," Lydia said. "You're starting to sound like me."

"God forbid."

As they looped back toward the café, Rowan saw the black sedan was gone. But its absence felt too deliberate, like it had slipped into another shadow rather than driven away.

"So what now?" Lydia asked.

"Rourke's analyzing the badge," Rowan said. "CJ's pulling River Bend property files. And you said you kept all your old notes?"

Lydia tapped her satchel. "Every page. Including one your father gave me after the Carter case. I was too green to know what it meant."

"What kind of note?"

"A ledger reference. Parcel 18B. 'Assignment withheld.' Does that ring any bells?"

A cold knot formed low in Rowan's stomach. "Eighteen B was circled in Sterling's development map. One of the plots that refused to sell."

Lydia nodded. "Then we're getting close to something."

Gus stepped onto the sidewalk, wiping his hands on a rag. "You two solving the whole world out here, or coming back for dessert?"

"What's the special?" Rowan asked.

"Cherry cobbler."

Lydia groaned. "Just pie with an identity crisis."

Rowan shook her head. "We'll take two to go."

They reached the cruiser as thunder rolled again, closer now, humming like the river under storm winds.

Lydia paused by the door. "For the record," she said, "if you die chasing this, I'm writing your obituary first."

"Spell my name right," Rowan deadpanned.

"No promises."

"You're incorrigible."

"Occupational hazard."

Rowan started the engine. "You still want redemption, Lydia?"

Lydia leaned down, rain beginning to fleck her glasses. "Always. But I'll settle for the truth."

She stepped back as Rowan pulled away. The first drops of rain scattered across the windshield, each one splitting into tiny mirrored rivers.

Half a block down, a car door closed softly—

A camera shutter clicked once—sharp, deliberate—

And the rain swallowed everything else.

Chapter 8

The Flood Warning

The Bottoms didn't appear on any official Cedar Valley map. It was a whispered place, a forgotten appendix clinging to the town's underbelly—a place where the river bent too close and too deep, and where the soil had swallowed more than its share of stories.

The cruiser bumped down a gravel road, dust billowing behind them like a ghostly escort. The air was thick with the scent of stagnant water and something older—decaying vegetation, iron, and rot that clung to the back of the throat.

CJ coughed beside her. "Cheerful spot."

"It keeps the riffraff out," Rowan said, though the line felt brittle in her mouth. Her father used to say the same thing whenever a call came from The Bottoms, a tone somewhere between warning and resignation. Stay sharp down there, Ro. Even the river holds its breath.

Truth was, The Bottoms didn't keep the riffraff out. It kept everyone out—law, progress, and any scrap of hope.

Fields stretched in uneven patches on either side, littered with the bones of old farmhouses. Sagging porches leaned at drunken angles. Windows stared like empty sockets. Rusted mailboxes listed toward the road, names long washed away by rain and time. The river, somewhere just beyond the tree line, whispered low and steady—its voice always there, even when unseen.

"My grandpa used to tell stories about this place," CJ said. "Said it was cursed. That the river takes what it's owed."

Rowan raised an eyebrow. "The only curse here is neglect."

But her grip on the wheel tightened. The air had a particular stillness—too quiet, too knowing. Even the insects seemed to hold their breath. A wind moved through skeletal trees, soft and deliberate, like breath down the back of her neck.

They passed a half-submerged tractor, its frame rusted orange, its tires half-swallowed by mud. A barn lay collapsed in on itself nearby, vines draped through the ribs of its rafters. Everything here looked abandoned mid-fight, like someone had tried to win against the land and the land had simply outlasted them.

"Dispatch, Hayes," she said into the radio. "Entering grid sector Beta-Nine, The Bottoms. Request backup from state patrol, ETA thirty minutes. Advise caution."

"Copy that, Detective," came the reply through static. "Be careful out there."

Rowan slowed the cruiser as the road narrowed to a single lane. The canopy closed overhead, slicing sunlight into thin, pale beams. The gravel under the tires shifted and cracked like brittle bones.

"There," CJ said, pointing. "The Hemlock place."

The house rose from the weeds like something the earth hadn't finished burying. Paint peeled away in curling strips. The porch sagged like an old spine. A rusted swing set stood in the yard, its chain groaning in the breeze like a ghost trying to speak.

Rowan cut the engine. "This is it."

CJ swallowed. "This place gives me the creeps."

"Good," Rowan said, stepping out. "Means you're paying attention."

The heat hit her first—wet and dense, laced with mildew and something sour. Each step through the overgrown yard released another wave of decay. The porch boards gave beneath her boots with a tired sigh.

The front door hung partially open. Cool air seeped out, carrying the smell of damp wood and mold. Rowan hesitated, hand drifting toward her flashlight.

"Let's check the perimeter first," she murmured.

They split—CJ right, Rowan left—circling the warped skeleton of the house. Flashlights skimmed shattered windows and furniture reduced to pulp by rain. Rowan spotted faint impressions in the mud—drag marks?—but the pattern was broken and half-swallowed by weeds.

Behind the house, the yard was waist-high with choking weeds. A crumbling stone well leaned crooked in the center, its rim slick with moss, its mouth swallowed by shadow.

"Check the outbuildings," Rowan called quietly. "I'll take the well."

CJ nodded and angled toward the shed.

Rowan approached the well, boots sinking slightly in the spongy ground. She knelt, sweeping her light across the rough stones. Far below, water glimmered faintly. The air drifting up was cold and metallic, the smell of iron and secrets that had aged in the dark.

Her beam caught something small embedded in the mud along the rim—metal glinting faintly. She reached down with her gloved hand and freed it.

A locket. Tarnished, heavy, half-eaten by rust. She wiped the face clean. Inside, behind a cracked sliver of glass, was the faded image of a young woman—smiling, bright, forever seventeen.

Rowan's breath hitched. The resemblance to Emily Carter was uncanny. Too uncanny.

Her thumb trembled. Was it Emily's? Another girl's? Or something left as a warning?

"Hayes!" CJ's voice cracked through the quiet, urgent. "I found something!"

Rowan pocketed the locket and sprinted toward the shed.

CJ stood in the doorway, pale under the flashlight glare. "Tracks," he said. "Fresh ones."

Rowan stepped inside. The air reeked of mildew and old oil. Tools hung from bent nails, shadows long and sharp across the walls. On the dirt floor, tire tracks carved deep grooves leading from the shed's rear wall toward the fields.

She crouched, running her fingers along one tread. "These match the tracks from the riverbank."

CJ nodded. "Which means whoever was there—"

"Was here first," Rowan finished. "Or came back."

Wind pushed through a gap in the boards, stirring dust in ghostly spirals. The swing chains outside creaked in a rhythm that felt too deliberate.

"Let's see where they go," Rowan said.

They followed the tracks into the overgrown field, flashlights weaving through the dark. The earth was soft, sucking at their boots. A chemical tang—gasoline—hung faintly in the air. Even the river seemed to pause, listening.

CJ tripped on a root and swore. "You ever get the feeling we shouldn't be here?"

"Every damn day," Rowan said.

At the far edge of the field, the tracks stopped abruptly near a patch of disturbed earth. Leaves and branches had been scattered over it—a rushed attempt at concealment.

Rowan knelt, brushing debris aside. The soil was loose—recently turned.

"Someone's been digging."

CJ scanned the tree line. "For what?"

"Let's find out."

She took a trowel from her kit and dug. The dirt yielded too easily. A few inches down, the blade struck something solid.

Metal.

She cleared soil from a tarnished object, exposing an old badge—corroded, unfamiliar.

The initials were faint but readable: J.B.

CJ leaned in. "Who's J.B.?"

"Not anyone in our department," Rowan said. "Not now, anyway."

"Could it have been your dad's old division?"

"No," Rowan murmured, stomach tightening. "His was newer. This one's decades old."

The badge felt cold, heavier than its size should allow. The soil beneath it was darker, damp in a way that suggested more than rain.

Before she could speak again—

A twig snapped.

Rowan froze, hand dropping to her weapon. Another snap—deliberate.

CJ whispered, "Hayes..."

Rowan swept her light toward the trees.

A figure stood there, half-concealed by branches. Tall. Still. A dark hoodie merging with the night.

"Police!" she barked. "Show me your hands!"

The figure didn't move. Only the faint rise and fall of breath betrayed life.

Rowan advanced, gun drawn. "Hands! Now!"

The figure lifted one arm. Something glinted—a metallic flash.

A gun.

"Drop it!" Rowan shouted.

The barrel shifted.

A shot cracked through the night.

Rowan dove, dirt exploding near her shoulder. CJ hit the ground beside her, cursing. Another shot—then silence.

Rowan rolled behind a fallen fence post, heart pounding hard enough to bruise.

"You see him?" she hissed.

CJ shook his head. "Gone!"

She scanned the tree line. Empty. Too empty.

She crept closer. Her flashlight swept branches and fog. Nothing but shadows.

Except... the faint smell of river water. Fresh. Recent.

"Think he was guarding the site?" CJ asked.

"Maybe," Rowan said. "Or maybe he was waiting for us."

CJ shivered. "You think he'll come back?"

"He already has."

She lifted the bagged badge. The initials glimmered faintly: J.B.

"Whoever he was," she whispered, "he didn't want this found."

CJ swallowed. "You think it ties back to Carter?"

Rowan didn't answer. The wind carried the river's scent—mud and metal, old and restless.

"I think it ties back to everyone," she said softly.

They hiked back to the cruiser in silence. The porch swing creaked in the rising wind, rhythmic and mocking. Rowan felt watched the entire walk, though she never turned quickly enough to catch anything but shifting shadows.

Lightning flickered on the horizon, illuminating the fields in a stark, breathless flash. For a heartbeat, Rowan thought she saw another figure watching from the porch.

Then darkness reclaimed everything.

Rowan climbed into the cruiser. The headlights carved two thin tunnels through the fog.

"Let's get the badge to Rourke," she said quietly.

CJ nodded, rubbing his arms. "And the gunman?"

"We'll find him," Rowan said. "He just told us where to look."

As the cruiser rolled forward, gravel hissing beneath the tires, the Hemlock house sagged back into darkness. The swing chains groaned in the wind—steady, mournful—like a lullaby for things the river refused to keep.

Chapter 9

The Riverbank

The rain hadn't stopped since morning. By noon, Main Street was a river in everything but name—gutters choking, storm drains gurgling, the steady hiss of downpour turning the town's chatter into static. Rowan's wipers beat a losing rhythm across the windshield as she eased the cruiser past the courthouse. Lightning stitched the sky above the clock tower and, for a heartbeat, the wet brick glowed like a warning.

"Radio says the river's up six inches in the last hour," CJ said, squinting at his phone. "State's calling it precautionary."

"It's never precaution when the river's involved," Rowan said.

She swung into the loop at City Hall. Rain flattened against the steps in sheets, bouncing off the stone like thrown gravel. By the time she and CJ crossed the lobby, they were dripping and silent, the smell of wet wool and paper rising around them.

Marge, the receptionist, didn't look up as she buzzed them through. "He's expecting you," she said in the tired, even voice of someone who had learned years ago to leave her opinions at home.

Mayor Daniel Pike's office was warm and dry and arranged like a photograph—flag in the corner, sepia prints of Cedar Valley when the paint was still proud, a wall of handshakes and ribbon-cuttings. He stood at the window with his hands in his pockets, watching rain rope down Main.

"Detective Hayes," he said without turning. "You're soaked. You should be home, not wading through this mess."

"I've seen worse," Rowan said. "I doubt you called me in to discuss the weather."

Pike turned, and the smile arrived before his eyes did. "I called you in to give you counsel."

"I don't take counsel from suspects."

"Careful," he said softly, as if the word itself might bruise. "Words like that do damage. To reputations. To budgets. To entire departments."

Rowan didn't sit. "You've pressured me to bury evidence. You leaned on my dispatcher. You sent your staff to 'help' at scenes where they didn't belong."

"I sent them to serve their town," Pike said, moving behind his desk and resting his fingertips lightly on the polished wood. "Cedar Valley survives on trust, Detective. You erode that, you erode everything."

"The bigger picture is a dead girl," Rowan said. "And a link to one who's been dead for twenty years."

Pike's mouth tightened. "The bigger picture is a community. Businesses that stay or flee. Families that choose to raise their children here or not."

"Progress built on secrets isn't progress," Rowan said. "It's rot with better signage."

The crack showed then—a flash of anger, quick and clean, before his face went smooth again. "Your father understood the line between duty and destruction."

"My father understood what it meant to drown in other people's decisions."

"That's enough," Pike snapped, stepping around the desk. "You're jeopardizing this town's future. You're stirring up old ghosts and pretending you don't hear the living."

"Sometimes the living are the ghosts," Rowan said.

The quiet that followed was so sharp Rowan could hear Marge shift in the outer office.

Pike drew a breath, slow and theatrical. "Be careful, Detective. Sometimes what you call justice is just another kind of flood."

Rowan's hand was already on the knob. "Then you'd better start stacking sandbags."

She left him staring at the glass like the water might obey.

Outside, the sirens began as a rumor and became a chorus—one, then two, then all of them, their wail twisting through the rain like thread. Not the noon test. The flood tone. A long, rising cry that lifted the hair on Rowan's neck.

CJ was already on the radio, voice clipped and loud over static. "Dispatch, Jenkins—confirm flood advisory."

"Confirmed," Dispatch replied. "Levee sensors tripped near the east bend and The Bottoms. Requesting volunteers for sandbag staging at Fairgrounds Lot B and east-bank access. EMS on standby."

Rowan pulled up her hood. "Let's go."

The fairgrounds lot looked like a battlefield improvised from habit. Trucks idled with hazard lights blinking. A stack of pallets had become a wall; a Bobcat grumbled in low gear, ferrying sand. Volunteers formed a chain—farmers in seed caps, teenagers in soaked hoodies, church ladies in plastic ponchos and determined faces. The boy from Main Street, the one who'd splashed them with his bike, jogged past with a bag half his size, sneakers slapping water.

"Double stack along the curve!" someone yelled. "Keep it even!"

CJ stepped into the flow like he'd been born to it, lifting until his arms shook, shouting directions when someone faltered. Rowan fell into line, wet burlap heavy in her hands, grit grinding through her gloves. Rain worked into her collar; mud sucked at her boots; river smell—metal and moss and something old—curled through everything like smoke.

An old man with a face like a dried apple grunted as he passed her a bag. "Clock's four minutes slow," he said. "Always is."

Rowan smiled without meaning to. "We'll buy it some time."

A high school girl with blue hair slipped in the mud. Rowan caught her elbow, righted her, felt the quick squeeze of gratitude before the chain lurched forward again.

"Levee's up another half foot," CJ called, eyes on the feed from the county sensor app. "We've got a weak spot by the cottonwoods."

"Take the Bobcat," Rowan said. "Dump base gravel and run a third line. I'll get more bodies."

"On it."

The town had learned this choreography the hard way—years ago, and then again, and again. Still, the river always added new steps. Rowan moved with it, kneeling in the rush of water seeping through her laces, stacking, shoving, sealing. Her muscles burned. Her heart hammered in her ribs in time with the slap-slap of bags hitting the growing wall.

"Breach!" someone yelled from down-curve. "Breach on the inside!"

Rowan ran. The world narrowed to the hiss of rain and the roar of brown water pushing through a six-foot wound and clawing at the ground beyond. Two men in seed caps fought to wedge bags into the biting gap and the river answered by shouldering them back.

"Truck!" Rowan shouted, and a pickup lurched into place, bed rattling with weight. She stepped into the flow before she could think better of it—cold to the thigh, silt grinding in her socks—grabbing one side of a bag while the farmer grabbed the other. Together they levered it into the hole. Then another. And another. The river shoved; she shoved back. Her knee slid; a hand—blue-haired girl, fierce as a saint—hooked her jacket and kept her upright.

"Hold it," Rowan said through her teeth. "Hold—"

It held. Denied its shortcut, the water frothed and sulked and slid, hunting for another weakness.

Rowan sagged back, breath burning. Her radio crackled. "Hayes—County Seven east of the bend. We've got a stalled pickup with an elderly driver inside. Water rising."

She met CJ's eyes. His hair dripped into his eyebrows. "Go," he said.

They left the levee to a dozen hands and a borrowed prayer and jumped into the cruiser. The wipers stuttered, then surrendered to streaks. Out past the last row of houses, the fields had converted into a broad, churning lake, broken only by fence tops and the dark shoulders of logs turning end over end.

"There," CJ said, pointing.

The truck's roof made a stubborn line through the water, headlights puddled and pulsing like a tired heartbeat. Rowan stopped short of the ditch, killed the engine, and grabbed the rope from the trunk.

"Anchor that to the post," she said. "If I go, you haul me back or you let me float to Davenport. Those are your only two options."

"That's not funny," CJ said, looping the rope with quick, surprisingly neat hands. "On you."

She tied the rope around her waist and tested the line. The water was faster than it looked—always faster than it looked. By the second step it tugged; by the third, it pulled; by the fourth, she was leaning into it like a fight.

The man inside pounded the glass, skin parchment-pale behind the fog of his own breath.

"Unlock it!" Rowan shouted, water stealing half her voice.

He fumbled; the door stuck; then it gave with a sucking lurch that sent a sheet of water into her chest and the old man into her arms.

"Can't swim," he gasped, voice thin with shock.

"You don't need to," she said, dragging him sideways, turning so her body took the current first. "You just need to walk like you're stubborn."

The river disagreed. A wind-driven wave slammed into her hip. The rope bit and her foot slipped on what wasn't ground anymore but moving water skin. Balance vanished.

Dark closed over her head. Cold rushed into her mouth, under her eyelids. For a heartbeat she felt the river's old certainty: The river takes its own—not words, but pressure.

Hands. Upward. Light.

CJ's arm locked around her, the old man's weight awkward between them. "I've got you!" CJ yelled. "I've got you, I've got you—move!"

They staggered to the lip of the road in lunging, graceless steps. Other hands appeared—volunteers, a firefighter with a mustache carved from oak, the blue-haired girl again, a woman in a PTA sweatshirt—pulling, hauling, telling them they'd done good in a language made of breath and mud.

Rowan collapsed on the shoulder. Rain drilled the puddles around her into lace. The old man sat hard beside her, started to shake, then began to cry like someone who had put off crying for too many years.

"What's your name?" Rowan asked, catching her breath.

"Earl Hemmer," he said. "I—my cows—"

"Cows are waterproof," CJ said, dropping on his other side. "That's science."

Hemmer snorted, then laughed, then cried harder. When the EMS crew took him, he clutched Rowan's sleeve with a grip that startled her and said, "Thank you," like it was a secret.

They watched the ambulance crawl up the hill, taillights flickering against the rain. The world smelled like gasoline, wet earth, and relief.

"Here," CJ said, producing a cigarette from his soaked jacket.

"You don't smoke," Rowan said.

"I just became a flood smoker," he said, striking a match cupped against the wind. The flame flared weakly, leaned, and took. He put the cigarette between her lips like a joke. She shouldn't have, but she did, the smoke threading through the damp like a thin line of warmth.

"The river's taking again," CJ said after a while, eyes on the bruised water pushing at the fence line.

Rowan exhaled, watching the smoke turn to fog and vanish. "Then we take something back."

The sirens shifted pitch—less wail, more command. The volunteer fire chief—Coulter, beard in wet knots—strode toward them with the posture of a man trying to outrun his own years.

"Hayes. Jenkins. East-bank wave is holding for now. City wants to know if we open the high school as a shelter."

Rowan stood; her knees disagreed, but she ignored them. "Open it. Call Pastor Linda to run sign-in. Call the librarian—she'll know who needs prescriptions, and the school nurse can lock them up. If the power cuts, the generator in the shop room is flagged 'don't touch.' Touch it."

Coulter nodded, already repeating orders into his radio. "Word from State: if the curve overtops, we evacuate blocks three through seven."

Rowan's phone buzzed. Messages stacked like incoming waves: a photo of her and Lydia walking under the Gazette window, captioned: DETECTIVE HAYES MEETS WITH DISCREDITED REPORTER—QUESTIONS SWIRL. An anonymous number: YOU'RE IN OVER YOUR HEAD. A screenshot of a social post: MAYOR: HAYES SEEKING "PERSONAL CLOSURE" AT TOWN'S EXPENSE.

CJ saw the screen and swore. "He's running a smear in a flood."

"He's scared," Rowan said. "Scared people double down. They build higher walls. Or they run."

A patrol unit nosed into the lot and Patel climbed out, jacket half-zipped, hair plastered to her forehead. "We've got a debate on Mill Street," she said. "Half the block wants to evacuate, other half says they'll ride it out."

"Who's holding out?" Rowan asked.

"Mrs. Vang with the six kids wants to go. Wexler—the nephew, not the old man—says stay. Says the town cries wolf."

"Tell Mr. Wexler the wolf has a boat," Rowan said, tugging her hood up again. "And it's coming."

They rolled toward Mill Street with the lights off. No point blinding people already staring into bad weather. The rain had lost some force, but the sky stayed the color of nickel and wind sheeted across open blocks in petty, relentless slaps.

On Mill, two clusters had formed—one around a minivan with its hatch open and Rubbermaid bins half-packed, the other around a man on his porch holding a beer like a talisman.

"Ma'am," Rowan said to Mrs. Vang, "we'll give you an escort to the high school."

"Bless you," the woman breathed as two kids clambered into the back of the van and three more argued about the dog.

"Wexler," CJ called, climbing the porch steps, "we're advising mandatory evacuation if the river overtops."

"It won't," Wexler said, staring at the street that wasn't water yet and already was. "Never does on this block. We're on a hump."

"Water doesn't care about humps," CJ said mildly. "It cares about slope. And we just lost six inches of bank."

Rowan stepped up beside him. "We don't want to come back for you in the dark."

Wexler looked at her, something loosening at the corner of his mouth. "You pulled Earl out."

"We did."

He sighed, a long exhale that sounded like surrender. "I'll pack a bag."

"Good man," Rowan said.

Back at the levee, the line had become muscle memory. Sandbags passed. A thermos made the rounds and nobody asked what was in it. Teenagers cursed; old women pretended not to hear. Pastor Linda handed out ponchos with the command of a field general and a hug for anyone too wet to refuse.

Rourke texted: BADGE "J.B." PRE-1950. COUNTY DEPUTY REGISTRY SHOWS JONAH BRETT, DECEASED 1948. CHECK ARCHIVES.

Rowan stared at the name until the letters blurred and then snapped back into focus.

Jonah Brett.

CJ read over her shoulder. "We've got another ghost."

"Not a ghost," Rowan said, feeling the tilt inside her that meant the next step would hurt. "A pattern."

"Hayes!" someone yelled. "We need you at the curve!"

They went. The curve roared. The wall held. The rain slackened to a steady, sullen drip, the kind that could last for days.

By evening, the high school gym shone with generator light and damp humanity. Cots lined the basketball court. Volunteers ladled soup into paper bowls. A girl in a red sweatshirt read to a cluster of toddlers from a laminated early reader while three men argued quietly about whether the 2008 flood had been higher.

Rowan stood by the doors and watched, the weight of her wet jacket pressing into her shoulders like hands. Outside, the air smelled of diesel, bleach, and cornfields after too much water. She took off the jacket, wrung the cuffs, and put it back on because there was nowhere it belonged more than on her.

"Detective," Pastor Linda said, appearing beside her with a cup of something that wasn't quite coffee and wasn't quite tea. "Drink. You'll insult me if you don't."

Rowan took a sip. Warmth unwound along her ribs. "Thank you."

"You look like your father when he hadn't slept."

"He didn't sleep much," Rowan said.

Pastor Linda nodded, eyes kind and unblinking. "He carried a lot so other people didn't have to."

"Sometimes he carried the wrong things."

"That's the trick of it," Linda said, patting her sleeve. "The river takes what you're holding, not necessarily what you should be."

CJ appeared with two blankets, one of which he draped over her shoulders without comment. "Levee captain says we've bought ourselves twelve hours," he said. "Maybe more if the rain passes east."

"Then we use them," Rowan said. "Recorder's office at first light. Parcel 18B. Assignment file. And I want audit logs—who accessed what, when."

CJ nodded. "I'll call ahead. Not that Marge will love it."

"She never loves it," Rowan said, and felt, to her surprise, the corner of her mouth twitch.

They stepped back outside into the quiet between storms. The river muttered beyond the tree line, restless but contained—for now. The courthouse clock struck the hour and then, as always, lagged and struck again four minutes late, trying to catch up.

CJ fished in his pocket. "One last criminal act," he said, offering another cigarette.

Rowan accepted, cupped the match, and watched the flame flare—a small, precise defiance. They stood shoulder to shoulder, smoke loosening into the damp air.

"The river's taking again," CJ said softly.

Rowan watched the dark line where water met land. "Then we'll take something back," she said, and flicked ash into a puddle like a vow.

Behind them, the gym doors swung open and laughter spilled out, thin and brave. A boy chased his sister down the hallway in socks, slid, fell, popped up grinning. Someone cheered for reasons that had nothing to do with weather. The town, bruised and busy, did what towns do—it held.

Rowan tipped her head, listening. Somewhere far off, thunder rolled, more warning than threat. Closer, a camera shutter clicked once—sharp, deliberate—and then the night swallowed the sound whole.

Chapter 10

The Assignment File

The rain hadn't quit. It had just changed its voice—softer now, a constant murmur against the windows of the Cedar Valley Gazette office. Inside, the world felt smaller: ink-stained, caffeine-fueled, and heavy with ghosts.

Rowan stood by the window, watching rivulets race each other down the glass. The newsroom's fluorescent light buzzed overhead, reflecting off stacks of old newspapers that leaned precariously like ancient tombstones. Lydia Bass moved behind her in the dimness, cigarette dangling from her lip, typing one-handed on a yellowed keyboard that had outlived three editors and probably half of Cedar Valley.

"Damn rain," Lydia muttered, peering through the grime. "River'll be up to its old tricks again."

"Feels like it never stopped," Rowan said, still watching the water slide across the glass. "Just took a break long enough for us to forget what it could do."

Lydia snorted. "You sound like my ex-husband. He used to talk about the river like it was a living thing. Said it had moods." She stubbed her cigarette out in an ashtray already crowded with butts. "I told him it didn't have moods—it had victims."

Rowan turned toward the desk, where Lydia's chaotic universe sprawled across every surface: overflowing manila folders, paper clippings, coffee rings fossilized into the wood. Somewhere under it all, Rowan knew, were the bones of a story her father had started and someone else had buried.

"Here," she said, tapping a faded clipping Lydia had tossed aside. The headline shouted in jagged type: MILL CLOSES AFTER TRAGEDY! A photo showed a much younger Daniel Pike beside his uncle, both in their Sunday best, both looking grim.

"You know this one?" Rowan asked.

"Old news," Lydia said, reaching for her glasses. "Mill shut down after a flood. Pike's uncle went belly-up. Half the town went unemployed for a year."

"Read the article," Rowan said.

Lydia sighed, but humored her. "Okay… worker named Thomas Bell disappeared. Presumed drowned. Body never recovered." She looked up, unimpressed. "Happens."

"Keep going," Rowan said, sliding over another article. "Martha Crane. Scaffolding accident. 'Tragic misstep,' coroner said."

Lydia arched a brow. "You think Pike's uncle was pushing people into the river now?"

"I think there's a pattern," Rowan said evenly, and placed a third clipping beside the first two. "John Peterson. Tractor overturned near the riverbank, 1998. My father ruled it an accident. But I remember him being… uneasy."

"Uneasy how?"

"He came home that night and sat at the kitchen table for hours without touching his dinner," Rowan said quietly. "Kept saying, 'The river doesn't take by accident.'"

Lydia stared at her a moment, the smirk fading from her face. "You think all this ties to Pike?"

"I think all this ties to something," Rowan said. "The mill, the river, the land. And Pike's family has their fingerprints on every bit of it."

The storm outside deepened. The ceiling fan creaked with each slow rotation, stirring the smell of ink and nicotine.

Lydia reached for another cigarette but didn't light it. Instead, she began sorting through the growing pile of clippings like a card dealer at the end of her rope.

"Well," she said after a beat, "if you're right, you're poking at the biggest hornet's nest in town."

Rowan's gaze fell on a headline buried near the bottom of the pile: LOCAL BOY STILL MISSING – FAMILY PRAYS FOR ANSWERS. The photo was grainy, but the name printed below it stopped her cold.

"Billy Joe Carter," Rowan said quietly. "Emily's brother."

Lydia leaned closer. "That was—what—five years after Emily vanished?"

"Five years," Rowan confirmed. "He went missing out by The Bottoms. Same story: car abandoned, no body found."

Lydia rubbed her temple. "Christ, Rowan. You're digging up a whole graveyard."

"Someone has to." Rowan's voice was calm, but it carried an edge that silenced even the rain for a moment. "Emily. Sarah. Billy Joe. They all deserve better than rumors and obituaries."

Lydia exhaled smoke she hadn't realized she was still holding. "You ever think maybe your father was right not to stir this up?"

"No," Rowan said, eyes hard. "I think he wanted to. I think he was stopped."

That landed like a blow. Lydia looked at her for a long moment before speaking. "Alright," she said finally. "You've convinced me. Let's go grave-robbing."

They spent the next few hours drowning in paper. Lydia knew her archives like other people knew prayer books—by touch, not order. She dragged ledgers from under the desk, drawers, and even one from a filing cabinet labeled PIE CONTEST 1987 – DO NOT TOUCH.

Rowan flipped through brittle pages, her fingers blackened by dust and ink. "You ever think of digitizing these?" she asked.

"Don't speak blasphemy in my office," Lydia said. "These papers are older than most marriages in town. And twice as interesting."

She leaned over Rowan's shoulder as they worked through a stack of financial notes from the late nineties. The mill's ledger showed loans, payouts, unexplained "safety reimbursements." The numbers told a story of their own—a slow siphoning of life and money disguised as progress.

"Look at this," Lydia said suddenly, stabbing a finger at a date. "1997. The mill takes out a massive loan from First Cedar Valley Bank. Guess who's on the board at the time?"

Rowan didn't even have to check. "Daniel Pike."

"Bingo," Lydia said, eyes sharpening. "And the loan gets approved the same day John Peterson dies in that tractor 'accident.' That's one hell of a coincidence."

"I stopped believing in those," Rowan said. She turned the page, the paper soft as cloth from age. "And look at this—entries marked 'river disposal.' Chemical waste."

Lydia frowned. "You're saying they were dumping it in The Bottoms?"

"I'm saying they were hiding something down there," Rowan said softly. "And when people found out, they disappeared."

Thunder cracked close enough to rattle the windowpanes. The lights flickered once, thought about it, and held.

Lydia flipped to another section, scanning with a speed born of long practice. "Your badge ghost showed up in my files too," she murmured. "Jonah Brett—county deputy, drowned in '48. Official story is he fell into the river on patrol. His widow wrote three letters to the editor saying he was chasing someone."

"Letters get printed?" Rowan asked.

"One did," Lydia said. "Two didn't. The two that mentioned Sterling by name."

The realization settled between them, weighty and wet as the storm outside. The mill hadn't just poisoned the town's politics—it had poisoned the land and written a casualty list in water.

"Those missing people," Lydia said, voice shaking just a little. "If they got sick, started talking—"

"They were silenced," Rowan finished.

They sat in silence for a moment, listening to the rain thrum against the roof like a heartbeat. Lydia looked pale under the flickering light.

"You know what happens when you publish a story like this, right?" she said. "You don't win awards. You lose advertisers. Maybe your job. Maybe worse."

Rowan looked down at the papers spread before them—headlines, names, a silent ledger of a town that had traded its conscience for convenience. "Then we make it count."

It was nearly midnight when the last lead surfaced. Lydia had dug through another layer of chaos—an old subscription ledger, mostly unpaid balances and address changes—when she froze.

"Rowan. Look at this."

She held up a crumbling page. The handwriting was neat and formal, a record of advertising clients. Beside Sterling Mill was a notation in blue ink: Assignment – Filed. See Clerk's Ledger, Parcel 18B.

The ink smelled faintly like the sheriff's office used to smell in the '90s—old thermos coffee, paper warmed by fluorescent lights, the mill's whistle drifting through cracked windows at noon. Cedar Valley had sounded different back then, before the river took its first big bite.

Rowan's pulse kicked. "That's the same parcel listed in my father's notes," she said. "The one he circled and wrote follow the money."

Lydia grinned, teeth flashing in the dim light. "Well, I'll be damned. The paper kept better records than the county."

"Where's the clerk's ledger kept now?" Rowan asked.

"Recorder's office," Lydia said. "Basement level. Still has the original deed books. They don't like people poking around in there—too much mold, too many secrets."

"Perfect," Rowan said, gathering the papers into her bag. "We'll start there."

Lydia reached over and gripped her wrist. "Rowan. Be smart. The Pikes won't like you sniffing around old deeds. They built their empire on paper—paper's the only thing that can burn it down."

Rowan's phone vibrated on the desk, cutting through the tension. The caller ID read: CJ Jenkins.

"Hayes," she answered, breath steady but heart hammering.

"Detective," CJ said, voice urgent over the crackle of rain and static. "You'd better get down here. We found something."

"Where?"

"South bank," he said. "Just past The Bottoms. It washed up after the surge."

"What is it?"

There was a pause. "A lockbox," CJ said. "Old, metal, rusted shut. Looks like it's been buried a long time."

Rowan felt her pulse thrum in her ears. "Any markings?"

"Yeah," CJ said slowly. "There's an engraving on the lid. R.H."

Her father's initials.

Rowan's voice came out a whisper. "Don't open it. Not yet. I'm on my way."

She ended the call and grabbed her coat from the back of the chair. The rain outside had picked up again, relentless. Lydia watched her, eyes narrowed.

"R.H.," she repeated. "Robert Hayes."

Rowan nodded. "Looks like the river just gave something back."

Lydia rose, stubbed out her cigarette, and grabbed her own coat. "Then let's go fish our ghost out."

"You don't have to come," Rowan said.

Lydia's smile was sharp and tired. "If you die chasing this, I'm writing your obituary first."

"Spell my name right," Rowan said.

"No promises."

They stepped out into the storm together. The wind tore at their coats, the rain blinding in sheets, the air metallic with the smell of the river rising again. Somewhere beyond the courthouse, the sirens wailed a new warning—part flood, part reckoning.

Rowan tightened her grip on the doorframe for a moment before stepping fully into the rain.

The Cedar River was awake.

And it was starting to talk.

Chapter 11

What the River Returned

The floodlights threw hard white cones over the south bank, turning the river into a jittering strip of tin. Mist hung low and stubborn, drifting in and out of the beams like something that had decided to breathe. CJ waited by the ambulance turnout with his hands jammed into a pair of borrowed work gloves, a poncho flapping around his knees. Beyond him, volunteers in reflective vests picked through flood debris with rakes, piling branches, fence wire, and the occasional orphaned trash can into soggy pyramids.

Rowan parked behind the rescue truck and stepped into the damp hush beneath the sirens. The rain had eased to a drizzle that smelled like iron and algae and old tires—The Bottoms on a night the world couldn't be bothered to end.

"Over here," CJ called, lifting his chin toward the water-line. His breath came out in little ghosts in the light. "We pulled it from that eddy. Caught under the roots."

He led her down a shallow slope slick with new mud. A knot of volunteers made room, and there it was on a tarp: a metal box the size of a thick briefcase, rust blooming across its edges, mud lacquered into its seams. A padlock clung to the hasp like a barnacle.

Rowan crouched. The lid wore a faint engraving, half-eaten by time. She wiped across it with her sleeve. Two letters rose in the light, shy and severe: R. H.

The sound the river made grew louder in her head, crowding out the generator's rattle and the wet slap of boots behind her. Her father's initials. The box felt suddenly heavier than its size allowed as if something inside had massed up over the years, weight collected from every unasked question.

Some part of her had always believed the river kept a private archive of everything Cedar Valley tried to forget. Tonight, standing ankle-deep in its leavings, she had the unnerving sense that it had decided to start returning files.

"Where exactly?" Rowan asked, without taking her eyes from the letters.

CJ pointed to a snag of willow roots just beyond the gravel. "Flood dropped it there. Patel spotted the corner after we hauled the branch out. We thought it was just junk until I saw the engraving."

"Anybody else touch it?"

"Just me and Patel. We moved it onto the tarp. Kept the mud where it was. Figured you'd want it that way."

"You figured right," she said. "Get me bolt cutters."

Patel jogged off toward the truck. Rowan blew a slow breath through her nose and let the cold take the back of her throat. The box was old-town hardware-store steel—nothing fancy, nothing ornate. Standard padlock, pitted but intact. The coat of river silt had protected the seams in places; years in the bottom grit had kept it from opening on its own.

Patel returned, shoulders hunched against the drizzle. "Cutters," she said, handing them over.

Rowan tested the hinge on the jaws, set them against the lock, and tightened. The padlock fought like all old things that mattered do—by refusing to acknowledge the present. CJ added his hands to the handles, and together they leaned in. The cutter flexed. The lock let go with a metallic pop that echoed off the water and sent a bird up out of the darkness, complaining.

CJ exhaled. "That felt like a sin."

"Everything that matters does," Rowan said.

She didn't open the box. Not right away. She reached up on impulse and flicked her flashlight off, then signaled to CJ and Patel with a small circle of her index finger. They followed suit. The floodlights still burned, but their corner of the bank slipped a shade darker. Rowan let her eyes adjust until the silver of the river separated from the wet black of the bank.

The habit was older than her badge. Her father had taught it on a summer night when the air had tasted like bug spray and peppermint. *You don't just look at what you're holding, Ro. You look at who's holding you.*

Upstream, on the levee's crest, a shape stood where there was no reason to stand. Too still for a volunteer, too patient for a passerby. Not a posture so much as a presence: waiting for news without wanting to hear it said.

"Levee," Rowan murmured.

CJ followed her gaze. "You want me to—?"

"Not yet," she said. "If they're watching, it's because they need to. Let's make them work for what they think they'll see."

She clicked her light back on, and the world came forward again. Mud, metal, the ancient smell of river rot. Her hands didn't shake, exactly, but they weren't steady either. She slid the latch free and lifted the lid.

Inside, the air was dry—a fist of stale closeness that rose and then fell like a kept breath released. Layers, packed and careful, lived there. A folded oilcloth. An envelope tied with string. A small black notebook elastic-banded shut. An old micro-cassette recorder, the kind secretaries used before time learned to stream. And beneath those, the edge of something hard and rectangular wrapped in waxed paper.

"Bag and tag," Rowan said, and Patel passed her the evidence bags, the Sharpie already uncapped. They worked in a quiet choreography—Rodgering item numbers, noting condition, leaving the order undisturbed. When Rowan lifted the oilcloth, a smell of old gun grease and cedar shavings rose like memory.

She set the recorder aside. The waxed paper parcel was heavier than it looked. She unwrapped it carefully, teasing it apart where it had fused.

A photograph lay inside, protected by the paper's stubbornness. Four faces in sun-faded color, their edges scalloped like it had once lived in a wallet. Two she knew instantly: her father, younger and slim-shouldered in his uniform, and Frank Wallace beside him, not yet soft at the jaw, squinting into the light. Between them, a girl in a floral dress—Emily Carter, seventeen for all time. And on the far edge, half-turned, mouth already sliding into a smile he hadn't paid for, Gideon Pike.

Lydia's voice, from another day, threaded up through Rowan's skull: He could charm a church committee and bleed a contractor dry in the same afternoon.

CJ leaned close, breath fogging the plastic. "That's Pike Sr., isn't it?"

Rowan nodded. Her father's hand was on Emily's shoulder in the picture. Protective or possessive? The camera didn't care. The camera didn't know.

Beneath the photo lay a folded map of the river bend—parcel numbers handwritten in two different inks. One neat and impatient (her father's). One blockier, more theatrical (she'd seen it on a ledger: G.P.). Parcel 18B circled in red. Two neighboring lots circled as well. In the margin near all three, someone had written the same word: contingent.

Rowan's chest tightened. The oilcloth had kept everything intact. Which meant someone had expected to open it again. Someone who hadn't gotten the chance.

She slid the map into a bag and picked up the black notebook. The elastic snapped when she eased it off. Inside, her father's handwriting marched down the first page in a tighter, more private script than his reports. Initials, dates, arrows:

H.S. – mill / river

G.P. – bank, board, "development"

F.W. – on scene / wants out

J.B. – asks wrong questions → river

At the bottom, underlined twice: **If I can't finish, someone has to.**

"Roll call of the old guard," CJ murmured over her shoulder. "Sterling, Pike... Wallace, Brett."

"And whoever thought the river was a filing system," Rowan said. She closed the notebook carefully, as if the ink could still smear, and bagged it.

She set the map aside and untied the string around the envelope. The paper had gone soft with age, the kind of softness that made it travel dangerously close to dissolving. Inside lay three things: a key taped to an index card with the neat label "RECORDER BSMT – LEDGER CABINET," a photocopy of a check from Sterling Development LLC to the county clerk—filing fees circled—and two lines in her father's handwriting at the bottom of the page:

Let the river keep it.

If you're reading this, Pike will already know.

Her throat went tight. The words brought with them the smell of pine cleaner and coffee gone cold, the scrape of a chair on kitchen tile, the rasp of her father's voice when he thought she was asleep. *Let the river keep it, Ro. Some truths drown better than people.* And beneath that, the warning he'd never had the guts to say out loud.

She wanted to be furious. She wanted to throw the whole box into the water and watch it vanish the way it should have years ago. Instead, she slid the note back into its envelope as if not to wake something sleeping.

"Recorder's basement," CJ said softly, pointing to the key. "We finally have a door to open."

"And a reminder we're not the first ones who tried," Rowan said.

She picked up the micro-cassette recorder. Its casing was scuffed, but the tape inside was intact. She thumbed the eject switch. The spool showed the lazy, magnetic brown of possibility.

"Batteries?" Patel asked.

"In my bag," Rowan said. Patel passed them over. Rowan slid the compartment open; two AAs clinked home; the machine's tiny red eye glowed. She pressed Play.

At first there was only the thick whisper of tape moving and the tiny motor's insect whine. Then a room arrived around them—hollow, with the bounce of plaster walls. A chair scraped. A male voice, careful and tired: her father.

"—on the record," Robert Hayes said. "You say it on the record."

Another voice, lower, familiar enough to kick Rowan's heart out of rhythm: Frank Wallace. "It wasn't supposed to be her."

The words she'd heard as a child came back to her in a perfect, sick mirror. She could see the hallway of their old house as if she were inside it again: the night light pouring lemon over the baseboards, her father's office door open to a sliver, smoke curling through, a man's back bent forward, both of them arguing their voices into whispers so they wouldn't wake her. It wasn't supposed to be her.

On the tape, her father said, quiet and hard: "Who was it supposed to be, then?"

A beat. Then Wallace, defensive. "You know how these things go. Pressure. Timing. You look the other way once and it gets easier to keep looking."

"Names," her father said. "We don't leave this room without names."

The tape hiccuped. A second voice joined, thin with nervous bravado: Gideon Pike. "Bob. Let's not pretend you don't understand how towns operate. You write your reports; I keep the lights on. Everybody wins."

"You kill girls," her father said. He didn't raise his voice. He didn't have to.

A chair scraped again; a fist hit wood. "Watch your mouth," Pike said, the smile gone. "We're talking about order."

The recorder clicked. Silence swallowed the edges of the floodlights. CJ's eyes were on Rowan's hands; Patel's on the shape at the levee above them.

Rowan rewound a finger-width and played it again. Same scrape, same ruinous phrase.

"It's genuine," CJ said. "This isn't spliced."

"It's old," Patel added. "Listen to the hiss. No modern file sounds like that."

Rowan stopped the tape and sat back on her heels. The figure on the levee had moved two steps closer while they'd been listening—or she had imagined it? The mist made distances lie. A car door thunked closed up on the road, not near enough to matter, near enough to be counted.

"Bag the recorder," Rowan said. "And the tape stays with me."

Patel nodded. They worked through the rest of the box's contents in order—photograph, map, check copy, key, the little notebook, the oilcloth that smelled like her father's hands after he'd cleaned his shotgun on October Sundays. Rowan labeled each bag with the surety of a woman who refused to let the past keep cheating.

When she finally slid the empty box back onto the tarp, a square shadow remained in the bottom—the outline of one more thing she hadn't removed. She scraped gently with a gloved finger and found a brass tag riveted there, tarnish trying and failing to eat the lettering. Property of Cedar Valley Sheriff's Office – Evidence Retention. A number stamped beneath.

"Jesus," CJ whispered. "He checked it out under evidence."

"Or never checked it in," Rowan said.

They carried the box up the slope as one, the volunteers parting and pretending not to look and failing. The floodlights buzzed overhead like a thousand stubborn insects. On the levee, the watcher had gone—or stepped back beyond the light. A small relief tried to arrive and didn't.

By the trucks, Lydia appeared, hair pinned up in hopeless defiance of the weather, glasses fogged. "I came as soon as CJ texted," she said, breathless. "Tell me you found a story."

Rowan lifted the bagged recorder. "I found a voice."

Lydia peered, then exhaled a humorless laugh. "Your father always did prefer tape to trust." Her eyes slid to the levee and narrowed. "You've got company."

"Had," Rowan said. "Let's not give them a second show."

They worked fast. CJ logged the chain; Patel signed; Lydia scribbled parcel numbers onto a napkin she produced from a pocket like a magician, then immediately lost it and found it again with a curse. The key went into Rowan's breast pocket. Its teeth bit through the thin fabric as if reminding her it existed. The notebook's page of initials replayed behind her eyes like a list of unfinished business: H.S., G.P., F.W., J.B.

"Recorder's office is closed," CJ said.

"Not to keys," Lydia said.

"Not tonight," Rowan answered. "We're soaked, we're loud, and we're being watched. We go in at first light. Fewer eyes, fewer excuses."

"Assuming the basement isn't under water," Lydia said.

Rowan glanced toward the river. In the floodlight, the water looked almost obedient—hunched within the banks they'd forced on it. Debris turned slowly in the eddies like thoughts that wouldn't stay gone.

"If it is," she said, "we'll pump it." She tucked the photo deeper into its bag and slid it into a hard case. "If they buried proof in paper, the river tried to help."

"And Wallace?" Lydia asked quietly. "He was in that room. He's on your father's list. You going to talk to him?"

Rowan thought of the tremor in his voice on the tape. Of the way her father had said, Names. "After the basement," she said. "We start with the ledgers. Then we go to the men who tried to survive them."

They loaded the evidence into the truck. CJ climbed into the passenger seat and wrung his poncho onto the gravel; water slopped, made a small dark continent.

"You okay?" he asked gently, not looking at her when he asked it.

"I don't know the last time I was," Rowan said. She closed the truck door and, for a moment, leaned her forehead against the cool glass. On the other side, the river kept moving like a thought that wouldn't be argued out of existence.

They rolled out with the lights off. The levee cut a low shape against the sky. A single taillight flared at the far end, then winked out. Rowan didn't say anything. CJ didn't need her to.

Downtown, the high school gym still hummed with generator light and a thousand small human noises—cots creaking, soup ladles thudding the bottoms of borrowed pots, kids discovering that echo is a game. Rowan pulled into the police lot instead, where the sodium lights painted everything the color of old coins.

Inside the station, the overnight desk officer looked from the dripping trio to the box and back again. "That from the river?"

"It is now," Rowan said.

"Locker?" he asked.

"Locker," she said, and signed for the key. The click and clunk of the evidence cabinet's tumblers felt like punctuation after a sentence too long to read aloud. She slid the box into the shelf and locked it behind a grate that had outlasted better stories than this one.

Lydia leaned against the wall and tipped her head back, eyes closed. "You know what happens when we print," she said. "Half the town will say your father was a hero for trying to drown the truth. The other half will say he was a coward for not letting it live."

"I know," Rowan said.

"Which side do you land on?"

Rowan didn't answer. Her hands smelled like river and rust and the faint, relentless sweetness of cedar oil. She reached into her pocket and drew out the key, held it up the way a person holds a relic in a church.

"I land on this," she said. "On doors we're done letting stay closed."

"And on names," she added, almost to herself. "Starting with the ones who were in that room."

CJ nodded once. "First light."

Lydia's mouth twitched. "If you die opening that door, I'm writing your obituary first."

"Spell my name right," Rowan said.

"No promises," Lydia said, pushing off the wall. "But I'll try."

They stepped back into the thinning rain. The courthouse clock tolled, then tolled again, catching up with itself as if embarrassed. Somewhere, a car engine started and then thought better of it. The river made the same old sound it had made before they were born and would make after they were gone—something between whisper and warning.

Rowan looked toward the levee and thought of the photograph, the girl in the floral dress, the men whose hands had been too sure, the note that had asked the water to do what men would not. She thought of the tape, of the phrase that would not leave her body: It wasn't supposed to be her.

"I know," she said to no one in particular, to everyone who had ever said it. "It never is."

She closed her eyes against the sting of the rain and opened them again to the work that was left. The morning would come. The basement would wait, or it wouldn't. Wallace would talk, or he wouldn't. The door would open, or it would learn what it meant to be opened.

What the river returned wasn't mercy. It was a ledger. And Rowan had decided, once and for all, to read it out loud.

Chapter 12

The Recorder's Basement

The world before dawn was a gray so complete it felt personal. The rain had eased, but Cedar Valley still wore the hangover of a storm—streets slick, drains gurgling, trees bowing under the weight of their own survival.

Rowan parked half a block from City Hall, her cruiser's headlights off. Beside her, CJ rubbed his hands together for warmth. Lydia sat in the back seat, thermos in hand, glasses fogged.

"You realize," Lydia murmured, "that breaking into a municipal building before sunrise is generally frowned upon."

Rowan didn't look at her. "Good thing we're not breaking in. We have a key."

Lydia snorted. "Yes, a key from a decades-old lockbox dredged up from the river. That's totally the same as a warrant."

Rowan shot her a look in the rearview mirror. "You can wait in the car."

"Hell no," Lydia said, tightening her coat. "If this basement eats you alive, I'm getting the story firsthand."

CJ smiled faintly, but the humor didn't reach his eyes. "Let's move before we start a paper trail of our own."

They crossed the square, their boots whispering against the wet brick. City Hall loomed ahead—stoic, self-important, and dark except for the dim orange glow of an emergency light near the clerk's entrance. Rowan's breath clouded in front of her as she slid the key from the river lockbox into the lock. It resisted, then turned with a satisfying click.

For a flicker of a second, she heard her father's voice in her head: Let the river keep it.

She turned the knob anyway.

"After you," she said, pushing the door open.

The hallway inside smelled of mildew and lemon cleaner fighting a losing battle. A few framed photos lined the walls—ribbon cuttings, holiday parades, the mayor shaking hands with anyone who'd stand still long enough. Each frame gleamed faintly as the flashlight beams passed.

CJ swept the hall with his light. "Basement door should be at the end, right?"

Rowan nodded. "Behind Records."

They moved carefully, their steps echoing off the tile. The silence was thick enough to feel, interrupted only by the slow drip of water from somewhere unseen. When they reached the stairwell, the smell changed—wetter, heavier.

Lydia wrinkled her nose. "Oh, that's promising."

Rowan descended first, one hand on the rail. The beam of her flashlight found the landing, then the next flight. The deeper they went, the more the air pressed down—damp, metallic, threaded with the faint sweetness of mold.

At the bottom, water covered the floor in a thin, shivering sheet. Their reflections warped as they stepped off the last stair.

"Welcome to the swamp archives," Lydia muttered.

Rows of file cabinets stood like tombstones, some tipped, some already surrendering to rust. Paper floated in the water like pale leaves. Rowan's flashlight glinted off the brass tags on the nearest cabinet.

"Assignments," she said. "This is it."

She pulled the key from her jacket pocket, wiped it on her sleeve, and knelt beside the cabinet. The lock was old—the kind designed when people still believed locks could keep out curiosity. The key slid in without protest, turned with a heavy metallic sigh.

The drawer resisted, swollen from moisture. CJ crouched beside her and pulled with her. It gave suddenly, sending a wave of cold water lapping against their boots.

Inside: folders, hundreds of them, some so waterlogged they'd fused together. Rowan lifted one gingerly, her gloves slick with mud. The folder label read RIVER BEND DE-VELOPMENT — 1993–1994.

Her pulse spiked. "Got it."

Lydia waded closer, flashlight beam trembling slightly. "Tell me there's a payoff in there."

Rowan opened the folder on top of an overturned crate, using her flashlight for light. The papers inside were warped but legible—contracts, deeds, transfer agreements. Parcel numbers leapt out at her. 18B. 18C. 19A. The same three lots circled on the map from the lockbox.

"Here," CJ said, pointing. "Assignment of deed—signed by Harold Sterling."

Rowan traced the signatures with her eyes. Beneath Sterling's name was another, written in tighter, surer strokes. Gideon Pike.

Lydia let out a low whistle. "Father of our esteemed mayor. Signed, sealed, and delivered. You've got him, Hayes."

"Not yet," Rowan said. "Keep reading."

She turned the next page.

It wasn't there.

A torn edge ran jagged across the paper where a document should have been. Only a corner remained, a single handwritten notation at the bottom: Filed with supplemental agreement.

"Where's the supplement?" CJ asked.

Rowan rifled through the folder—pages missing, out of order, the smell of mildew growing stronger. "It's been pulled. Too clean. Maybe last week."

She tilted the folder so her flashlight caught the imprint left in the water residue. The rectangle where the missing page had rested was pale, cleaner than the sheets around it.

"Someone came down here and cherry-picked the one thing that could tie Pike to my father's investigation," she said. "Subtle."

Rowan stared at the empty space until her jaw ached. The key in her pocket felt heavier. "They knew we'd come looking."

A faint sound answered her—the creak of a door above them. All three froze.

CJ's voice dropped. "You locked the door behind us, right?"

Rowan nodded slowly. "Yeah."

Another sound followed—the soft rhythm of footsteps descending the stairs. Not hurried. Careful. Someone who knew the layout.

Lydia's eyes widened. "Please tell me that's the janitor with a bad sense of timing."

Rowan motioned for silence. She snapped the folder shut, slid it into her bag, and killed her flashlight. The others followed suit. The basement plunged into darkness, broken only by the faint shimmer of a flashlight beam sweeping the far wall from above.

The steps paused halfway down. Water rippled near the landing.

Rowan's pulse drummed in her ears. The smell of the river was stronger now—silt and cold and something old enough to remember its own crimes.

She leaned close to CJ and whispered, "Back stairwell. Go."

They moved slowly, wading through the water, each step deliberate. Lydia's breath came ragged but quiet. The beam from the intruder's flashlight arced across the room, catching the glint of metal and water, grazing the top of the cabinet they'd opened.

The steps resumed. Closer.

CJ reached the back stairwell door and tried the handle. Locked.

Rowan mouthed, "Key." He shook his head—it wasn't the same kind.

The beam moved again, now sweeping the center aisle. Whoever it was knew where to look.

Rowan's hand went to her weapon, the leather of the holster slick against her fingers. She glanced at the row of filing cabinets, calculated the line of sight.

A shadow crossed the beam—tall, lean. Male. A raincoat, dark hood up.

Lydia made a small, involuntary sound—a gasp disguised as breath.

The figure stopped.

Then the light clicked off.

For a heartbeat, the dark felt absolute. Then came the sound of movement—slow, deliberate splashes across the water. Coming toward them.

Rowan raised her weapon. "Police!" she called, her voice cutting through the dark. "Identify yourself!"

No answer. Just the sound of another step.

Then, suddenly, a door slammed somewhere behind them, and light flooded the stairwell.

"Rowan?" A voice called—one she recognized instantly. Patel. "You down here?"

Rowan exhaled so sharply it hurt. "Patel! Basement! Someone else is—"

She turned back toward the aisle, but the footsteps were gone. The water stilled, ripples fading into nothing. Whoever had been there had vanished, leaving only the whisper of settling debris.

Patel appeared at the bottom of the stairs, flashlight slicing through the gloom. "The hell happened? Thought I saw movement from outside."

Rowan lowered her weapon, heart still hammering. "You did. Someone was down here. Watching."

CJ ran a hand through his damp hair. "They knew exactly where to look. The file's missing pages, Patel. Clean tear, recent."

Patel swore softly. "Whoever it was must have heard you unlock the door. Maybe followed you in."

"Or never left," Lydia said, glancing toward the black mouth of a maintenance tunnel branching off the far wall. "That doesn't look OSHA-approved."

Rowan followed her gaze. The tunnel was narrow, carved into the concrete decades ago for wiring and drainage. The grate covering it hung loose. She crouched and shined her light inside. Footprints. Muddy. Leading inward.

"CJ," she said quietly, "call it in. Get two more units down here. And a camera."

He nodded and stepped aside to radio.

Lydia stood beside her, staring into the tunnel. "You think that's where your father's ghosts went?"

"I think that's where our suspect did," Rowan said. "And I'm done letting them walk away."

Patel frowned. "You want to follow them down there?"

Rowan holstered her weapon. The echo of her father's taped voice scraped across her memory: You look the other way once and it gets easier to keep looking. "Not tonight," she said. "We don't chase shadows. We mark the way and come back with light."

By the time they surfaced, dawn had broken—a bruised pink bleeding into the clouds over Cedar Valley. Rainwater pooled in the cracks of Main Street, reflecting the courthouse dome and the bare branches that fenced it in.

CJ finished securing the perimeter while Patel briefed the arriving officers. Lydia leaned against the cruiser, scribbling in her notebook despite the drizzle.

Rowan stood on the curb, staring at the courthouse steps. The river was out of sight from here, but she could feel it—the quiet pull of something vast and patient beneath the town's foundations.

CJ joined her, rubbing his eyes. "You think the missing page is what your dad was hiding?"

"Maybe," she said. "Or what he was protecting."

Lydia looked up from her notes. "You really think he was protecting Pike? After what you heard on that tape?"

Rowan shook her head. "Not Pike. Someone else. Maybe someone caught in the middle. Maybe Emily. Maybe whoever signed that 'supplemental agreement' and didn't live long enough to regret it."

The thought hung between them, heavy as the humidity.

Patel approached, rain dripping from her cap. "Units found tire impressions behind the building. Fresh, from last night. Two sets. One matches city fleet tread."

"Maintenance trucks?" Rowan asked.

"Or mayor's," Patel said. "They share a pool."

Lydia muttered, "Of course they do."

CJ zipped his jacket, shoulders hunched. "So Pike's people are cleaning up while we're still getting our boots on."

Rowan looked at the courthouse dome again, the first weak sunlight catching the weathervane. "Let them clean. We'll see what they missed."

She reached into her jacket pocket and touched the key again, the metal still cold against her skin. The same key that had opened her father's box. The same key that had unlocked a door meant to stay shut. Somewhere in the evidence locker, the J.B. badge and her father's tape waited, their silent weight leaning against this moment.

Lydia closed her notebook with a snap. "What's next, Detective?"

Rowan's gaze drifted toward the river valley beyond town. "The maintenance tunnel," she said. "If Pike or whoever's behind this used it once, they'll use it again."

"Lovely," Lydia said dryly. "Nothing like chasing corruption through ankle-deep sewage to remind a girl why she got into journalism."

CJ smirked. "You could've stayed in the car."

"And miss the glory?" Lydia said, lighting a cigarette. "Not a chance."

Rowan watched the smoke curl upward, merging with the morning fog. "We'll regroup at noon. Patel, get the lab to prioritize what we pulled from that folder. CJ, see if the recorder's office has a log of who accessed archives in the last week. Names, time stamps, key cards—if it exists, I want it."

CJ nodded. "On it."

Lydia blew out smoke. "And me?"

Rowan's lips curved just slightly. "You dig where I can't. Off the record, for now. Old subscription lists, donation rolls, any mention of parcel 18B. And Jonah Brett—J.B. doesn't stay a set of initials."

Lydia smiled, all teeth. "Music to my ink-stained ears."

They broke apart as the sun tried, weakly, to claim the morning. The courthouse clock chimed seven times, each strike echoing across the wet square.

Rowan stood for a long moment after the others left, listening to the water still gurgling through the storm drains. It was the same sound she'd heard in every flood season—steady, unbothered, relentless.

She looked toward the river's direction, though she couldn't see it from here. "You can keep your secrets for now," she murmured. "But I'm coming back."

The wind shifted, carrying the faintest scent of silt and something older. It almost sounded like the river answered—not in words, but in a low, persistent murmur.

Rowan took it as agreement.

Chapter 13

The Turmoil Beneath

By noon, the sun had vanished again, leaving Cedar Valley washed in a dim, pewter light. The courthouse square smelled of damp stone and diesel. Rowan stood beside the maintenance tunnel entrance behind City Hall, where the grate still hung loose from the night before. Mud smeared the concrete lip, and fresh footprints had already half-filled with water.

CJ crouched beside the opening, flashlight clipped to his vest. "Whoever was down here didn't bother to cover their tracks."

Patel shifted the equipment bag on her shoulder. "Or they didn't have time. The water's rising again."

Rowan looked toward the river. It was out of sight, but she could hear it—a dull, steady roar threading through the low clouds like distant thunder. The flood they'd just barely held at the levee felt closer underground than it did topside.

"We go in," she said. "Take what we need and get out before this turns into a swimming lesson."

She descended first, boots scraping the narrow rungs of the ladder slick with condensation. The tunnel swallowed her in silence. The air was close and metallic, cold enough to raise goosebumps. A thin sheet of water moved sluggishly across the floor, reflecting the tremor of their flashlights.

CJ's voice echoed behind her. "You sure about this? I read once that most bad decisions start with the words 'we go in.'"

"Then let's make it one of the good ones," she said.

At the bottom, they could just stand upright. The concrete walls wept moisture, a slow, constant drip that sounded almost alive. Faded paint on the wall read City Works 1951. Rusted pipes ran overhead like the exposed ribs of some sleeping creature.

The beam of Rowan's flashlight revealed a junction ahead. The tunnel split—one branch veering toward the courthouse foundation, the other sloping west toward The Bottoms. The smell of the river was stronger that way, full of silt and rot.

CJ's light caught something on the wall—a handprint, smeared in mud. Below it, scratched into the surface with a piece of metal, were the letters R.H.

Rowan's pulse quickened. "He was here."

Patel turned toward her. "Your father?"

She nodded, tracing the letters with her glove. "Robert Hayes. This wasn't random."

Jonah Brett's badge, the J.B. stamped in brass, the evidence box from the river with her father's note—all of it lined up in her head like incomplete coordinates pointing down, not out.

They followed the west tunnel. It narrowed, forcing them single file. The sound of their boots sloshing through water mixed with the slow hiss of air escaping from old seams in the pipework.

After a dozen yards, Rowan's light fell on something wedged against the wall—a tin lunchbox, dented and orange with rust. She pried it free, mud breaking loose in ribbons. Inside was a small roll of undeveloped film sealed in plastic, a folding pocketknife, and a sheriff's patch worn almost to threads.

CJ whistled softly. "That's ancient. Fifties, maybe earlier. Lines up with our friend Jonah Brett."

Rowan turned the patch over. The stitching still faintly spelled out Cedar County Sheriff's Dept. "Whoever left this wanted it hidden, not lost."

They kept going until the tunnel opened into a circular chamber. The ceiling rose high enough to stand upright. Light filtered down through a rusted grate far above, a pale shaft that caught motes of dust drifting like snow.

"Looks like a drainage nexus," Patel said, sweeping her beam around.

The floor was littered with debris—branches, broken glass, the hollow shell of a bicycle tire. In one corner, a heavy steel door waited, padlocked and streaked with rust.

Rowan's light skimmed the surface. Someone had scratched words near the latch. Let the river keep it.

She froze. "That's my father's handwriting."

CJ swallowed. "He was here all right. The question is—what was he trying to keep?"

Patel took out a pry bar. "Guess we're about to find out."

The lock resisted, groaning as she worked the bar under the shackle. The sound echoed down the tunnel, loud as thunder. When it finally snapped, the noise startled even Patel.

Rowan hesitated a heartbeat before pushing the door. It opened with a moan of metal against concrete, releasing a breath of air that smelled of oil, river silt, and old paper.

The room beyond was small, lined with shelving and toppled file cabinets. A desk sat broken in one corner, drawers spilled open like entrails. Faded city maintenance logs clung to the walls in soggy layers.

CJ's flashlight found a cluster of photographs tacked up with rusted nails—black-and-white shots of the mill, the riverbanks, the Carter farmhouse. The faces of men in work clothes stared back from another image, blurred by time.

Rowan stepped closer. In the center hung one color photo: her father, Sheriff Robert Hayes, shaking hands with Harold Sterling and Gideon Pike in front of the mill. The caption scrawled on the back read, River Bend groundbreaking, May 1993.

Her throat tightened. "He was part of it."

"Or they wanted it to look that way," CJ said quietly.

Patel ran her light along the shelves. "You'll want to see this."

Boxes sat stacked in the corner, their labels faded but legible: WEXLER LEDGER (COPY), CARTER CASE—EVIDENCE HOLD, DISPOSAL RECORDS 1993–94.

Rowan pulled the top box toward her. Inside were photocopies of deeds, handwritten notes, and a small cassette sealed in plastic. The label read: Interview – Emily Carter (Prelim).

Her breath caught. "He talked to her before she disappeared."

Patel dug a handheld recorder from her kit and snapped the tape into place. The player hissed to life, and a girl's voice—young, fragile—filled the chamber.

"It wasn't supposed to be me."

Rowan's heart stopped for a beat. The echo of another phrase—It wasn't supposed to be her—ghosted through her memory, layered over a childhood doorway and Frank Wallace's voice on the tape from the river box. The words wrapped around each other like current; nobody was ever supposed to be the one.

On the recording, her father's voice cut in: calm, weary. "Emily, who told you that?"

A pause. The faint sound of crying.

"Mr. Pike. He said my family was supposed to sign the papers. Said they didn't, and somebody had to fix it."

Rowan's pulse thudded in her ears.

"He said he'd take care of it," Emily whispered. "Said the river could wash anything clean."

The tape clicked, then static.

Rowan stared at the player, willing more words to come. "That's it?"

Patel checked the counter. "That's all there is."

CJ looked around the room. "If your dad recorded that, why hide it instead of using it?"

"Maybe he tried," Rowan said. "And someone stopped him. Or he realized the people who should care were the ones writing the checks."

Her gaze skimmed the DISPOSAL RECORDS box. The river hadn't just carried bodies—it had carried chemicals, money, leverage. A whole ledger, disguised as water.

Before anyone could answer, a distant clang echoed through the tunnel—the sound of metal on stone. They froze.

CJ whispered, "Please tell me that's the pipes expanding."

Rowan killed her flashlight. The chamber fell into darkness. From somewhere beyond the doorway came the faint rhythm of footsteps splashing through shallow water.

Patel drew her sidearm. "Someone followed us."

Rowan's voice was a whisper. "Stay low. Back wall."

They crouched behind the toppled desk. Light flickered outside the room—a flashlight beam sweeping slow arcs across the chamber. It stopped on the door, lingered, then moved on.

A man's silhouette appeared in the threshold. Tall, wearing a raincoat. The hood obscured his face. He took two steps inside, scanning.

CJ's grip tightened on his flashlight, ready to swing. Rowan shook her head sharply.

The man knelt, examining the broken padlock on the floor. His voice was barely audible over the dripping pipes. "Too late."

Then he turned and walked back into the tunnel, the beam of his flashlight bouncing off the low ceiling until it disappeared around the bend.

For a long time, none of them spoke.

Finally, Patel exhaled. "I'm starting to think your father had the right idea—let the river keep it."

Rowan retrieved the cassette and tucked it into her pocket. It felt heavier than it should. "Not this time."

They left the room quickly, retracing their steps to the junction. The water was higher now, rippling around their calves. The tunnel breathed like a living thing.

Halfway back, they heard Lydia's voice echo faintly from the entrance. "Hayes! You down there?"

"Here!" Rowan called back. "What's going on?"

Lydia's flashlight appeared above them as she crouched near the ladder. "You're not going to like this. City truck just pulled out of the alley—no plates, tinted windows. Whoever was driving it was watching the grate."

"Pike's cleanup crew," CJ muttered.

Lydia handed down a damp manila envelope. "They dropped this when they peeled out."

Rowan opened it. Inside were photographs—telephoto shots taken from a distance. Her car. CJ leaving his apartment. Lydia at the Gazette. Even a grainy image of her father's old house, the porch light burning.

"They've been following us," she said quietly.

Patel glanced toward the street above. "Then let's not make it easy for them."

They climbed out one at a time. The sky had turned the color of pewter again, the air thick with the promise of more rain. The courthouse clock struck two, each chime echoing across the empty square.

CJ wiped water from his face. "We've got a tape that implicates Pike, a missing file, and now surveillance photos. That's not a coincidence."

"No," Rowan said. "It's a message."

Lydia wrung rain from her hair. "What kind?"

"The kind that says we're getting close."

They crossed the square toward the cruiser, the wind carrying the smell of the river even this far uptown. Rowan paused at the curb and looked back at City Hall. The building's brick face looked solid, trustworthy—until you knew what was buried beneath it.

She felt the cassette through her jacket pocket, its edges cold and solid. Emily Carter's voice echoed in her head, fragile and resigned.

It wasn't supposed to be me.

Jonah Brett's badge. The ledger in the mill. The payments to the Carters. Parcel 18B. Her father's taped argument with Pike and Wallace. All of it stacked up like sandbags against a flood of lies.

CJ started the engine, and the cruiser's headlights cut through the fog. "Where to?"

"Back to the station," Rowan said. "We log the evidence and make copies before anyone else gets a chance to erase it."

"And after that?" Patel asked.

Rowan's gaze drifted toward the swollen line of trees that hid the river from view. "We go back to The Bottoms. If Pike dumped bodies, proof, anything—it's there. And now we know Emily was part of the bargain they tried to make with the water."

Lydia groaned softly. "You realize every horror movie ever made starts with someone saying that."

Rowan managed the faintest smile. "Good thing we're not in one."

CJ eased the cruiser onto Main Street. Rain began again, light at first, then heavier, drumming against the roof in a relentless rhythm. The wipers beat time to Rowan's thoughts—steady, certain, impossible to drown out.

As they turned toward the bridge, she caught sight of the river below, swollen and dark, pressing hard against its banks. It moved like something alive, purposeful. For a moment, she thought she saw a shimmer near the bend—a flash of silver, maybe light on water, maybe something else entirely.

The current carried it away before she could be sure.

Rowan leaned back, voice low. "You've kept your secrets long enough," she murmured. "Now it's our turn."

The river didn't answer, but the sound of the rain grew louder, as if it approved.

Chapter 14

The River's Price

The rain hadn't stopped, not really. It only changed its rhythm—soft, hard, soft again—like the river deciding how quickly it wanted to confess. By dawn, Cedar Valley looked bruised. The courthouse lawn gleamed like glass, and the square smelled of wet leaves, diesel, and the faint sweetness of crushed corn from somewhere downwind.

Rowan parked near the levee, wipers chattering, jaw set. The cassette lay between her and CJ in a clear evidence bag, the label in her father's block letters: Interview: Emily Carter (Prelim). It seemed to vibrate with its own pulse, as if waiting for the right nerve to press.

"You ever get the feeling the whole town's holding its breath?" CJ asked, both hands wrapped around a Styrofoam cup that had long gone cold.

"It's been holding it for twenty years," Rowan said, staring at the swollen river. "Maybe today it exhales."

A civil-defense siren moaned low, then rose. On the radio, a calm voice clipped through static: "—county officials reporting a second levee breach along the west bank. Evacuation for River Bend advised. Repeat, residents in River Bend, move to higher ground immediately."

CJ groaned. "The river's taking attendance."

"Then we don't let it call our names," Rowan said. She killed the engine. Rain thrummed on the roof like impatient fingers.

They jogged toward the staging area where volunteers stacked sandbags in a frenzied assembly line. National Guard trucks idled, headlights cutting pale tunnels through mist. A woman in a church windbreaker handed out ponchos with the authority of someone who'd organized a hundred potlucks and three floods. "You two—detectives?—take these. You'll be soaked through in five."

"We're already soaked through," CJ said, shrugging into his.

Lydia Bass materialized like a rumor, hair slicked to her forehead, camera clutched to her chest in a plastic wrap.

"You're late," she said. "North levee's flirting with disaster. The mayor's flirting with Channel Eight."

"Any sign of Pike in person?" Rowan asked.

"Just his grin," Lydia said. "He's promising sandbags and salvation. He'd hand out forgiveness if it came in cases."

Patel jogged up, radio pressed to her ear. "We've got a pickup stuck halfway to the trees near the bridge. Driver won't leave. Says he'll take his chances with the river."

"Who is it?" Rowan asked.

"Dale Krantz."

CJ blew air through his teeth. "The River Rat."

Rowan was already moving. "Let's make sure he doesn't become river bait."

They slid into the cruiser and barreled toward the bridge, tires hissing on waterlogged asphalt. As they crested the rise, the world narrowed to brown water and bent trees. The river had swollen beyond its usual boundaries, tugging at roadside ditches like a thief testing windows. The pickup sat nose-down, rear wheels spinning uselessly in the current. Its headlights threw shaky cones across the flood, illuminating branches, a plastic trash can, the shiny white underbelly of a drowned refrigerator.

Rowan splashed toward the driver's side, cold water surging around her shins. "Krantz! You need to get out of the truck! Now!"

The window cracked open a few inches. Dale Krantz's face, all windburn and stubbornness, leaned into the gap. "You people always show up when there's a camera," he yelled. "Where were you when they were dumping? Where were you when the trucks came at night?"

"We're here now," Rowan said, fighting to keep her voice level. "The levee's going to break. You have to move."

Krantz's eyes glittered with rain or rage. "They're under there!" He jabbed a finger toward the churn. "The ones who wouldn't sell. The river's got 'em. Your precious Pike made sure."

CJ tried to take some of the heat out of it. "Dale, nobody's arguing with you. We just need—"

The levee upstream made a terrible, animal sound, a bass groan that shivered through asphalt into bone. Rowan looked up in time to see the wall bulge and then tear like wet paper.

"Move!" Patel shouted.

The flood hit in a single, body-sized shove. Rowan went down hard, lungs evacuated by panic and impact. The current caught her, spun her, slammed her shoulder against the truck. Cold knifed through her clothes. She heard CJ curse, felt Patel's hand clamp his jacket, then her wrist. For a dizzy, infinite second she wasn't sure which direction was up.

A sharp, frantic sound cut through the roar. Barking—high, terrified, relentless.

Rowan twisted. In the bed of the pickup, a brindled dog skittered, claws hammering metal, water climbing fast. Something in her body moved before her brain did. She kicked away from the truck, half-swimming, half-falling along the side until she could reach the bed. The dog lunged; she grabbed its scruff and the edge of the bed in the same motion. For a heartbeat her boots found nothing and the water tried to take her. Then Patel's hand was there again, iron on her forearm, hauling her and forty pounds of shaking dog up the embankment.

The truck groaned like a ship, lifted, twisted, and vanished in a froth of brown. The sound it made going under was obscene, metal grinding stone.

"You're insane," CJ panted, eyes wide. The dog, drenched, leaned into his chest like he'd always been its person.

"Occupational hazard," Rowan rasped, on hands and knees, trying to remember how to breathe. The world smelled like mud and oil and terror.

Behind them, the water chewed the road and spit it out, piece by piece. A line of cottonwoods along the far bank swayed and then toppled all at once, roots clawing air as if that would help. People yelled from the staging area. A siren yowled, then died. Somewhere a child cried and someone shushed him with a voice that wasn't certain.

They made it back to the cordon on shaky legs, the dog pressed to CJ like a wet lantern. A paramedic thrust a blanket at Rowan. "You're gray," he said. "Sit down before you fall down."

"I can't," she said, but she let him drape the blanket anyway. Lydia appeared and stuck a microphone in her face. Rowan raised one eyebrow and Lydia pulled it back with a snort.

"Had to try," Lydia said, eyes full and hard. "You look like something the river chewed and changed its mind about."

"Nice to be loved," Rowan said.

By noon the rain settled into a petulant drizzle. The river, sated for the moment, slumped against its banks. Crews worked in the raw aftermath: pumps thumped; shovels thunked; someone passed out sandwiches wrapped in wax paper that tasted like salt and fatigue. The square felt emptied out—like a carnival packed up too fast, leaving behind a few unlucky tent stakes and a smell you couldn't blame on anyone.

Rowan stood on the courthouse steps with Lydia, both wrapped to the knees in emergency blankets. Lydia handed over a thermos that had seen more action than most marriages. "Drink before your teeth start playing castanets."

Rowan took it and didn't taste the coffee. "You ever think maybe this town doesn't want to be saved?"

"Oh it wants it," Lydia said. "It just prefers to be saved quietly."

Patel trotted up from the river, mud up to her calves, hair stringing water. Behind her, two volunteers carried a plastic tub wrapped in tape. CJ followed, limping slightly, the rescued dog now wearing a child's T-shirt like a cape.

"They found this wedged under the bridge piling," Patel said. "Almost lost it when the pump hiccuped."

CJ set the tub down. Inside: a swollen ledger, a clump of waterlogged files, a tarnished photo frame with no glass. The ledger's cover had once been expensive—good leather, good ink. Now it was a sponge.

Rowan peeled it open gently. The pages sucked and released, the ink bleeding in places, stubborn in others. The crest at the top of each page still showed through in gold leaf: Sterling Development.

Patel held out a waterproof envelope. The county seal, smeared but defiant, clung to one corner. "This was floating near it."

Rowan slit it open with a fingernail. Inside lay a single sheet of paper: thin, brittle, perfect. The missing assignment agreement.

Her father's signature sat beside Harold Sterling's and Gideon Pike's. The letters were patient, controlled, familiar. Beneath, in sharp darker ink, three words: Filed under duress.

For a second, the world tilted. Sound went away, color went with it. There was only the pen stroke and the hand that had made it—the hand that had lifted her to the top of the fridge to watch fireworks, the hand that had squeezed her shoulder when he had nothing safe to say.

"Why would he sign it?" CJ asked, voice careful.

Rowan traced the lower margin. Another note, so faint you had to want it to be there: Truth comes due.

"He didn't bury it," she said. "He banked it. In the one place that outlasts men."

Lydia looked toward the river, her mouth a tight line. "He hid it in the current."

"Or left it where the current could eventually carry it back," Patel said. "That's a hell of a gamble."

Rowan slipped the page into a fresh sleeve. Her hands had stopped shaking. "He gambled on time. And on me."

Across the square, a portable generator coughed, caught. The courthouse clock chimed six times and then, true to habit, chimed again, late to its own count. A volunteer shouted something about more sand. The dog sneezed and sneezed again, indignant.

"Where's Pike?" Rowan asked.

Lydia checked her phone, shielded it from the drizzle with her coat. "City Hall. Seven o'clock. He's doing his 'Cedar Valley Strong' routine."

Patel said, "We could walk this straight into the county attorney's office and let the machine grind."

"The machine is why we're here," Rowan said. She turned toward City Hall, its windows glowing like a story that wanted to be heard. "He's hidden behind rooms and committees long enough. He can answer under the lights."

"Bold," Lydia said. "Reckless. Absolutely my kind of stupid. Let's go."

The press conference drew them as if it had heat. Reporters huddled under tents, umbrellas bumping, rain ticking a bright rhythm against nylon. Cables ran like snakes through puddles. Pike stood at the podium, sleeves rolled, chin up, the wind combing his hair with just enough disrespect to make him look human. He had the voice of a man who'd taught himself to sound like a father and a general and a televangelist all at once.

"—and our thoughts are with those displaced," he said. "We will rebuild. We always do."

Rowan stepped from the crowd and onto the low riser. Cameras swung. Umbrellas tilted. A dozen people said her name at once, all of them in different ways.

"Mr. Mayor," she said.

His smile didn't break, it shuttered. "Detective Hayes," he said warmly enough to frost glass. "We're grateful you're here. These are times for unity."

"Then you won't mind a little truth." She stood beside the podium, not behind it. She held the sleeve with the agreement so that only he could see it.

For the first time since she'd known him, his eyes moved before his mouth did. The recognition was there—fast, clear, then buried.

"An old administrative form," he said gently, for the microphones. "A footnote in a complicated history."

"An assignment transferring the Carters' land to Sterling Development," Rowan said, loud enough for the front row to hear but not the back. "Signed by you. Signed by my father. Filed under duress."

A wiry man in a Channel Eight jacket leaned in. "Under duress?"

Rowan didn't look at him. She looked at Pike and said, "Your supplemental agreement went missing from the recorder's basement last week. We found the rest. And this."

CJ stepped forward and set a small weatherproof speaker on the edge of the podium. He pressed a button. The hiss came first, thin and insistent. Then Emily's voice, soft but arrow-true: It wasn't supposed to be me.

Reporters stopped writing. Someone's umbrella folded in a gust of wind and nobody helped because every pair of hands had something in it that suddenly felt dumb. The rain got quiet. Or maybe everything else did.

Who told you that? her father's voice asked, steady, tired.

A Mr. Pike, Emily whispered. He said my family was supposed to sign the papers. Said they didn't, and somebody had to fix it. He said the river could wash anything clean.

The tape clicked on air like a door closing. Then there was only rain again and the glazed sound of people remembering how to breathe.

"That is a fabrication," Pike said, a laugh clinging to the underside of his words like algae. "Easily done with modern technology. We live in an age of slander."

Lydia barked a humorless laugh. "That tape is older than half the crowd."

Rowan held his gaze. "It's a thirty-year-old microcassette pulled from a rusted locker in a maintenance tunnel," she said. "My father's voice. Emily Carter's voice. Both naming your family and your project."

He leaned toward her. Close enough that the crowd couldn't hear, but every camera saw the angle of his jaw. "You think you can drown me with a fairy tale and a broken toy?"

"I don't need to," she said softly. "The river's already rising."

He turned to the crowd to reclaim them. "Ladies and gentlemen, I—"

Lydia's voice cut across him like a thrown rope. "Mayor Pike, did you or your father ever threaten Emily Carter or her family regarding the River Bend acquisition?"

He glared at her, then turned the glare into a smile so expertly it would have earned him applause under any other sky. "Absolutely not. Those accusations are cruel to the memories of good people."

"Then you won't mind answering a few more," Rowan said. "Where were you the night Emily disappeared? Why was a page removed from the recorder's file last week? Why is there surveillance of me, my partner, and Ms. Bass in a city envelope dropped by a city truck?"

The crowd became a hive. Questions stung the air. Flashbulbs stuttered. Somewhere a deputy shouted for space and got none.

Pike put his hands up in a gesture that had saved him a dozen times. "Cedar Valley, please. This is a time of crisis. We must come together."

Rowan stepped closer to the microphones. She didn't raise her voice. She let the quiet around it do the lifting. "We are together," she said. "Right now. All of us who live here. And we deserve to know who decided this river had room for our dead."

That was when the first chant started. It wasn't loud. It wasn't organized. It was just three people who had lost something and found their tongues at the same time: "Answer her. Answer her."

It spread the way things do in towns—sideways, then forward, then back. People who'd come for a photo op found themselves in a story they couldn't leave without choosing a part.

Pike's aides pushed through with the practiced panic of people who had carried him out of fires before. Deputies angled in, one hand extended to Rowan, the other to the mayor. Patel surfaced at Rowan's elbow, a small island of calm. "You've made your point," she murmured. "Let the paper eat him now."

Rowan didn't move. She looked at Pike until the camera lights bleached his face to paper. "You can't bury a river," she said. "It remembers."

He was smiling again when the deputies took his arms. He always remembered the smile, even when he couldn't manage the truth. His mouth kept it up as they led him down the steps. It looked like a decision from far away. Up close, it looked like a man whose face had forgotten the right shape.

The square exhaled. The chant dried up. People started talking about coffee, about cots, about whether the church basement had power. A volunteer walked past with a mop on one shoulder like a rifle.

CJ rubbed a hand down his face, leaving a clean streak among the mud. "You think that did it?"

"It opened a door," Rowan said. "There's more on the other side. There's still a missing page, and someone who knew that tunnel better than we do."

They found quiet at the edge of the square where the railing overlooked the river. The water had lost its white teeth and gone back to the slow gnaw. Pieces of someone's fence moved past like tired punctuation. A blue cooler bobbed, then decided against drowning and lodged in a snag.

Lydia lit a cigarette and cupped it from the wind. The ember made a small, stubborn star. "If you die chasing this," she said, "I'm writing your obituary first."

"Keep it short," Rowan said.

"Two words," Lydia said. "Raised hell."

CJ leaned his elbows on the rail. The dog—claimed by a pair of teenagers who swore he was theirs and named him Buckshot—slept curled at their feet, paw twitching at a flood he would only ever half-remember. "You think the river's finally done talking?" CJ asked.

"The river never shuts up," Rowan said. "We just forget how to listen."

A towboat's horn drifted upriver, low and plaintive. Beyond the trees, sirens wound down and then, almost shyly, stopped. The courthouse clock decided it was eight and told everyone, twice.

Rowan touched the sleeve in her coat pocket—the agreement her father had signed and argued with in the same breath. She pictured his hand, the ache in it after too many pens and too many nights. She pictured him in that tunnel, choosing a hiding place that would outlast men and lies.

"The river takes its own," she said.

Lydia looked at her. "And tonight?"

"Tonight it gave one back."

They stood there until the cold found the seams in their blankets and the night decided to be just night again. Then they turned toward the lights, toward coffee that would taste like victory and pennies, toward paperwork and statements and the long, slow process of turning a story into consequence.

Behind them, the river kept moving—never content, never finished, patient in a way people couldn't afford to be. It held what it would, released what it chose, and whispered the rest along the banks for anyone who wanted to learn its language. Rowan listened until the words inside her settled into place.

Tomorrow there would be questions and lawyers and arguments about what counted as proof and what counted as faith. Tomorrow there would be the county attorney and the recorder's office and a dozen men who would swear they never heard a thing. Pike still had allies; the man in the tunnel still had no name. But tonight the water had given her a page and a voice, and that felt like enough to begin.

She tightened the blanket around her shoulders and started walking.

Chapter 15

After the Flood

The morning after smelled like wet metal and lilies left too long in a vase. Fog clung to the river like a second skin, softening the sharp lines of the levee and the courthouse dome into something the eye could almost forgive. A gull—lost this far inland or just opportunistic—wheeled once over the muddy water, thought better of it, and veered away.

Rowan stood on the levee in boots that squelched when she shifted her weight. The river had fallen a little. Not much. It sulked inside its banks, churned a huff of brown at a stump, nudged a half-submerged shopping cart out of the reeds, then changed its mind and let it stay. Behind her, the square was waking with the creak of plywood and the cough of generators. Someone laughed too loudly—shock venting as humor—and someone else answered with a tired, automatic "hush."

"You look like you slept on gravel," CJ said.

"I slept on an evidence locker," Rowan said. "Gravel would've been a luxury."

He handed her coffee in a church-printed foam cup. The lid had split somewhere between the fellowship hall and her hands and leaked a dark comma onto the back of his knuckles. He didn't notice. The world had quietly rewritten what counted as mess.

They walked the levee together while the fog drew back like a curtain that hated mornings. On the far bank, the cottonwoods wore rag banners of torn plastic and river grass. A lawn chair leaned against a sycamore like a hungover guest.

"Dog made it through the night," CJ said. "The teenagers named him Buck. Then Buckshot. Then they argued about hyphenation and fell asleep in the gym bleachers."

"Any word on the Krantz pickup?" Rowan asked.

"Downstream, wrapped around a piling," CJ said. "Dale's mad we cut it loose. Told Patel he could've salvaged the carb. Then he cried for five minutes. Said he dreamed of trucks with no faces."

Rowan tipped the coffee to her mouth. It tasted like tar and reassurance. "Today'll be paperwork and people," she said. "County attorney. State lab. Reporters."

"And sand," CJ added, nodding toward a line of volunteers moving bags from a pallet to a wall with the slow rhythm of folk song. "And stories about angels. People love those after a flood."

"People need those," she said.

They cut through the square. The statue of the soldier in front of the courthouse seemed to be shivering in the damp. Someone had wrapped a garbage bag around his rifle like a raincoat for a child. Flyers were taped to a folding table—missing pets, missing heirlooms, missing days of work. A boy in a plastic fire hat listed each item on a clipboard and drew a smiley face next to every promise to help, whether he believed it or not.

In the gym, the air was wet breath and floor polish. The basketball hoops wore the same resigned expression as every hoop in every emergency shelter. Families camped in systems that only made sense to the people inside them: a pallet of cots near the bleachers, a quilt fort under the scoreboard, a row of folding chairs that had become a kitchen with a hot plate and a coffee maker and mugs that said things like #1 GRANDPA and TOO BLESSED TO BE STRESSED. Rowan recognized three women from her mother's pie committee stirring oatmeal in a drum pot as if they'd been born mid-stir. They'd been waiting their whole lives to be essential this way. They were very good at it.

"Detective Hayes," Pastor Linda said, as if greeting a parishioner who had finally come to her senses. "You'll want eggs? We can scramble like the devil and still call it holy." She winked, then sobered. "Thank you for last night. I heard about the Krantz situation. And the... other thing."

Rowan nodded. Thanks had always sat strangely on her shoulders. "We all did what we had to."

Lydia appeared from a tangle of cots with a notebook, a camera strap digging into her shoulder. A kid with a gap-toothed smile trailed her like a junior stringer, clutching extra pens.

"Morning, hard news," Lydia said. "You look like you fought a river and then made it apologize."

"It owed us," Rowan said.

Lydia jerked her head toward the front doors, where two TV vans lined the curb like beached whales. "They want a sound bite. I told them they could have one when I'm done getting the story the river told instead." She made a face—the expression she reserved for municipal spin and poorly made pie. "Any word on Pike?"

"Arraignment this afternoon," CJ said. "Patel says the phones haven't stopped. Half the town wants to post his bail. The other half wants to tilt the courthouse so he slides into the river."

"Here," Lydia said, and handed Rowan a copy of the Gazette. The paper had been printed in a rush—ink a shade too heavy, columns slightly skewed—but the headline cut clean:

THE RIVER'S DUE

Beneath it, a photo from the press conference: Rowan standing a half-step off the podium with a sleeve in her hand, Pike's smile mid-fail, rain tightening the scene into something almost biblical.

"Redemption looks good on you," Lydia said, embarrassed by her own sincerity. She brushed it off with a joke. "If you must know, I used a thesaurus for 'due.' Considered 'reckoning,' but I didn't want to give the church ladies heartburn."

"Let them earn it," Rowan said, folding the paper with care and tucking it under her arm as if it were breakable.

An elderly man waved from a cot by the free-throw line. He had a farmer's weather map of a face and a knit cap that said IOWA in block letters. "Detective," he called. "My truck floated away, but I got my wife's biscuit recipe. That count as a miracle?"

"It counts as lunch," she said, and watched him laugh until he coughed and patted his chest.

CJ had already peeled off to help move a crate. He scooped up a kitten from beneath a bleacher on the way and handed it to a girl who clutched it like a soft fact. Outside the gym doors, a Guard kid with a jaw like a corn crib let an old lady sit in his truck to warm up while he told her stories about a flood that happened before he was born. Her face smoothed out as he talked. Some people knew the right lies to tell when the truth was too heavy.

"County attorney wants you at ten," Patel said from behind Rowan, and it was exactly ten. Patel had the gift of appearing when the clock did. "He's bringing someone from the AG's office. They're going to argue about who gets the glory and who gets the headache. I told them you don't care."

"I don't," Rowan said.

"They want the tape and the agreement."

"They can have copies," Rowan said. "Originals stay with me until chain-of-custody forms are signed by someone whose name my father would've circled."

Patel's mouth twitched. "You want to be careful how many ghosts you let pick your battles."

"I'm all out of careful," Rowan said, and Patel didn't nod so much as stop not-nodding.

The county attorney wore a tie with little wagons on it and the look of a man whose coffee had not done its job. The assistant AG had perfect hair and a briefcase that probably came with instructions. They sat in what used to be a social studies classroom—peeling map of Iowa, a faded poster about the importance of voting, a chalkboard still ghosted with an equation no one remembered writing.

"There's no question the mayor's in trouble," the county attorney said, hands folded on the table like he was about to bless it. "The recording, the ledger, the document. But the homicide angle—" He glanced at the AG rep. "That's a bigger lift."

"He didn't have to strangle anyone to do a murder," Rowan said. "He set it up and he cleaned it up. He broke the town so it would fit in his pocket."

The AG rep adjusted his cuff like he was setting the minute hand of a watch with his heartbeat. "If we go to trial on conspiracy or felony murder, we'll need more than a thirty-year-old tape and a single document that could be argued as coerced."

"'Filed under duress' is a confession without the comfort of a bench," Lydia said from the doorway, uninvited, notebook already open.

"This is confidential," the AG rep said.

"So is every family's grief," Lydia said, leaning against the jamb like that settled it.

Rowan slid the plastic sleeves across the table. "You have your copies. You'll get your lab reports. You'll get the chain on the ledger pulled from under the bridge. You'll have Patel's sworn statement about the recorder's basement and the missing pages. If you want more, the river can probably cough something else up if we ask nice."

"Relying on miracles is for Sunday," the county attorney said gently.

"Then think of it as silt," Rowan said. "It builds. One layer at a time."

They wrangled for an hour. They wanted ownership and words like jurisdiction and phrases like best for the community. Rowan recognized the old cadence—softeners over hard edges, the civic balm that made bleeding look like blushing. She kept her voice even and her jaw unlocked. She said no when she had to and yes when she could without losing a truth.

When she stepped back into the hallway, Lydia blew out a breath like a woman who'd held it since '93. "They'll take a piece and claim the whole."

"They can have the work," Rowan said. "We keep the promise."

"What promise is that?" Lydia asked.

Rowan didn't answer. She knew what she meant: a promise to Emily, to the girl who'd trusted her father with a secret and a fear. To the version of Sheriff Hayes who had signed a document because a bigger wrong would have grown in that signature's absence, then had the nerve to write himself a rebuke at the bottom. To a town that had chosen not to know because knowing came with cost.

She went to the station because her key still fit the door and because her hands needed something to do that wasn't clenching. The evidence room smelled like dry cardboard and the ghost of bleach. On top of the locker, someone had balanced a vase with three daffodils that had survived the rain by sheer opinion. The front desk had a pie cooling on a trivet that said LIVE LAUGH LAWSUIT.

She took the long way to her office. Past the wall where the department hung pictures—a fish CJ had caught as a kid, Patel's academy class, a Polaroid of the sheriff's holiday party where someone's antler headband had drooped into their pudding. Her father's picture hung near the end. His smile in it was smaller than the ones he'd given her at breakfast but real enough to lend warmth to the hallway.

"Morning," said the rookie on phones, a kid with a haircut that still looked like a decision. "We've had six calls about rumors Pike's skipping bail. We've had eight about a raccoon in the library. We've had one from Mrs. Ellison asking if the flood invalidates her parking ticket."

"Tell her the river takes its own," Rowan said. "But the meter doesn't care."

Her office smelled the way it always had: dry paper, pencil shavings, the ghost of her father's Old Spice sunk into the wood from the days she'd done homework in here while he read reports and pretended to be surprised when she got the answers right. On a high shelf, a shoebox with the word LAKE written in her mother's hand held snapshots whose corners had made permanent decisions about curling.

In the bottom drawer of the filing cabinet, behind policy manuals and a stack of forms that felt like a sleeping porcupine if you reached without looking, lay a small cigar tin with three pennies inside. One of her father's old superstitions: pennies to pay the ferryman, pennies to remind you nothing was free. She shook the tin. The pennies clicked like bones. It didn't sound sad. It sounded like continuity.

She checked the tape again, as if it might have evaporated in the night. Emily's voice stayed right where it was, a small persistent lantern in a room that had finally been aired. Rowan made another copy on the department's ancient deck because making copies calmed her. The machine wheezed and clanked and declared itself victorious with a thunk.

After lunch—the gym kind: a sandwich heroic in its dryness and a cookie that regretted its life choices—Rowan drove to the cemetery on the hill. The road up was still damp where shadow had made a truce with sun. The wind smelled like clover and iron. Graves wore flags and peonies and the complicated dignity of names in granite.

Her father's stone was exactly where it had always been, in the row where sunrise got first say. She stood with her hands in her pockets and tried to make both halves of herself quiet—the one that wanted to list evidence, the one that wanted to say, You could have told me.

"I found the note," she said at last. "Filed under duress. Truth comes due." She paused, then smiled at the absurdity and the grace of talking to rock. "You were always more patient than me."

She took his badge from her pocket—the one he'd worn when he was still invincible to her and mortal to everyone else—and set it on the stone for a second. The metal was warm. The sun had found it. She didn't leave it; she wasn't ready to let the world walk up and take something that belonged to their house. But the act of setting it down felt like an honest thing.

"I wanted you to be clean," she said. "You weren't. Neither am I. But you were brave. Brave enough to sign, and braver to write the part that made you look small."

Wind moved through the oaks and made a sound like distant water in a culvert. A hawk, unimpressed by human epiphany, rode a thermal into somewhere else it needed to be.

She went home long enough to change her shirt and lose an argument with the water heater, then back to the square in time to see a rainbow try out a draft of itself over the river. It wasn't a good rainbow—the colors faint, the arc incomplete—but it had the nerve to exist. People pointed with their chins, as Midwesterners do in the presence of spectacle.

Mayor Pike's arraignment filled the courthouse like a rehearsal dinner for a family that had run out of polite topics thirty years ago. Reporters took their places along the aisle, pens already angry. The county attorney spoke on record enough to sound courageous and off record enough to sound employed. Pike came in with his jaw set to Determined and his eyes set to Weather This. He did not look at Rowan. He looked at a point half a foot above her left shoulder, a trick taught to television by politics and to politics by fear.

It took less time than it should have and more than anybody had patience for. Bail was argued like a philosophy and set like a compromise. Charges were read like a poem nobody wanted to memorize. When it was over, the world did not tilt. The river did not rise. The courthouse clock, four minutes slow, nodded to itself in satisfaction.

On the steps, a man stopped Rowan to tell her his wife had slept for the first time in years and he didn't know whether to thank her or be mad that it took this much. She said she understood and meant it. A girl with the complicated braid of someone who made art with hair handed her a drawing of the river with eyes. The eyes were not kind, but they were fair.

"We're alive," CJ said, which seemed like news worth writing down.

"Barely," Rowan said, and felt the weight of the word shift inside her from complaint to gratitude.

They walked to the levee again in the late sun. The rainbow had faded to rumor. The river reflected a sky that had decided to be blue, then thought better of it and settled on unpolished pewter. Somewhere a radio played a hymn; somewhere a hammer put a roof back where it belonged.

"Tomorrow," Lydia said, appearing like a coda, "I'm running a second-day piece. Not the mayor. The volunteers. The small brave things. Your dog rescue goes in the sixth paragraph. Don't argue; heroes go below the fold."

"Make sure you spell Buckshot right," CJ said.

"It's hyphenated," Rowan added, deadpan, and all three of them laughed like people who had unclenched enough to remember how.

They stood there until the light decided it was done with them. When they finally turned to go, Rowan looked back at the bend where the river made its slow, chicken-hearted curve and the cottonwoods wore the night like a shawl. She didn't ask anything of it. She didn't curse it. She acknowledged it the way you acknowledge an old neighbor you will never quite know.

"The river takes its own," she said—not as a warning or a wound this time, but as an admission of jurisdiction. Then she added, because she had earned the right, "And sometimes, when it's ready, it gives us just enough to keep going."

The fog had burned off. The town smelled like damp earth and hot engines and coffee that had sat—the smells of recovery. Lights came on in windows like the slow applause of houses. They followed the sidewalk toward work that would not end and chose not to resent that fact.

Behind them, the river kept its counsel and its course, unbothered by men or headlines, rocking its secrets in the dark as if soothing an old, difficult child. It would never be solved. It didn't need to be. It only needed watching.

And the town, for the first time in a very long time, was watching back.

Chapter 16

The Reckoning

The courthouse smelled like damp wool, lemon cleaner, and nerves. Rainwater still dripped from the hats and coats hanging near the door, and the air carried that heavy, humid thickness of a town that had been holding its breath for too long. Rowan paused just inside, letting her eyes adjust to the dim light. The fluorescent bulbs buzzed overhead, matching the hum in her own veins.

CJ trailed her by a few steps, tugging at the knot of his tie as if it might choke him. "You sure about this, Hayes?" he asked quietly. "It's not too late to let the state handle Pike."

Rowan adjusted her badge. "It's my town too."

He nodded, subdued. "Doesn't mean you have to bleed for it."

"I already did," she said. "Now it's the town's turn."

As they moved down the marble corridor, whispers trailed after them.

"That's Hayes' daughter," someone murmured. "The sheriff's girl."

Another voice answered, "Bob Hayes never would've dragged this mess out into daylight."

The words stung, but she didn't slow down. Every generation chose what kind of silence to keep.

They reached the heavy double doors of the courtroom. Lydia Bass waited outside, pen tucked behind one ear, reporter's notebook clutched like a weapon.

"You ready?" she asked.

"No," Rowan said. "But that never stopped me before."

Inside, the room was half full. Townspeople sat shoulder to shoulder—shop owners, farmers, retirees, kids too young to remember Emily Carter but old enough to have heard her name in whispers. The air buzzed with shuffling papers and nervous coughs. On the front bench, Mayor Daniel Pike sat beside his attorney, posture perfect, expression carved from something trying hard to look like calm.

Lydia slipped into the back row, tapping her recorder once before setting it down. CJ took a seat near the aisle, flipping through his notes, but Rowan stayed standing until the bailiff nudged her to sit.

The judge entered—a tall man with a tired face and a voice like gravel in a riverbed. "Court is in session," he said. "The State of Iowa versus Daniel Gideon Pike."

The prosecutor rose. "Your Honor, the state will show that the defendant, Mayor Daniel Pike, knowingly participated in the concealment of multiple crimes tied to the River Bend development. These acts include obstruction of justice, evidence tampering, and conspiracy. Furthermore, we will show that his father, Gideon Pike Sr., directly benefited from the deaths and disappearances connected to those properties."

A low murmur rippled through the crowd. Pike didn't move. His eyes remained fixed straight ahead, a politician's mask that had outlived its use.

The first exhibit came quickly: the ledger. Projected on the screen, it looked almost harmless—neat columns, tidy handwriting, sums that would have meant nothing to anyone who hadn't spent months chasing ghosts. But to Rowan, those numbers glowed like scars. H.S. for Harold Sterling. G.P. for Gideon Pike. Payments to the Carter family, to the

Petersons, to names that had once belonged to real people and were now only headstones and rumor.

CJ's foot tapped beneath the table. Lydia's pen moved in small, rapid strokes.

Next came the recording—the one Rowan had found sealed in her father's lockbox. The judge leaned forward, brow furrowing. When the tape began, the sound was scratchy at first, like rain on a tin roof. Then her father's voice rose out of the hiss.

"Filed under duress. Truth comes due."

A chair creaked somewhere in the back. Then another. The room grew still as Emily Carter's trembling voice broke through—young, terrified, asking someone not to tell her parents, not to ruin everything. Not all the words survived the static, but the meaning did.

When the tape ended, silence hung in the room like smoke. Pike's jaw twitched. His hand clenched once, then relaxed, fingers trembling.

The prosecutor let the quiet sit before speaking again. "Your Honor, this recording was recovered from a sealed evidence box belonging to Sheriff Robert Hayes, dated 1994. The state crime lab has verified its authenticity. What you just heard corroborates testimony suppressed during the original Carter investigation."

The defense attorney stood, voice sharp. "Your Honor, this is prejudicial hearsay. There's no proof my client was aware of this recording, nor that it pertains to any alleged wrongdoing by him or his administration."

The judge's gavel rapped once. "Overruled. Continue."

For the next two hours, witnesses paraded through the stand—county clerks, bank tellers, a retired developer who couldn't meet Rowan's eyes. They spoke of signatures that didn't match, contracts that vanished, payments that didn't add up. Every thread led back to Pike. Sometimes in straight lines, sometimes in loops, but always to the same name.

At recess, Rowan stepped into the hall. The air was cooler here, the marble echoing with stray footsteps. She leaned against the wall, palms pressed flat against the stone to stop them from shaking.

"Hard day for justice," a voice murmured behind her.

She turned. Pike stood at the far end of the corridor, his lawyer nowhere in sight. His tie was loosened, his face drawn tight with anger and something that looked almost like fear.

"You think this makes you a hero?" he asked, voice low. "You think this town will thank you for what you're doing?"

"I don't care if they do," Rowan said.

"They'll turn on you," he hissed. "Same way they turned on your father."

Her breath hitched, but she didn't look away. "Maybe. But at least I'll be facing the right direction when they do."

For a moment, he looked ready to say more. Then he shook his head, muttered something she couldn't catch, and walked back toward the courtroom doors. The echo of his shoes faded down the hall.

When the session resumed, the defense called Pike himself to the stand. His lawyer coaxed him through a careful narrative—his years of public service, his pride in Cedar Valley, his father's shadow. He played humble, earnest, even broken. For a few minutes, Rowan almost believed him.

Then came cross-examination.

"Mr. Pike," the prosecutor began, "you've told this court you knew nothing of the payments recorded in the Wexler ledger?"

"That's correct," Pike said, voice steady.

"And you had no knowledge of the chemical dumping in The Bottoms?"

"None."

"You weren't aware of the false land deeds, the missing parcel transfers, the fact that your own father's company profited directly from those deals?"

"I trusted the process," Pike snapped. "I didn't review every line of paperwork."

The attorney nodded slowly. "And when Detective Hayes presented you with evidence linking your family to the Carter case—"

"I told her to let it go," Pike blurted.

The words hung in the air. He realized his mistake a half-second too late.

The prosecutor tilted his head. "You told her to let it go."

Pike's lips parted, closed. "I meant—to let the authorities—"

"The same way your father told Sheriff Hayes to 'let it go' in 1994?" the attorney pressed.

The courtroom stirred. Someone whispered, "God help us," under their breath.

Pike's face flushed crimson. "This is a farce," he shouted. "You think you can rewrite history? My family built this town!"

"No," the prosecutor said quietly. "They buried it."

Pike slumped back, breathing hard. The room exhaled in unison.

Lydia's camera clicked once—sharp, echoing. Rowan turned slightly and saw her watching through the lens, eyes fierce and sad all at once. Lydia had covered too many stories where the truth arrived too late.

Not this time.

The trial adjourned near dusk. Rain streaked the courthouse windows, soft but relentless, as though the sky itself refused to look away. Rowan sat until the benches emptied, then gathered her notes and walked into the hall.

CJ caught up with her at the door. "Well," he said, "that's one way to ruin a career."

Rowan managed a tired smile. "Mine or his?"

He shrugged. "Depends who writes the headline."

They stepped out into the cooling evening. The square glistened under streetlights, puddles reflecting the courthouse clock—four minutes behind, stubborn as ever. Across the street, Lydia stood under an awning, talking into her phone. When she saw them, she waved.

"You two coming for pie," she called, "or planning to stand there like tragic statues?"

"Pie sounds decent," CJ said.

"Lemon," Lydia added. "For luck."

Rowan hesitated, glancing back once at the courthouse. Through the rain-streaked glass, she could just make out the faint silhouette of Pike being led away in handcuffs. For the first time in months, her breath came easy and stayed that way.

CJ followed her gaze. "Think the river's finally done taking?" he asked.

Rowan slipped her hands into her coat pockets. "Maybe not," she said. "But it's changing what it keeps."

They crossed the square toward the diner. Steam fogged the windows, and the neon sign buzzed faintly, the only defiant color in the washed-out night. Inside, the hum of voices was low, tentative—a town rediscovering its own language after years of silence.

When Lydia slid the pie across the table, Rowan laughed quietly. "You really think lemon brings luck?"

Lydia grinned. "No. But it tastes like hope."

Outside, rain mingled with the river's steady whisper—no apology, no promise, just endurance.

And for once, that was enough.

Chapter 17

Where the Mill Once Breathed

The flood smell lingered even after the sun returned. It clung to alleyways and the hems of jeans and the undersides of porch steps—silt and rot and the metallic ghost of rain. Cedar Valley moved through it the way people move through a shared memory: carefully, telling each other as they went where the footing held.

Rowan parked near the gym and walked the long way to the square. The morning had come out wide and blue, a deliberate apology. A crew from the county had already scraped the mud line off the courthouse steps; the sandstone shone two shades lighter where last night had been erased with stubborn brushes and hose water. The courthouse clock, newly cleaned and no wiser, still lagged four minutes.

In front of City Hall, a makeshift table crowded with clipboards and Sharpies stretched between two sawhorses. A volunteer in a ball cap and a knee brace handed out forms with the officious cheer of an usher at a wedding.

"If you're here for claims, line A; if you're here for sandbags, line B; if you're here to yell, I'm taking lunch at noon," he announced to no one in particular.

CJ stood at the end of line C, holding a coffee in each hand and a leash looped around one wrist. Buckshot sat at his feet wearing a bandanna in a pattern that wanted to be llamas and failed. The dog looked up at Rowan and yawned like a man who had watched a long movie and refused to admit it made him cry.

"You look like you slept for an entire hour," CJ said, handing her a cup.

"Fifty-three minutes," she said. "But I dreamed of pie charts, so technically it counts double."

He grinned. "Patel wants us at the recorder's basement at ten. Warrant's signed. She said to bring gloves and a bad attitude."

"I never travel without both," Rowan said. "Where's Lydia?"

"Wrote through the night," he said. "I think she's sleeping on the Gazette couch. Or she became ink and climbed into the press."

"Either way," Rowan said, "she earned it."

They crossed the square together. An older couple in matching windbreakers waved them down and pressed a foil-wrapped loaf of banana bread into Rowan's hands like it might keep a ship afloat.

"For keeping the river from taking more," the woman said.

Rowan accepted it with the same awkward grace she reserved for commendations and casseroles; both belonged to other people's ideas of heroism.

By ten, the recorder's basement had that particular chill of rooms designed for paper rather than people. The lights flickered once and chose resilience over drama. Rows of metal shelves rose from concrete, box labels facing out in tidy loops: DEEDS 1990–1994; PLATS 1980–1985; LIENS—MISC. A damp mark the size and shape of an old flood darkened the lower two feet of the far wall.

Patel met them at the door, warrant in hand. "We're looking for missing parcel sheets from River Bend, any indexes for the assignment agreement, and whatever else smells like bleach and fear," she said. "Rosa from the clerk's office is our guide. She knows this basement better than her own kitchen."

Rosa was a woman small enough to be underestimated and loud enough to correct the error on sight. "We had a mouse problem down here once," she said, leading them past a shelf with an apology of traps on it. "They learned not to like paper. I told them their literacy would be their undoing."

They found the file drawer where the River Bend plats should have been. Half of the tabs sat in the slot with no manila hanging behind them—as if someone had performed a magic trick with no applause. CJ peered into the empty space as though the right act of squinting might conjure a missing deed.

"Here," Rosa said, tugging open a drawer lower down with a grunt. The smell bumped them like a memory: mildew and reels of old microfilm. "Overflow. Or that's what the last clerk called it when I asked why we were filing by sediment layers."

Rowan pulled a box marked CORRESPON-DENCE—ARCHIVE and set it on a steel table. Inside, letters sank into one another like roof shingles after a hailstorm.

She sorted with gloved fingers, her mind making room for small facts the way a river makes room for pebbles in spring.

A memo on deputy letterhead—1983—regarding a "temporary bridge closure to accommodate heavy equipment travel." A stamped envelope addressed to the Gazette returned for insufficient postage, the corner bearing a wet thumb smear fossilized into the paper. Two copies of a tract map, one with border notes in someone's careful architect's hand: reroute, mitigation, residents—offer relocation. The second map was almost identical, except the notes at the bottom read: residents—remove.

"You seeing this?" CJ asked, leaning over her shoulder.

"I wish I weren't," she said.

Patel's phone trilled. She angled away, murmuring in the tone reserved for county attorneys and organized fires. "He did what?—No. He doesn't get to make a statement from the steps. He's a defendant, not a weatherman."

Rowan kept sorting. The stack of small horrors grew in a neat pile at her left elbow. Then she felt it: a thin envelope that didn't match the weight of the others. She lifted it. The paper had a waxy sheen, the seal broken and resealed with clear tape.

Inside lay a black-and-white photograph, the kind made by a copier that had put in years without complaint. Four men stood on the riverbank in summer suits with their jackets off, sleeves rolled: Sterling; Gideon Pike, younger and broader; a county board chair whose funeral Rowan had attended out of respect and curiosity; and her father. He stood a half-step away from the others, weight on one foot, tie crooked. Frank Wallace hovered at the edge of the frame, head turned to the side as if expecting bad news to come from there. In the left margin, a hand had written a date and a time in blue pen. In the right margin: keep for later.

Her mouth went dry. She set the photo face down and told herself that her father's distance was not happenstance. People who wanted to live with themselves left a half-step when they could.

On the next shelf down lay a box stamped with a crooked ink label: BADGES—RET. The tape had loosened in damp; the lid shrugged when she touched it. Inside, tarnished stars slept in tissue paper. Someone had penciled initials on the edge of each wrap. J.B. had two packages.

She unwrapped the first. A badge with a cracked enamel field and an eagle whose head had become more suggestion than bird looked back at her, number 17. The back was stamped **Bledsoe, JOHN**. The second wrapping held not a badge but a thin rectangle of leather. Inside, a photograph of a young man in a uniform too stiff for his bones and a girl with a ribboned ponytail, both squinting into light.

"J.B.," CJ said softly, reading over her shoulder. "John Bledsoe."

"Deputy, 1969 to '79," Rosa supplied without looking. "Died in the flood that took the old Cedar bridge. Or that's the story they put on the plaque."

Rowan turned the leather holder over in her hands. A smear of dark on one corner had bled into the grain and set, like dried river in spring. The boy's eyes in the photo were too sure of the future; the girl's were too sure of him. On the inside flap, as if added in a moment alone, someone had written in pencil: **keep her away from the water.**

CJ pointed at the box label. "Why would his badge be here and another badge with his initials be... out there," he said, meaning buried in a field like a secret that had tried and failed to keep itself.

"Because someone took the badge from his body before they put him in a story," Rowan said, as much to the room as to the two people she trusted in it. She slid the leather back into its sleeve. The past wasn't done with them. It had just moved upstream.

They logged what they could and left the basement to Rosa, who had already started to draft a new index in a notebook with a kitten on the cover. "I like kittens for hard work," she said. "They sharpen the edges of my kindness."

On the square, the day had decided to be July after a week of April. Humidity rose off the bricks in a sigh. Volunteers lifted soaked carpet out of the library and leaned it against bike racks like tired animals. Someone's boombox played a song about forgiveness a few decades too old for the kids dancing to it. A baby slept on the courthouse lawn with his mouth open, the kind of sleep people lose forever after ten.

Lydia caught them by the gazebo, a grin carving dusk into her face despite noon's insistence. "You look like you found something that makes me want a cigarette," she said. "Give me a chance to be virtuous and I'll manage it half the time."

Rowan told her about Bledsoe. Lydia's eyebrows arched toward conspiracy, then flattened—less delight than sorrow.

"'69," she said quietly. "That was the flood with the church roof that floated two blocks. My mother kept a picture of it taped inside a cookbook. Said it explained everything you needed to know about water and religion."

"Could be another story we inherited," CJ said.

"Oh, we inherited a library," Lydia said. "We're just now learning to read."

News moved faster in Cedar Valley when it was late to arrive. By afternoon, someone had strung a line of paper lanterns between trees on the river path. Folks called it a vigil and a potluck and a clean-up party in turns—Cedar Valley preferred an event to a ceremony. Kids decorated sandbags with Sharpies; each bag acquired a cartoon face, most of them cheerful and a few of them thoughtfully mean. The church ladies set out aluminum pans of casseroles that all introduced themselves as comfort. A guitar arrived, and two teenagers who had never agreed on anything agreed on the chords to "Angel from Montgomery."

Rowan found Lucas near the lamppost where they had argued once about something neither of them would admit had been love. He wore a river worker's tan and the old blue jacket he'd kept in the boat for fifteen years. Mud had gotten into the seams and stayed there, like fidelity.

"You planning to do that disappearing thing again?" he asked, half a smile lifting the side of his mouth that used to find hers easily.

"Probably," she said. "Seems to be my best move."

"You're good at it," he said, and then, to save them both, added, "Saw the paper. Saw the TV. Saw Pike try to talk with his eyes. Didn't work out for him."

"Paper's Lydia," Rowan said. "TV is luck. The rest is the river."

He tipped his chin toward the bend. "She did her part," he said. "You did yours."

"I signed nothing," Rowan said. "On purpose."

"Your father signed and wrote a refusal at the bottom," Lucas said. "That's the most honest thing a man can do with a pen."

They stood in an easy silence that had taken a decade to earn. A boy tried to skip a stone and nearly hit his own sneaker. The stone took one hard hop and then bit water. He raised both hands to the sky as if to lay claim to it anyway.

"Your boat still runs?" she asked.

"Mostly. She coughs like a pack-a-day smoker in the morning. She's better by noon."

"Take me out tomorrow," she said. "I want to look at where the old bridge was. The badge—"

"Bledsoe," he said, nodding, because this was who he was: a man who knew names and currents. "Yeah. That's a story for a different tide."

The vigil grew not louder but more certain. A line formed for prayers; some people joined. A line formed for pie; everyone joined. CJ argued gently with a kid about whether Buckshot would enjoy a piece of fried chicken; Buckshot rendered judgment by eating half and sitting down for the rest.

Rowan carried two paper plates and stopped at the levee. Evening had put its hand over the bright of the day and softened everything. The water moved with its usual shrug. This was the hour when the town looked best at being itself. The arguments and reconciliations, the debts and credits, the small braveries. They lay out on the lawn like quilts.

"Detective," a voice said at her shoulder.

She turned to find Eve Rourke, hair still in its workday knot, hands clean, eyes tired. The doctor rarely came to gatherings; pathology made a person careful with crowds.

"I got lab confirmation on the fibers in the knot," Eve said. "Pre-2000, as we thought. We also found secondary DNA on Sarah's bracelet."

"Secondary," Rowan said. "Not Wallace."

"No. Female. Partial. Too degraded to match without a miracle. But it's there."

"Emily," Rowan said quietly.

"Or someone who helped pull her from the world," Eve said, the kindness of her voice a blade wrapped in velvet. "I don't know which story is more merciful."

"I don't either," Rowan said. "Thank you."

Eve hesitated, then reached out and touched Rowan's forearm—a quick, careful gesture, like a veterinarian petting a dog in a burn ward. "You did it," she said. "Whatever comes next, you did this part."

Rowan nodded and watched her walk back into the crowd, where people like Eve faded by choice and tended by instinct.

Twilight found the river in a different mood. It slowed at the bend the way a thought slows when the mind is tired enough to tell the truth. Lanterns flickered against water in hesitant versions of stars. The courthouse clock announced eight and then considered the possibility of eight again. A breeze found the lantern line and made the paper skins shiver.

Lydia came up with a folded newspaper and placed it against Rowan's elbow. "Tomorrow's run," she said. "Front page is Pike's hearing. Below the fold is Bledsoe. You get one quote and it makes you sound gruff and noble and tired in a way that will flatter only you. You're welcome."

"What about you?" Rowan asked.

Lydia gazed over the water as if it might quote her back. "I got my own redemption," she said. "Buried in a column inch. People who know will know. People who don't will think I'm still loud. Both kinds will be right."

"Are you going to sleep now?" Rowan asked.

"In another life," Lydia said. "I'm meeting a source whose shoes I don't trust but whose fear I do. If he's good, we'll have language for the next part."

"Next part?" CJ asked, appearing like a punctuation mark made of coffee and dog hair.

Lydia handed him a napkin. "There's always a next part," she said. "Ask the river."

They drifted back into the crowd. A soft cheer went up from somewhere near the bandstand; a child had made it across the grass without falling and his mother had decided courage required applause. A string of small applause followed, for no reason other than practice. It sounded like rain remembering and being kind about it.

Later, when the lanterns had all been carried home in paper bags that left a trail of wax kisses along the sidewalk, when the casseroles had been reduced to edges and argument, when CJ had convinced Buckshot that the world did not owe him a third dinner, Rowan walked the river path alone.

At the spot where the boardwalk gave way to dirt, she stopped. She took her father's badge from her pocket and set it on the railing. The metal caught the thin sliver of moon and held it like a coin. She took the photocopy of the assignment agreement and read the bottom line again: **Filed under duress. Truth comes due.** It had been an apology and a dare, and she had taken both.

A car rolled past on the street above, the kind of car that belonged to a person who had never learned the sound of gravel under tires. Headlights slid over the cottonwoods and tried to make them confess; the trees offered no comment. Across the river, something large moved in the dark—deer, probably, or a person who liked riverbanks at night because they felt like the truth no one else would listen to.

Rowan tucked the badge away and pulled out the leather holder that had belonged to John Bledsoe. She opened it and ran her thumb over the penciled line inside: **keep her away from the water.** It wasn't a prayer. It was a failed instruction. She thought of the girl in the photo with him—unknown to her, but not to someone. Names were part of the work.

Her phone buzzed. A text from Patel: *Arraignment moved up. Defense rattled. Be ready at nine.* Another from the county attorney: *State AG wants joint presser. Smile.*

A third from a number she didn't recognize: *I have something that belonged to Emily. Meet me where the mill used to breathe. Midnight.*

She stared at that last line until the words separated from meaning. *Where the mill used to breathe.* The part of her that had gotten used to being hunted lifted its head and sniffed the air. The part of her that knew a trap from a chance weighed the hour and the place and the signature, which was nothing but absence.

Lucas would tell her not to go alone. CJ would insist on coming. Lydia would remind her that mysteries favored the patient and the prepared, not the brave and the dumb. Her father, if ghosts offered guidance, would say what he had said when she was nine and wanted to take a shortcut through the culvert: *There's the way we take when we have time, and the way we take when we don't.*

She typed back: *Thirty minutes.* Then, instead of every threat and warning she wanted to add, she wrote: *If you're lying, the river will keep your secret only as long as it has to.*

Buckshot materialized out of the dim with CJ at the end of his leash. "You've got the look," he said.

"What look?"

"The one you get when a bad idea dresses up as a plan."

"You free?"

"I'm a public servant," he said solemnly. "I'm never free."

"Bring your flashlight," she said.

Lydia stepped out from behind a cottonwood, having learned her craft in towns where privacy meant you asked before you told. "If I pretend I'm going home," she said, "I expect you to pretend you believe me."

"Go home," Rowan said.

"Liar," Lydia said fondly, and handed her a small recorder anyway. "Press this if anyone decides to monologue."

They walked together as far as the turn that would take them back to the square. Lydia peeled away with a wave. CJ fell into step beside Rowan like a man who had decided this particular trouble was worth his stupid ankle, his stubborn heart, and his pension.

The path to the old mill was soft with leaves and the dust of buildings that had disliked becoming memory. The river muttered to itself in the dark. Fireflies wrote their brief sermons. Somewhere an owl took attendance in a register voice.

"You think it's real?" CJ asked.

"Everything's real," Rowan said. "Some of it is also true."

They stepped into the clearing where the mill had once hulked against the water and threatened to fall in just for the relief. Nothing remained now but pilings and the story of noise. The river's surface took the moon and broke it into the pieces water prefers. On the far bank, a form detached itself from shade. Tall, a little hunched, careful with the way it placed its feet.

"Detective Hayes?" the figure called softly. A man's voice, hoarse with smoke or guilt. "Come alone?"

"Never," she said.

He stepped into the light. Not Pike. Not Sterling's ghost. Not a deputy who had learned to hate and hide. A maintenance man she recognized from City Hall—late fifties, thin enough to owe someone an apology. He carried a shoebox like a person carries a small animal they mean to set free.

"I stole records," he said, without preamble, voice shaking so hard the words rattled. "I didn't want to, but they told me to burn them and I couldn't. I put them in a vent. I figured the building would keep them honest longer than men would. But then the flood—" He looked at the river as if it kept an appointment book. "I thought the water would eat what I did."

"It doesn't eat everything," Rowan said. "Sometimes it just softens the edges."

He held out the box. "There are schedules. Lists. Names. People they paid to look away. People they paid to push. A letter from Gideon Pike to Sterling about Emily. I read it and then I didn't sleep for a week."

"Why now?" CJ asked.

The man tried to smile and failed. "Because you said it out loud," he said to Rowan. "The thing about the river. It takes its own. I don't want to belong to it."

He put the box in her hands like surrender and absolution weighed the same.

A sound cracked the air—twigs under a boot, close enough to be human, quiet enough to be practiced. Rowan pivoted. The dark offered no face. CJ's light sliced a clean white blade through leaves and found nothing but leaves, willing to testify to anything if asked in the right tone.

"Go," Rowan said to the man, eyes still on the dark. "Go the long way. Walk where there are windows and porch lights. Don't stop unless you meet a dog you know by name."

He nodded and vanished up the path with the odd light step of a man who had been frightened for so long he had taught his body small ways to kiss the ground and not be heard.

Rowan and CJ stood a long minute, listening to the river that had done them the courtesy of not drowning the truth this time. Somewhere upstream, a fish slapped the surface as if putting a period at the end of a sentence it had not read.

"When this is over," CJ said, "when we file this and testify and argue and sleep like criminals in church—what then?"

"Then we start over," Rowan said. "There's a badge from 1969 and a girl in a photograph who didn't make the paper. There's a letter from a farmer that never got mailed. There's—"

"Always a next part," he finished for her.

"Always," she said.

They walked back toward the lights, two shadows in long coats with a dog. Behind them, the river slid past, carrying sticks and secrets and the reflections of lanterns that had not been put away as neatly as their owners had intended. It was not done with them. It never would be.

That was the bargain of living next to water: you learned to hold what you could, you learned to let go of what you must, and you learned the sound of a story arriving soaked and late and still worth telling.

Chapter 18

The River's Ledger

The river went back to pretending it was ordinary.

Two weeks after the flood, Cedar Valley wore its damage like a denim jacket—patched, frayed, still serviceable. Mud had retreated to the places mud preferred. Sandbags sat in neat, reproachful pyramids where lawns used to be. The air smelled like hot asphalt, mowed grass, and the faint, stubborn tang of mildew under fresh paint.

Rowan stood on the courthouse steps, watching a crew rehang the flag that had come down in the storm. The sandstone was fully scrubbed now; only a faint line at shin height betrayed where the water had flirted with the entrance.

"Clock's still four minutes slow," CJ said, coming up beside her with a file under one arm and a plastic cup of something iced and questionable in the other. "Town can change its mayor faster than its habits."

"Some habits keep us honest," Rowan said.

He followed her gaze to the clock. "You headed to the grand jury room, or planning to melt here like a tragic statue?"

"On my way," she said. "Thought I'd see how the building looked when it wasn't trying to drown me."

"Less dramatic," he said. "Still drafty."

Inside, the courthouse hummed with a quieter tension than trial days. No TV vans. No protestors. Just the murmur of jurors in their good clothes, the shuffle of overworked staff, the particular briskness lawyers got when they smelled history and job security at the same time.

The county attorney met her outside the paneled door that used to lead to a judge's chambers and now housed an oversize table and undersize coffee pot.

"You know how this goes," he said, straightening his wagon-print tie. "You walk them through the timeline. We play the tapes. We show the ledger pages. We add the new material from the shoebox. They ask questions. We all pretend the law is tidy."

"It isn't," Rowan said.

"I said we pretend," he replied. "You ready?"

"No," she said. "But that never stopped me before."

Inside, twelve faces turned toward her—farmers, a high school secretary, a man who ran the hardware store, a woman who did not say she was the mayor's cousin but carried his jawline like a debt. The room smelled like coffee, carpet cleaner, and nerves.

She swore in. She told the story again.

How the lockbox had surfaced from the river. How her father's handwriting had waited three decades to be read by someone who wouldn't flinch. How Emily Carter's trembling voice and Gideon Pike's easy threat had been captured on a microcassette that outlived men, administrations, and a building remodel. How a maintenance man with more conscience than power had hidden schedules and letters in a vent because he'd been told to burn them and couldn't.

They played the tape. Even in this smaller room, even after hearing it more times than she could count, something in Rowan's chest tightened when Emily said, *It wasn't supposed to be me.*

The county attorney moved to the next exhibit: pages from the Wexler ledger, the assignment agreement, photocopies of the shoebox finds. He slid one letter into the center of the table as if laying down a card he'd been waiting his whole career to play.

"From Gideon Pike to Harold Sterling," he said. "Dated three weeks before Emily Carter disappeared."

He nodded to Rowan. "Detective Hayes?"

She read, because someone had to.

"'If the Carters won't sign,'" she began, the words sour on her tongue, "'we remind them what they stand to lose. The girl is... amenable. Make sure Sheriff Hayes understands the stakes. He knows which way this town floats.'"

A juror sucked in a breath like they'd been slapped.

Rowan laid the page down. "Signed: Gideon Pike."

The room went quiet enough to hear the ancient air conditioner struggle in the wall.

"Questions?" the county attorney asked.

A man in a seed-corn cap raised his hand, then remembered where he was and dropped it. "You're saying your dad knew," he said. "About the pressure. About your friend. About the river deals."

"Yes," Rowan said. There was no point in trimming it. "He knew enough to be dangerous. And not enough to be safe."

"And he... signed anyway," the man said, looking down at the copy of the assignment agreement—the one with Robert Hayes's neat signature and the three words *filed under duress* like a curse and a confession.

"He signed," Rowan said. "And then he hid the proof where he thought the river and time would keep it until someone could use it without getting killed for the trouble."

The mayor's cousin's mouth tightened. "That sound like courage to you?" she asked. "Or cowardice?"

Rowan met her eyes. "Both," she said. "Most decent things are."

The grand jury questions came in their slow, careful way.

Was she certain the tapes hadn't been altered? Yes—the lab work was in the folder in front of them.

Was she certain the maintenance records and schedules weren't forged? Yes—the ink and paper dated out. The shoebox contents matched originals still in City Hall's system, where no one thought to look.

Was she certain her personal feelings about her father and Emily and this town weren't coloring her testimony?

"Yes," she said—and then, because she'd promised herself she would never lie to a room on purpose, added, "As certain as anybody here is about anything that happened twenty years ago and ruined people we liked."

They let her go after an hour.

In the hallway, CJ waited with his back against the wainscoting, staring at a poster about civic pride and jury duty.

"Well?" he asked.

"They're thinking," she said. "You can hear the grinding if you stand close enough."

He pushed away from the wall. "You done for the day?"

"With talking," she said. "Not with thinking."

"Good," he said. "Lucas is outside with the boat. Says the river owes him overtime."

The launch ramp still smelled like oil and algae and old panic. The cedar planks had warped at the edges from the flood and settled into new complaints.

Lucas's boat idled in the shallows, the engine making a low, familiar grumble. He stood at the stern, lines in his hands, hat pulled down against a sun that meant well and overshot.

"Got you a present," he called as they walked down. "State owns it, but I'm the one stuck reading the manual."

He jerked a thumb toward the squat gray unit mounted near the console. "Side-scan sonar," he said with mock reverence. "Brought in for post-flood debris surveys. I convinced them a grumpy river worker and two law enforcement types could be trusted not to crash it into a log."

CJ eyed the device. "You understand how to operate it?"

"Absolutely not," Lucas said. "But luckily, she does."

Eve Rourke sat on the bow, sleeves rolled, hair tied back with the pragmatic efficiency of someone who spent her days around reluctant bodies. She balanced the sonar's tablet display in one hand and tapped it with a stylus like she was disciplining an unruly student.

"Turns out reading shadows on a screen isn't that different from reading shadows in an MRI," she said. "Less screaming. Usually."

Rowan stepped onto the boat, the familiar lurch underfoot a reminder that solid ground was a suggestion in this town, not a promise. Buckshot followed with less grace and more enthusiasm, claws scrambling on metal, tongue lolling.

"You sure you want the dog?" Eve asked.

"Evidence hound," CJ said. "Unofficial, but dedicated."

Lucas eased them off the trailer. The boat slipped into the main channel with the practiced reluctance of anything that worked for a living. The river looked calmer now—wide, scuffed, pretending it had never done a wild thing in its life.

"Old bridge site first," Rowan said.

Lucas nodded. "You'll get your haunted tour. If Bledsoe's out there, this thing'll see him before we do."

They motored upstream, past the new bridge with its concrete shoulders and smug guardrails, toward the bend where the old iron span had given up in '69. The banks here were older—less manicured, more honest. Cottonwoods leaned in with the reckless trust of trees that had never learned not to.

Eve studied the sonar readout as the boat eased over the invisible scar where the bridge had once anchored.

"Bottom's uneven," she murmured. "Old pilings. Debris field. Give me another pass."

Lucas circled, slower. The engine's hum took on the rhythm of a lullaby sung while watching for snakes.

On the screen, the riverbed appeared in grayscale: ridges and hollows, logs like sleeping creatures, a refrigerator or maybe a car hood sulking in the silt.

"Here," Eve said, tapping.

A long, clean rectangle showed near the edge of the beam—too straight and too smooth to belong to nature. Metal. Big.

"Could be a chassis," CJ said. "Could be a section of bridge."

"Depth's fifteen feet," Eve said. "Current's slower here than downstream, but not kind. You want a dive, you're going to need more than good intentions and a rope."

Lucas made another pass. The rectangle stayed where it was, patient. A few yards downstream, a smaller object sat half-crooked in the silt. Eve zoomed in.

"Another metal echo," she said. "Not car-sized. Footlocker? Trunk?"

Rowan felt something tighten in her chest. The river was a collector, never a minimalist.

"We'll get the state dive team," CJ said. "Make them earn their hazard pay."

"Already texted Patel," Eve said. "Told her to bring coffee and liability waivers."

Lucas cut the engine. For a moment they drifted, the boat turning lazily in the current. The town looked different from here—less neat, more precarious. You could see where the water had licked at the edges of yards, where hung laundry had surrendered and fallen, where someone had painted a line on their garage wall and written NICE TRY under it.

"You ever think about leaving?" Lucas asked, squinting toward the horizon.

"Like moving?" CJ said. "Or like witness protection?"

"Either," Lucas said. "Both."

Rowan watched a branch turn in the eddy, spin once, then commit to downstream. "When I was a kid, I thought I'd go somewhere with mountains," she said. "Something taller than the courthouse dome. Somewhere the water stayed politely in pools you could see the bottom of."

"And now?" Lucas asked.

"Now I know the mountains have their own rivers," she said. "And they talk less nice."

CJ snorted. "That our official tourism slogan now? 'Cedar Valley: At Least the River's Honest'?"

"I'd put that on a brochure," Eve said.

They let the silence sit after that—the good kind that didn't need mending. Buckshot curled against CJ's leg, snoring in damp, contented bursts. A heron lifted off the bank, wings beating slow, each flap a counted thing.

"Mark both targets," Rowan said at last. "Big rectangle, smaller box. If the river's kept something down here this long, I'd like a word with it."

Eve tapped the coordinates into the tablet. "Marked. Labeled: Possibly Terrible One and Possibly Terrible Two."

"Very scientific," CJ said.

The station felt smaller now, crowded with boxes labeled EVIDENCE, boxes labeled REPAIRS, and one labeled MISC that smelled suspiciously like baked goods. Someone had hung a new bulletin board near the break room: COMMUNITY THANKS. It already sagged under homemade cards, photos of sandbag lines, and a picture of Buckshot in a child's life jacket with the caption: OUR HERO — DO NOT FEED CHOCOLATE.

In her office, Rowan pulled a fresh case file from the drawer. The manila folder was blank and stiff, the cardboard equivalent of a deep breath.

Across the top, in neat block letters, she wrote:

CEDAR VALLEY – 1969 FLOOD / DEPUTY JOHN BLEDSOE (UNRESOLVED)

Underneath, smaller:

Possible related: bridge failure, missing persons, unassigned evidence.

She slid in a photocopy of John Bledsoe's old leather holder, the sonar printout of the rectangle under the old bridge, and a copy of the obituary that praised his "heroic service" and said nothing at all about how his badge had ended up in a field a county away.

On a Post-it, she wrote the line penciled inside his wallet—

keep her away from the water —and stuck it to the inside cover.

Her phone buzzed. A text from Lydia:

HEADS UP. GRAND JURY TRUE BILL ON 6 COUNTS. PLOT THICKENS, FILLS OUT, GETS INDEXED. CHECK YOUR EMAIL.

Rowan opened her inbox. The county attorney had sent the official notice: indictment on multiple counts of conspiracy, obstruction, evidence tampering, and accessory to felony homicide. Attached was a brief note.

We're moving forward. Thanks for giving us something to move with.

She sat back in her chair. The feeling that came wasn't triumph. It was more like finally straightening a picture that had been crooked so long everyone had started to lean with it.

CJ knocked and stuck his head in. "You see the bill?"

"Yeah."

He held up a printout of tomorrow's Gazette mock-up. **THE RIVER'S LEDGER**, the headline read. Below it, a photo of the river bending around town, lanterns reflected in the water like a second, trembling string of lights.

"Lydia says you get two quotes this time," he said. "Try not to sound too poetic. It scares the retirees."

"I'll do my best," she said.

He nodded toward the file on her desk. "New case?"

"Old one," she said. "Just finally getting a name."

He came in and dropped into the chair across from her. "You ever worry this never stops? We dig up one rot and find another underneath, and another under that, and pretty soon we're ankle-deep in ghosts with a shovel that's too small."

"Every day," Rowan said. "But if we stop digging, the ghosts start doing the shoveling. They're worse at paperwork."

He laughed, short but real. "Put that on the recruitment brochure."

She closed the file gently. "We get Pike. We follow Sterling's paper trail. Maybe we find what's under the old bridge. Maybe we don't. Bledsoe, Emily, Sarah—they don't get a do-over. The town does. That's what we're actually indicting: the habit of looking away."

"Think it'll stick?" he asked.

"It'll scar," she said. "Which is better than festering."

He stood, stretching until something in his shoulder complained about flood rescues and bad mattresses. "Lucas says if we're on the river at dawn tomorrow, he'll show us where the old bridge pylons still squeak. You in?"

"Yeah," she said. "Text me the time."

"As your attorney, I'm obligated to remind you we don't have attorneys," he said. "But as your partner: bring coffee."

When he was gone, the office felt briefly too quiet. Rowan opened the bottom drawer and took out the cigar tin with three pennies inside. She shook it. The faint clink steadied her the way nothing else did.

For the ferryman, her father had always said. *In case he gets greedy.*

She set the tin on top of the new file—a paperweight for things that wanted to drift.

By evening, the heat had softened into something almost kind. The square hosted its latest version of normal: kids chasing each other around the soldier statue, a food truck selling tacos, a busker coaxing respectable music out of a battered guitar.

Rowan walked the river path, hands in her pockets. The water moved with its usual shrug, taking tree limbs, a lost basketball, the reflection of the courthouse dome. A slight breeze carried the distant smell of grilled meat and cut hay.

At the spot where boardwalk met dirt, she stopped. That place had become its own mile marker—the point in her day where she checked in with whatever passed for faith.

She could see the mill site downriver, a darker shadow where nothing stood anymore. Somewhere beyond that lay the bend where the sonar had traced their new mysteries in grayscale.

Her phone buzzed. A text from an unknown local number:

Heard what you did with the river. About damn time. She never liked that bridge. — M.

Rowan stared at it, then smiled despite herself. *M* could have been anyone—Mabel from the bakery. Mike from the feed store. Martha Crane's sister. Or someone else entirely.

She typed back:

We're still listening. Tell her to keep talking.

She didn't hit send. Instead, she deleted the message, slid the phone back into her pocket, and let the not-sent words sit with all the others the river already knew.

Lights blinked on in houses along the bluff. One porch had a sign propped against the railing:

THANK YOU, FIRST RESPONDERS / RIVER NOT DONE WITH YOU YET.

Someone had drawn a cartoon wave with angry eyebrows.

"Same to you," Rowan murmured.

She took her father's badge out one more time, let it catch the last light, then put it away. The weight had changed—not lighter, just settled differently.

"The river takes its own," she said, quiet enough that only she and the water heard it. "And the rest of us? It leaves standing here with clipboards and subpoenas and casseroles, trying to earn the ground we're on."

The current rolled past, unbothered.

Tomorrow there would be more evidence, more lab reports, more arguments about venue and jury pools. There would be a dive team's cautious descent, the rise of old metal from silt, the careful cataloging of whatever the river decided to surrender.

Tonight there was just this: a town that had stopped pretending not to hear the stories under its feet; a detective with fewer illusions but better questions; a river that would never be solved but might, if watched long enough, be understood.

Rowan turned back toward the square—the lights, the noise, the work waiting with its endless, ordinary insistence.

Behind her, the river kept moving, carrying secrets and driftwood and the faint glimmer of lantern wax that refused to fade.

She listened, as she always had.

The difference now was simple and enormous.

She was listening on purpose.

Chapter 19

What the River Kept

By dawn, the river looked almost polite. Mist lay low over the water, thin as breath on glass. The new bridge rose out of it in pale concrete ribs; below, the current slid past like something that had decided—for now—to behave. The parking lot by the launch ramp, usually home to fishermen's trucks and the occasional bored teenager, was crowded with state vehicles: two dive-team vans, a mobile command trailer, and Patel's cruiser crooked at the edge like an exclamation point.

Rowan pulled in beside CJ and killed the engine. Buckshot, riding shotgun with the solemnity of a second-in-command, put his paws on the dash and huffed at the sight of strangers in dry suits.

"Stay," Rowan told him. "You're on morale duty."

He gave her the look he reserved for unreasonable orders and sat back with a sigh.

CJ met her by the back of the car, coffee in one hand, a coiled rope in the other. "Morning, Hayes. You look like you've been up since 1969."

"New case file insomnia," she said. "Bledsoe kept getting out of the folder and walking around."

"Maybe today we get him to lie down somewhere official," CJ said.

Patel stood near the trailer, talking with the dive team leader—a woman in her forties with a buzz cut, a clipboard, and the air of someone who trusted water about as far as she could throw it, and who had thrown it farther than most.

"Detective Hayes," she called as Rowan approached. "Sergeant Wynn, DNR dive."

Wynn offered a gloved hand. "You're our local trouble," she said. "Heard you stirred up a hornet's nest and then asked the river to deliver the rest."

"We're trying to spread the workload," Rowan said.

Wynn's mouth twitched. "We've loaded your sonar coordinates. Target One—large metallic object, approximately vehicle-sized, depth fifteen. Target Two—smaller, probably container. Current's moderate, visibility's bad. You watching from here or riding out?"

"Boat," Rowan said.

Patel gave her a look that managed to combine warning, resignation, and *you were always going to anyway.* "Stay behind the divers," she said. "And don't fall in. I'm out of heroism paperwork."

"Noted," Rowan said.

Lucas's boat bobbed at the dock, impatient as a dog held by the collar. He stood in the stern, adjusting lines. Eve was already aboard, a waterproof kit bag at her feet, hair braided tight and tucked under a cap that said IOWA STATE MEDICAL EXAMINER in lettering just smug enough.

"Got your pennies?" she asked as Rowan stepped on.

Rowan patted her pocket. "Three in the tin. One on my conscience."

"Sounds about right," Eve said.

Two divers from Wynn's team climbed aboard with them, rubber and neoprene creaking. One had a cartoon frog sticker on his air tank; the other had written NO DRAMA in Sharpie across his fin strap, which felt like tempting fate.

Lucas pushed off. The boat eased into the channel, joined by a second dive boat from upriver. The morning was quiet enough to hear the hiss and clack of gear checks over the engine.

"Old bridge site first," Wynn said from the other boat, loud enough to carry. "Vehicle mark, then we swing back for the smaller hit."

Rowan moved to the bow as they motored upstream. The town fell away behind them—courthouse dome shrinking, square turning to a smudge of brick and muffled noise. Ahead, the river narrowed and took on a more intent look, as though it remembered something here.

They passed under the new bridge. Rowan felt her shoulders hitch the way they always did under concrete—old habit, formed by years of driving below overpasses with the knowledge her father had died near one. Beyond, the banks grew wilder, cottonwoods leaning in, bank grass torn and re-sown by the flood.

"Right about here," Lucas said, nodding to Eve.

She watched the tablet, sonar sweeping in methodical bands below them. "Coming up... there."

The long, clean rectangle reappeared on the screen. Even in grainy grayscale, it had a wrongness to it, a geometry that didn't belong on a riverbed.

"Target One," Eve said. "Still sitting where we left it."

Wynn's boat took position slightly upstream, anchor dropping with a heavy splash. Wynn's voice crackled over the handheld radio clipped to Rowan's vest. "Current's going to want to throw us downstream. We'll run a jackstay between the boats—tensioned line. Divers follow it to the mark. No one goes wandering."

"Copy," Rowan said, though she wasn't the one who'd be in the water.

Lines arced out. Metal rang softly as clips caught. The two divers on their boat checked buckles, regulators, each other. Eve watched them with the cool focus of someone who knew exactly what could go wrong with a human body and had a list of ways to argue it back.

"You ever dive?" one of them asked Rowan, more for distraction than curiosity.

"Pool once," Rowan said. "Didn't like the part where I couldn't hear my own bad ideas."

"Best part," he said, and rolled backward off the gunwale with a splash.

His partner followed. Bubbles rose, then smoothed. The ropes took on a faint vibration as weight moved along them below.

Rowan gripped the rail harder than she meant to. Her brain supplied images she didn't need: the bridge collapsing in '69, cars and people going down together; the water in that old black-and-white newspaper photo lapping at receding taillights like a satisfied animal.

"Breathe," Eve said mildly beside her. "He's the one under. You hyperventilating doesn't help his oxygen mix."

Rowan sucked in a slower breath. The river smelled like it always did in summer—green and murky and faintly metallic, as if it had bitten down on something it didn't intend to let go.

The radio on the console crackled. Wynn's voice: "Team One at bottom. Visibility one to two feet. Beginning sweep to south."

Time became elastic. Thirty seconds stretched; two minutes yawned. Lucas kept a casual eye on the bank, but Rowan could see the set of his jaw.

"Contact," Wynn's voice said. "We have metal. Contour matches vehicle roofline. Hood buried. No bubbles from interior."

Eve muttered, "Good, that's... good," as much to herself as anyone.

The frog-tank diver's voice came through, muffled by regulator and water. "Passenger-side glass is gone. Frame's twisted. I'm at the rear quarter panel."

"Tag it," Wynn said. "Run your line fore to aft, see if we've got a full chassis."

A beat, then: "Affirmative. Full vehicle. Compact sedan. Mid-century, by the look."

Rowan didn't realize she'd been holding her breath until her lungs protested. "Bledsoe's year," she said quietly.

Eve's eyes softened. "Could be coincidence."

"Could," Rowan said. Neither of them believed it.

"Checking interior," came the diver's voice. "Front seat... debris, silt. No obvious occupant. Rear seat—"

Silence. A shift in the rope between the boats.

"Say again, One," Wynn said, voice flat.

"Rear seat," he repeated. "Remains. Skeletal. Seated behind the wheel well—like he was thrown backwards when—" He cut himself off. "Tagging. Pocket area. There's... some kind of wallet or badge case. I can't see details."

Rowan closed her eyes briefly. The world did its best to keep spinning. Somewhere, a heron squawked in complaint at being disturbed so early.

"Do not remove anything by hand," Wynn said. "Body and artifacts come up together. We'll use the lifting bag. Mark anchor points."

"Acknowledged," the diver said.

CJ touched Rowan's elbow. "You good?"

"No," she said. "But that never stopped me before."

The next half hour passed in a series of controlled violences—the heavy splash of the lift bag, the creak of lines as they took on weight, the slow, careful rise of something that had been down too long. The river complained in small ways: eddies thickening, bubbles coming up where they had no business being, a branch arriving just at the wrong moment to tangle a line until Lucas leaned over and swatted it away like a fly.

Finally, something broke the surface off the port side—a ghost of a shape under clouded water, then the murky outline of a car roof. Metal, once blue or green, now raw and rusted, breached like a surfacing whale. A dangling strap marked where the driver's door had once been.

"Easy," Wynn called from the other boat. "Let it settle."

The wreck bumped the hull with a hollow, exhausted sound. Divers rose beside it, faces half-hidden by masks. One of them thumbed up in the universal *we're still alive* gesture.

They lashed the car between the boats and eased it toward the ramp, the river dragging at it as if to reclaim what was being stolen back. Onshore, deputies and a tow crew in reflective vests waited, winch cable ready. The whole process felt reverent and a little sacrilegious.

Rowan stepped off the boat as soon as they nudged the concrete. The air on land was no steadier. Mud sucked at boots as the tow hook clamped on, metal shrieking softly.

"Keep it tarped," Eve said. "We don't need a crowd learning anatomy today."

A blue tarp spread over most of the car, leaving only the undercarriage and bent bumper exposed. The winch whined. The wreck rose, dripping river and silt, water pouring from the trunk and wheel wells in murky curtains. Something dark and small slid out and hit the ramp with a wet smack.

Rowan bent to pick it up before anyone else noticed. A hubcap, warped and stamped with a logo that had gone out of style before she was born. She set it aside.

The tow truck pulled the car onto the flatbed, tarp shivering.

Wynn turned to her. "We'll transport to your secure bay," she said. "We open it under controlled conditions. Chain of custody, photos, the works."

Rowan nodded. "I want to be there."

"That's the idea," Wynn said. "You took the river's statement. Now we read it."

They moved the operation to the secure garage behind the station—a concrete box that usually housed seized drug cars and the occasional boat the state refused to assign a budget to. Today, the air inside held only oil, dust, and a faint tang of bleach from some long-ago spill.

The flatbed backed in. Doors clanged. Buckshot, relegated to the squad room with a chew toy the size of his ego, barked once in indignant commentary.

"Okay," Eve said, voice gone even flatter than usual. "Here's how this works. We photograph before we touch, we photograph as we touch, and nobody puts anything in a pocket that isn't theirs."

Wynn's divers, now stripped of tanks and rubber and back in human-sized bodies, nodded. CJ set up a video camera on a tripod. Patel leaned against the wall, arms folded, eyes sharp.

Rowan stood at the rear quarter panel as they peeled the tarp back. The smell hit first—stale river, wet metal, the faint, unmistakable sweetness of old death. It was gentler than a fresh scene, but no less insistent.

The car was a '60s Chevy, four-door, windshield caved, as if something heavy had sat on its face. The driver's seat was twisted, its springs showing; the steering wheel bent.

In the rear, behind the driver's side, a skeleton sat slumped against what remained of the seat frame. The bones wore tatters of uniform fabric, color long leached out, and the ghost of a badge shape on the left breast where metal had once ridden.

Eve stepped in. "Hold," she said softly, and began her slow orbit with the camera. Every angle, every scrap, cataloged.

On the remains' left hand, something still clung near the finger bones—a flattened metal ring.

"Wedding band," Eve murmured. "We'll check against the inventory."

At the hip, half-buried in sediment hardened to something like clay, a leather rectangle jutted out.

Rowan felt her whole body go still.

Eve saw it too. "Wallet or badge case," she said. "Photograph, then we excavate."

It took ten minutes. Ten meticulous, gloved minutes of brushing and teasing and coaxing until the leather came free. It still held its shape, barely; water had been kinder to it than to most.

Eve set it on an evidence pad and opened it with a pair of forceps.

Inside, under a film of silt, lay a badge dulled to pewter. The enamel field was cracked. The number, when the mud washed away, shone through: 17.

Below it, stamped in smaller letters: BLEDSOE, J.

Next to it, protected by the closed flap for decades, was a photograph. A young man in uniform, hat crooked, grin tilted like he expected the world to tilt back. Beside him, a girl with a ribboned ponytail, squinting into light, hand threaded through his arm.

On the inside of the leather, the pencil-scrawled line had blurred but not vanished.

keep her away from the water

Rowan's throat closed. The room around her dimmed at the edges.

"That's him," Rosa said from the doorway.

Rowan hadn't heard her arrive, but there she was—the clerk from the recorder's basement, still in her work cardigan, eyes shiny. "I typed his name a hundred times when they did that memorial plaque," she said. "Deputy John Bledsoe. My mom cried every time she saw the picture in the paper. Said he was too young to know how brave he'd been."

"We'll need dental records," Eve said, gently steering the moment back to procedure. "Old files. Anything you can find."

"I'll find them," Rosa said. "Even if I have to raid the museum and the church basement both."

Rowan forced her voice to work. "Thank you," she said. To Eve. To Rosa. To the room. To the river, maybe.

Patel exhaled. "We'll log this as a recovery, not a fresh homicide," she said. "But whatever Bledsoe was doing out there—whoever he died for—ties back to our mess. That bridge didn't just fail. Somebody sent him into that water with more than patrol on his mind."

CJ pointed to the shattered windshield frame. "You thinking sabotage?"

"Or pursuit," Rowan said. "Or a bad decision forced by a worse one. Either way, it's a story we didn't know we had to ask about."

"Speaking of stories," Wynn said, glancing at the clock on the wall, "we still have your Target Two to clear. The smaller object."

Rowan blinked, dragged reluctantly back to the present. "The trunk," she said. "Footlocker. Whatever it is."

Wynn nodded. "You want to press your luck today?"

Rowan looked back at Bledsoe's remains—at the badge, the ring, the scribbled plea for a girl whose name she didn't know yet.

"I don't think luck is what we're dealing with," she said. "But yes. Let's see what else the river was holding onto."

They went back out after lunch, the sun higher now and the heat lying heavier on the water. Buckshot, demoted again to station dog, watched them leave from the squad room window with the air of a martyr.

This time, the sonar target appeared faster—a compact, boxy shape lying crooked in a deeper pocket of the channel.

"Depth twenty," Eve said. "Current's messing with the returns. Whatever it is, it's wedged."

"Could be an old tool chest," Lucas said. "Could be somebody's regretted boat project."

"Could be records," Rowan said. "Or it could be a whole lot of nothing." Her voice said she didn't believe in nothing, not anymore.

Wynn's team dropped again, smaller crew this time. The radio crackled: "Contact. Metal container. Approx four by two. Heavily encrusted. No obvious openings. Secured for lift."

The box broke the surface minutes later, clotted with river growth and a beard of stringy roots. They wrestled it onto the deck with grunts and curses, then onto the dock, then into the truck. It weighed more than it looked.

At the station, they repeated the ritual: photos, gloves, slow patience. The box turned out to be military surplus—an old ammunition or equipment trunk, olive paint leached toward gray. The latch had rusted almost shut.

"Ready?" Eve asked.

Rowan nodded. "On three."

They forced the latch together. It gave with a screech like a protest from another era. The lid lifted, grudging.

Inside, wrapped in layers of oilcloth and what had once been plastic, lay paper. Stacks and stacks of it. The top bundle's outer sheet peeled away in Eve's hand, but the ones beneath held.

CJ let out a low whistle. "Well, that's not tackle."

Patel stepped closer, eyes narrowing. "Hold it."

Eve froze, hands steady midair.

"Let me get the camera closer," Patel said. "Whatever this is, it's why someone tried to make sure the river kept it."

They documented the first bundle as it came out. The heading, once the mud was brushed aside, read:

STERLING DEVELOPMENT – INTERNAL MEM-
ORANDA, 1968–1970

The second:

CEDAR COUNTY BOARD – UNFILED MINUTES
(PROPOSED)

The third:

RIVER CORRIDOR RELOCATION PROJECT –
CONFIDENTIAL ESTIMATES / REVISED

At the bottom of the trunk, shorter than the rest and wedged into a corner, lay a thin, sealed envelope. Wax had crumbled from its flap, but the seal itself had once borne the county's crest. Across the front, in handwriting Rowan could have recognized blindfolded, were four words.

For when she's old enough.

Her hand shook as she lifted it.

"Emily?" CJ asked quietly.

"Or me," Rowan said. Her voice felt like it belonged to someone standing further away. "Or some other girl they thought they could bargain with."

"Chain of custody," Eve reminded gently. "We log it, we open it with the camera rolling, we all pretend we're made of patience."

"Right," Rowan said, dragging her mind back through the necessary steps. "Log it. Everything goes through the lab first. No shortcuts. Not with this."

Patel scribbled on the evidence tag. "We've got Bledsoe. We've got Sterling's internal sins. We've got a packet addressed to a girl and a grand jury that just found its spine," she said. "If Pike's people thought the river would bury this, they misread their geography."

Rowan looked again at the envelope. *For when she's old enough.*

"I think," she said slowly, "we're about to find out exactly how long the river considers 'old enough.'"

That night, long after the trunk had been locked in evidence and the car sealed in the bay, after Bledsoe's remains had gone with Eve to the lab and the dive team had driven north toward their next borrowed river, Rowan walked the path to the bend.

The water glimmered under a slice of moon. Somewhere upstream, a fish slapped. Downriver, beyond the shadows of the cottonwoods, she could just see the darker patch that marked the old bridge site.

She took the cigar tin from her pocket and shook it. The pennies rattled, small and stubborn.

"One for Bledsoe," she said softly. "One for Emily. One for whoever that girl in the photo was, the one with the ribbon."

She set the tin on the railing, just for a moment, then picked it up again. Some things you left to the elements. Some things you took back.

"The river takes its own," she said to the current. "But you kept them for us. Him. The papers. Whatever's in that envelope. You held on longer than you had to."

The river, being a river, didn't answer. It moved past her ankles of thought with its usual shrug, carrying sticks and silt and the faint, silver smear of the moon.

Behind her, the town glowed in windows and porch lights, a scatter of human insistence. Ahead, on her desk, waited a trunk full of other people's secrets and a letter that had crossed decades to land in her hands.

For the first time in a long time, the weight of what they still didn't know felt less like drowning and more like a tide she might be able to read.

"Okay," Rowan said. "We'll keep listening."

The river went on pretending it was ordinary.

She knew better now.

Chapter 20

The Letter That Didn't Drown

The envelope sat in the middle of the table like a small, polite bomb.

The conference room off the station's main hall had seen its share of arguments and potlucks and one surprise retirement party that had almost killed a deputy with cake. Today it smelled like coffee gone bitter, copier ozone, and the iron tang of anticipation. Outside the frosted glass, the station murmured in its usual rhythms—phones ringing, printers spitting, someone laughing too sharply at a joke that wasn't funny.

Rowan couldn't hear any of it properly. Her whole focus narrowed to the rectangle of paper between them.

For when she's old enough.

The ink had feathered a little where water had touched it, but the letters were unmistakable. Her father's hand. Neat, blocky, the same script that had written *Filed under duress* and *Truth comes due* in a margin meant to be ignored.

Patel sat to her left, a legal pad in front of her, pen poised. To Rowan's right, CJ had his notebook open and his knee bouncing just enough to vibrate the table. Across from them, the county attorney and the visiting assistant AG occupied their side of the wood like a two-man panel on whether history got to happen.

Eve stood near the door with a tablet and a camera, because of course she was documenting this. The envelope lay on a clean evidence mat, already photographed from every angle, the evidence tag clipped nearby with dates, times, and signatures in tidy lines.

"Department case number, Bledsoe file number, trunk ID…" Eve finished her quiet litany, then looked at Rowan. "Ready?"

"No," Rowan said. "But that never stopped me before."

The county attorney cleared his throat. "Just for the record," he said, "we all understand this may be personal."

Rowan kept her gaze on the envelope. "It already is," she said. "That's why you wanted me in the room."

He didn't argue.

Eve set the camera rolling, the tiny red light blinking. "You'll open it," she said to Rowan, "so the chain is clear. I'll hold the corners."

Rowan pulled on fresh gloves. The latex snapped softly, the sound too bright in the quiet.

Up close, the envelope looked older than she'd let herself see at first glance. The paper had that faint waxy sheen of county stationery from another decade. The seal at the back was half–eaten away, but enough remained of the crest to be recognizable—a badly drawn river and a too-proud eagle, the same one that sat over the courthouse door.

She slid a finger under the flap, slow, careful. The paper gave with a reluctant sigh.

Inside was a single sheet, folded in thirds. No thick stack, no hidden confession written on the back of a tract map. Just one page.

Her hands wanted to shake. She told them no.

"Read it aloud," Patel said quietly. "If you can."

If you can. The words tried to snag. Rowan unfolded the page.

The first thing she saw was the date.

June 14, 1969.

Her father would've been twenty-six. A deputy, not yet sheriff. The river that year had taken the old bridge and half the stories people were willing to tell.

Below the date:

For my girl, when she's old enough to know what kind of town she belongs to.

Her throat tightened. She heard, faintly and unhelpfully, his voice in memory—reading her bedtime story titles, calling her in from the yard, saying her name when she'd scraped a knee like it was an apology to the universe.

She forced herself through the rest.

You'll be grown when you read this, or else somebody made a mistake I can't fix from here. I'm writing it because I don't know which way the river will take me before I get to say any of this out loud.

She didn't read the words like a letter. She delivered them like testimony, because that was what they were now. Eve's camera caught every line, each pause when Rowan had to breathe around a sentence.

By the time you can understand this, you'll have questions. About the badge. About the bridge someone let fall. About the girl they whispered about instead of remembering properly.

CJ's pen had stopped moving. Patel's jaw worked once and then set.

Rowan read on.

He wrote about 1969—about how the river had been high and mean, and the board had wanted the old bridge open anyway because closing it meant admitting they'd pushed their luck too far with the new industrial traffic.

He wrote about John Bledsoe.

He was a good deputy. He didn't know how to look away. We had a call about barrels dumping upstream after midnight. Complaints from the Bottoms about smell and dead fish. John went ahead of me in the cruiser. I got held up at the station with a call from the board chair "reminding" me who signed our checks.

Rowan heard the quotes in the word even without the marks.

By the time I got near the bridge, I saw headlights go off the side. It looked like an accident. That's the story we told. It made everyone feel better than the truth— that he'd radioed in that he saw a truck backing up to the water and someone else's headlights right behind him.

Her eyes skimmed the paragraph she didn't speak aloud: the one where her father wrote that he'd heard Bledsoe's last words on the radio—*tell her to stay away from the water*—before the line went static.

She swallowed and picked back up where her voice could walk.

We didn't pull the car then. The river was high. They told us it wasn't safe, we'd never get a rig in there, better to let it be. The board wrote a plaque about brave service and the bridge's age. Sterling made a donation for a new span. The town took the story that hurt less.

A muscle in Patel's cheek twitched.

The letter shifted then, like a current catching on something harder.

That same year, Sterling and Gideon Pike came to me about land. They had plans for the river corridor. They said flood controls and jobs. I saw the maps; I saw the houses that would be in the way. They said most of those folks would be glad to go.

He wrote about "persuasion"—about meetings with families who didn't want to sell, about threats dressed up as zoning arguments. He wrote about Emily Carter's parents, and how the Carters had held out longer than most because the farm was all they had.

Gideon said the girl liked town, liked the new movie house, liked the idea of not milking at dawn. He said young people understood progress better than their folks. He said you can move a family easier if you move their heart first.

Rowan's hand tightened on the page.

Her father wrote that he'd thought it was talk—ugly, but empty. Until he got word about Emily the first time she'd gone missing for a night and come back shaking and stubborn, refusing to name who'd cornered her at the river's edge with big plans and bigger threats.

I tried to open a file on it. The board chair called me in. Gideon sat in the corner and smiled without teeth. They told me we'd lose the development if we made trouble. They told me nobody would build here if they thought the sheriff's office couldn't be "practical."

He wrote about the assignment agreement—the one she'd held on the courthouse steps, the one with his signature and *Filed under duress* at the bottom.

I signed because if I didn't, they were going to find somebody who liked the idea of using kids as leverage. I signed and then I wrote the truth where I knew it would outlast me if your mother or you ever wanted to use it. I recorded what Emily told me even after they told me to drop it. I kept copies of what they did with the river. I couldn't stop everything. I could make sure someone could see it later.

The words blurred. For a second she saw only the parentheses of his hesitation—those places where his pen had pressed too hard, leaving faint dents in the paper.

If you're reading this, then the river and time have done their work, and you've decided not to look away. I won't ask you to forgive what I did or what I failed to. I'll ask you to remember that sometimes cowardice and courage wear the same face in the mirror. Do what you can live with. Don't let them tell you silence is loyalty. This town is worth more than the men who tried to own it. So are you.

He signed it simply:

Your dad,

Robert Hayes

Rowan's voice went out on the last syllable. The air in the room seemed to thicken.

Nobody spoke at first. Eve's camera hummed faintly. Somewhere out in the hall, a phone rang three times and stopped.

The county attorney let out a slow breath. "Well," he said. "That's... certainly not nothing."

The assistant AG had the look of a man mentally building an exhibit list. "It corroborates the trunk documents," he said. "Places Sterling and Gideon Pike in conspiracy as far back as '69. Supports a pattern of coercion. And if we can tie this to board minutes, that's half a rack of indictments."

Rowan kept her eyes on the letter. "It also makes my father accessory to half of it," she said.

"That's not how a jury will read it," the AG rep said automatically.

Patel cut him a look. "You don't get to tell her that," she said. "Not yet."

Rowan folded the letter carefully along its old creases. The paper felt fragile but stubborn, like the town.

"He tried," she said. "He didn't do enough. Both things get to be true."

CJ finally spoke. "He gave you the road map," he said quietly. "Not perfect. But it got us to Bledsoe. To the trunk. To the Pikes. Emily's voice isn't yelling into a void anymore."

Eve stepped in to take the letter, her touch efficient but gentle. "We'll get it scanned and secured," she said. "Original in fireproof, copies for the file and the court. And you get your own copy when we're done doing the legal dance."

Rowan nodded. It was either that or shake.

The county attorney cleared his throat again. "With this and the trunk, we've got enough to expand the Pike indictment," he said. "We add historical counts—conspiracy related to the '69 flood cover-up, falsified board records, whatever Sterling's memos give us. Might not physically put Gideon in the ground any deeper, but it hits his estate and legacy. And it makes Emily's disappearance part of a larger pattern, not an isolated tragedy."

"What about Bledsoe?" Rowan asked. "He gets to be more than a plaque?"

Eve answered that one. "Dental comparison's already in progress," she said. "Preliminary match is strong. Once that's confirmed, cause and manner will go in his file. Even if we can't say sabotage or accident conclusively, we can say more than 'car went in river and we shrugged.'"

"And the girl in his photo?" Rowan asked, surprising herself with the urgency in her own voice. "The one in his badge case. The penciled line—keep her away from the water. Who was she?"

Patel's gaze softened. "Rosa's on it," she said. "Yearbook, church directories, whatever she can dig out. Somebody will remember."

Somebody. The river had kept the body. The paper would have to deliver the name.

The meeting bled into logistics then—subpoena schedules, how to catalog the Sterling memos, whether to bring in a special prosecutor for the historical portion so the locals wouldn't have to cross old friends and enemies.

Rowan answered what she had to, nodded when appropriate, said no when someone suggested the letter might be too "emotional" for a jury.

"It's evidence," she said. "They can decide how it makes them feel."

By the time the conference room emptied, the sun had shifted across the frosted glass, turning the light in the room a cooler white. Only CJ lingered, shuffling his notes into a stack that had lost any hope of staying straight.

"You okay?" he asked.

Rowan let out a breath she'd been holding since 1969. "That's a terrible question."

"Yeah," he agreed. "You okay-ish?"

"Closer," she said. "He knew more than I wanted. He did more than I feared. He still failed Emily and Bledsoe. And he knew it. I'm..." She searched for the word and found one that didn't quite fit but refused to be moved. "Relieved."

CJ nodded. "You thought he was clean. Then you thought he was dirty. Turns out he was human. Messy middle. Welcome to the club."

"You think I'm human?" she said, managing the corner of a smile.

"On odd-numbered days," he said. "Today counts."

They walked out together. At the front desk, Buckshot lay behind the counter with his chin on his paws, supervising Mrs. Ellison paying a parking ticket with an air of great moral offense.

"You know," Mrs. Ellison said, signing the receipt, "if the river washed my car two inches, it should wash my fines too. Biblical out there."

"The river takes its own," Rowan said. "But the meter doesn't tithe."

She took Buckshot's ears in both hands and scratched until his back leg thumped. His eyes closed halfway, bliss and indignation at war.

"Come on," CJ said. "Lydia's pacing outside like a reporter who heard the word 'letter' through three doors and a filing cabinet."

He wasn't wrong.

Lydia waited by the steps, phone in one hand, the other jammed into her jacket pocket. The day was warm enough not to need the coat, but she wore stress like a cold front.

"Is it everything I hoped and feared?" she asked by way of greeting.

"Yes," Rowan said.

"You going to make me work for it?" Lydia asked.

"Yes," Rowan said again. "But I'll give you the bones. You can hang the words."

They walked a slow loop around the square. Rowan gave her the outline—no quotes, not yet. The date, the bridge, Bledsoe, Gideon's letter to Sterling, her father's decision to sign and then sabotage the paper trail with truth tucked into the margins.

Lydia's pen moved fast, shorthand looping like river eddies. At one point she stopped, stared at the page, and scribbled out *cowardice* only to write it back in smaller, tighter letters.

"So your dad wasn't a saint and he wasn't a villain," she said. "He was a man with a pen and a set of bad options."

"Congratulations," Rowan said. "You've just summed up the county."

Lydia huffed. "You realize this blows up half the town's mythology. Sheriff Hayes, Last Decent Man. Pike the Elder, Self-Made Savior. Sterling, Philanthropic Tyrant. The way we tell it, those guys were marble statues. Turns out they were just... boys in bad suits making worse decisions."

"Write them as people," Rowan said. "Marble's for courthouses. People crack better on paper."

Lydia glanced at her, something like gratitude and challenge in her eyes. "You're getting good at this," she said. "You want a byline?"

"Absolutely not," Rowan said.

The afternoon slid past in motions that felt almost normal. Reports to finish, calls from the lab to return, an email from the dive team confirming the coordinates for a follow-up sweep near the mill site "just in case the river missed a spot."

By four, the station hummed with the low-level buzz of impending shift change. Someone had brought in a box of donuts that had been reduced to two plain and one maple that dared anyone to pretend they didn't want it.

Eve appeared in Rowan's doorway with a folder and a look that said, I know you're not done and I'm going to tell you something anyway.

"Dental's back," she said. "Bledsoe is Bledsoe."

Rowan let herself close her eyes for a second. "Cause?"

"Consistent with blunt force and drowning," Eve said. "Windshield frame into chest, water into lungs. No sign of pre-impact trauma. If there was sabotage, it was in what happened before the car left the road, not in the car itself."

"Accident weaponized by context," Rowan said.

"Pretty much," Eve said. "We'll write it up that way. You want to be there when we notify his surviving next of kin? There's a niece in Des Moines. Rosa tracked her down. She grew up on stories about him. Some right. Some... less so."

Rowan considered it, the weight of yet another family learning that the story that kept them upright needed rewriting.

"Yes," she said. "If she wants to meet the woman who dragged him out of the river."

Eve nodded. "I'll set it up. You okay?"

Rowan tilted her head. "That seems to be the question of the day."

"Good," Eve said. "Keeps you from pretending the answer's obvious."

When the office finally disgorged her into the early evening, the sky over Cedar Valley had gone high and clear.

The courthouse dome caught the light and threw it back in a dull bronze shrug. The clock, four minutes slow, told the wrong time with its usual conviction.

Rowan didn't head for her car.

Her feet took her instead to the cemetery hill.

The road up was dry now, the flood mud baked and cracked at the edges like a warning that had missed its moment. The air smelled of warm stone and cut grass, and underneath both, that faint sweet trace of lilies left too long in vases.

Her father's grave hadn't moved. Of course it hadn't. The wind toyed with the little flags someone had stuck near the veterans' row. An insect droned somewhere behind her shoulder, insistent but not quite annoying.

She stood there longer than she meant to, hands in her pockets, the letter's words echoing without needing the page.

Do what you can live with. Don't let them tell you silence is loyalty.

"I'm mad at you," she said finally, feeling faintly ridiculous and wholly sincere. "You know that, right?"

The stone didn't answer. The oak overhead shifted its leaves like an old gossip.

"I wanted you to be better than this place," she said. "Cleaner. Untouched. That's not fair. You were *of* it. You tried. You failed. You left me enough to finish. That's... more than most around here can say."

She took his badge from her pocket, its metal warm from the day. She set it on the stone again for a moment, next to the small bouquet someone had left—probably her mother, probably the same mix of wildflowers and grocery-store daisies she'd used for twenty years.

"The river takes its own," she murmured. "But you didn't let it take everything."

She picked up the badge again. Some things you loaned to the world. Some you kept.

On her way back down, her phone buzzed.

Lydia:

HEADLINE DRAFT: "LETTER FROM THE RIVER: HOW A DEAD SHERIFF HELPED INDICT A MAYOR." TOO MUCH?

Rowan thumbed back:

"DEAD SHERIFF" MIGHT UPSET THE PIE COMMITTEE. TRY "LATE."

A beat, then:

Lydia:

YOU'RE NO FUN. ALSO, GRAND JURY SCHEDUL-ING THE 2ND PHASE HEARINGS. THEY WANT YOU AND THE LETTER. BRING YOUR PA-TIENCE.

Rowan smiled despite herself. *The letter.* Like it was a person on the witness list.

She slipped the phone away and looked once more toward the river. From up here, it was just a strip of dull silver through the trees, deceptively narrow.

Tomorrow there would be more testimony. More meetings. More arguments with men who wanted the past to stay politely forgotten.

Tonight there was the simple, enormous fact that the river had kept a car, a badge, a trunk, and a letter safe long enough for her to find them.

The rest would be on her.

She headed back toward town, following the curve of the road down into the square. Lights were coming on in shop windows—the bakery, the hardware store, the Gazette office where Lydia's lamp would burn far later than the rest.

She passed the statue in front of the courthouse. Someone had tied a blue ribbon around the soldier's wrist. Another had propped a hand-lettered sign against the base: *WE SEE YOU NOW.*

The river, somewhere beyond the last row of houses, moved in its unhurried way, carrying sticks and secrets and the knowledge that some stories were finally being told on purpose.

For the first time in a long time, Rowan didn't feel like she was chasing its current.

She felt like she was walking beside it.

Chapter 21

Under the Lights

By morning, the river looked almost polite.

Sunlight brushed the surface in broken ribbons, catching on bits of branch and trash like the day was trying to apologize for the last six weeks. From the bluff above The Bottoms, the town looked stitched back together with tarps and plywood and stubbornness.

Rowan drank bad station coffee from a paper cup that had seen better days. The rim had a faint crack that leaked heat onto her fingers. She didn't move it. The sting helped.

Down at the maintenance lot, trucks idled in a row: county, state, and one with a logo she didn't recognize—green shield, blue wave. Department of Natural Resources. Or, as Lucas had put it over the phone: "The people who get mad when the mud glows."

Patel joined her at the railing, file folder under one arm, radio clipped to the other. Mud still clung to the soles of her boots in a permanent outline.

"Farmer called again," she said. "Wants to know when the circus is coming so he can move his cows."

"Tell him we'll try not to arrest any of them," Rowan said.

Patel snorted. "You're going to like him. He's got the exact amount of suspicion I like in a witness: medium-high and equal-opportunity."

Rowan nodded toward the cluster of trucks. "You get any sleep?"

"Two hours and a shower that lied about being hot," Patel said. "You?"

"Dreams," Rowan said. "About bridges and filing cabinets."

"On brand," Patel said. "County attorney wants a word before we go play in the dirt. State AG sent a deputy. He's already annoyed."

"Why?"

"He's in a small town and not on TV," Patel said. "Come on. Let's let him practice his concerned face."

The conference room in the station still smelled faintly of flood and dry erase marker. Someone had tried to make it cheerful with a vase of supermarket daisies in the middle of the table. They looked like they regretted the assignment.

The county attorney sat with his wagon-print tie askew, legal pad open, pen at the ready. Across from him, a man in a sharp suit and a sharper haircut scrolled through his phone. His briefcase sat on the table like a threat.

"Detective Hayes," the county attorney said, standing. "You know Deputy AG Morgan."

"We've emailed," Rowan said. "You sent the charming memo about venue changes and media sensitivity."

Morgan gave a brief, polished smile. "We appreciate your cooperation, Detective. Cases like this—small-town corruption, historic harm—they're delicate."

"Corruption, harm, river," Rowan said. "That about covers the last fifty years."

He didn't rise to it. "We've got indictment on six counts," he said. "Conspiracy, obstruction, tampering, accessory to felony homicide. Good work."

"It's not done," Rowan said.

"That's why I'm here," he said. "We've had preliminary outreach from Mayor Pike's counsel. They're sniffing around a plea."

The room seemed to tighten. Patel slid into a chair, watching his face like it was another kind of crime scene.

"Plea to what?" Rowan asked.

"Conspiracy and obstruction," Morgan said. "He pleads out, gives us a clean allocution on the record, and we retire the homicide-adjacent charges with... strong language." He steepled his fingers. "In exchange, we don't drag every board member and donor from the last thirty years into court. And your town gets to move on without becoming a statewide circus."

Rowan stared at him. "That's your pitch."

He spread his hands a fraction. "Juries are unpredictable. Elderly defendants garner sympathy. Memories fade. Documents get... nuanced on cross. A guilty plea on conspiracy and obstruction is not nothing."

"It also doesn't put the word 'death' anywhere near what happened to Emily or Bledsoe," Rowan said. "Or the others we haven't put names to yet."

"We can acknowledge harm in the allocution," Morgan said. "We can craft language that—"

"You can write a paragraph," she cut in. "Great. The Pikes have been doing that for decades."

The county attorney held up a hand, peacemaker. "Let's slow this down. We've got another piece coming in this morning with the barrels at the Wexler land. That changes leverage. Before we talk deals, we see what we've actually got."

Morgan nodded once. "Agreed. The environmental charges—if the DNR confirms contamination—that's another tool. Felony dumping, fraud, maybe federal involvement if we're lucky."

"If we're lucky," Rowan repeated. "We get more acronyms in the room."

He looked at her, measuring. "Detective, I understand this is personal. Your father, the river, the Carter case. But I have to see the whole board. What justice looks like for a town is sometimes different than what it looks like for one family."

Rowan met his gaze. "Then let me be clear: if you take a plea that writes the dead into footnotes, I'm testifying in every church basement and feed store from here to the state line. On my own time."

The county attorney winced, but didn't argue. Morgan's jaw ticked—annoyance or respect, hard to tell.

"Let's see what's in the field first," he said. "Then we can argue about adjectives."

The Wexler land had always looked slightly wrong to Rowan, even before she knew why.

From the road, it was just another patch of Iowa: rolling pasture, thin line of trees, a low rise where a house had once stood before a tax sale and a windstorm taught it humility. The grass grew in uneasy swaths, lush in some spots, stubbornly thin in others. Cows grazed at a distance, tails flicking, unconcerned with history.

The farmer who met them at the gate wiped his hands on his jeans and squinted like the sun owed him money.

"Name's Harlan Dittmer," he said. "I rent this patch off the county. They tell me you're here to dig up my cow pond?"

"Just the edge of it," Patel said. "You found a barrel lid?"

"Dog found it," Harlan said, hooking a thumb at a blue heeler that watched them with suspicious intelligence. "He likes to dig where the ground's wrong. Brought the lid up like a trophy. Figured I'd better call somebody before I grew a three-headed calf."

He led them along the fence line to a low, soggy spot where the pasture dipped toward a drainage ditch. Yesterday's rain had left a gloss on the grass. At the center of the dip, a circle of earth had slumped in: darker soil, bare in a ring, like something heavy had sat there too long and changed its mind.

The barrel lid leaned against a fence post. Rust had eaten the edges, but the stenciled logo in the center was still visible: STERLING DEV. CHEMICAL SERVICES. A series of numbers curved around the side.

"You didn't move anything else?" Eve asked, stepping carefully, soil sampler in hand.

"Dog tried," Harlan said. "I yelled. Dog listened. One of us is trainable."

The DNR guys—green vests, khaki pants, expressions of professional disappointment—set up a grid with small flags. One started probing the ground with a steel rod, muttering measurements. Another knelt to scoop soil into a plastic bag, double-gloved.

"Metal at two, maybe three feet," the rod guy said. "Hollow. Multiple hits."

"Plural," Rowan murmured.

"Of course," Patel said.

They brought in a small backhoe from the county shed. Harlan's heeler watched every move like he expected the earth itself to confess.

The first scoop peeled off the top layer of sod and set it aside in a neat square. The second bite hit something that rang dull and wrong.

"Okay," Eve said. "Hand tools from here."

They dug with shovels and care, muddy water seeping into the hole as if the river had sent a cousin. Within minutes, the curve of a drum emerged: blue paint under rust, the kind of industrial barrel that never held anything gentle.

"Markings," one of the DNR techs said, wiping muck from the side. "Sterling again. Same code series as the lid."

"And over here," the rod guy called from three feet away. "Another one."

They worked for an hour, uncovering the tops of five drums in a loose cluster, all very deliberately buried in the shallow bowl of the pasture. The soil around them stained darker, slicker.

The air had a sour tang now, chemical and sweet, underneath the usual mud and manure. Eve wrinkled her nose.

"You smell that?" she asked.

"Yeah," Rowan said. "What is it?"

"History," Eve said grimly. "And solvents."

The DNR team switched into full don't-touch-that mode—Tyvek suits, respirators, the whole kit. They took core samples of the stained soil, labeled them in careful block print.

Rowan stood at the edge of the tape, watching the drums emerge like relics from a faith nobody wanted anymore.

"Sterling's plant was supposed to neutralize waste," Patel said quietly. "Not plant it."

"Cheaper to let the land do the work," Rowan said. "As long as you don't mind what it grows."

Harlan jammed his hands deeper into his jacket pockets. "My father always said this ground had a mean streak," he muttered. "Cows got sick here more than they should. Vet said bad luck. Guess the vet was reading from an old script."

"Any people?" Eve asked gently. "Cancer clusters? Weird illnesses?"

Harlan's jaw tightened. "My brother died at forty-two with a liver that looked like he'd been drinking battery acid," he said. "Except he didn't drink. Doctor shrugged. Called it genetic. I call it Wexler."

Eve nodded once. "We'll get groundwater tests," she said. "You'll have answers. Maybe not the kind you want, but answers."

"That'd be a first," Harlan said.

One of the techs straightened, holding a smaller object wrapped in a gloved hand. "Got something wedged between the drums," he called.

He carried it up to the tape line. Eve took it, peeled back the plastic.

It was a metal tag, palm-sized, with a hole at one edge where it had once hung from something with a chain or wire. Mud streaked the surface, but the lettering underneath came through when she rubbed it with her thumb.

PROPERTY OF CEDAR COUNTY SHERIFF'S OFFICE

EVIDENCE – DO NOT REMOVE

Underneath, in smaller letters, a number. Rowan's stomach turned.

"Somebody threw a box of evidence in with the barrels," she said.

"Or chained a box to one before they rolled it in," CJ said. "Make sure it stayed sunk."

They scraped around the cluster more carefully. Between the second and third drum, they found splintered wood and the metal corners of what had once been a crate. Inside, barely holding together, were the ghosts of file folders: the impression of paper, clay-thick and unreadable.

"Lab's not going to like me," Eve said. "But I'll take it."

"Any chance of pulls?" Rowan asked.

"Maybe scraps," Eve said. "Letterheads. Signatures. Enough to show intent, not enough to make a neat PDF."

Rowan watched as they eased the crate remains into a tub, mud and all.

"Your father tried to hide evidence from Sterling and Pike," CJ said quietly. "Somebody did the opposite—hid evidence for them."

"Or from them," Rowan said. "If you worked here, saw what was going into the ground, and were scared enough to keep records off-site... this is where you'd put the originals if you knew the river was coming."

"Not exactly archival conditions," he said.

"Depends what you're hiding from," she said.

Morgan picked his way over from the trucks, holding a handkerchief over his nose. He looked at the drums with professional dismay.

"We've got enough here to bring environmental charges," he said. "Maybe fraud, depending on what the manifests say, if they even exist. This is good."

"Good isn't the word I'd use," Harlan said.

Morgan had the grace to look chastened. "Legally," he amended.

He turned to Rowan. "This bolsters the idea of a pattern. Pike's plea team is going to hate this. They wanted to close the book on River Bend as an old bad act. This keeps it open."

"Then you're not taking the deal," Rowan said.

His jaw worked. "I'm saying it gives us leverage to ask for more," he said. "If he wants to plead, he talks. On the record. About Sterling, about his father, about the dumping, about pressure on Sheriff Hayes and Deputy Bledsoe. No more 'vague community harm' and 'regrettable oversights.' Names. Dates. Direct answers."

"And if he won't?" Patel asked.

"Then we go to trial," Morgan said. "And roll these barrels into the middle of the courtroom if we have to."

Harlan's dog barked once, sharp, as if in agreement.

By late afternoon, the pasture looked like a crime scene and a construction site had a discouraging baby.

Barrels sat lashed upright on pallets, rims wrapped in plastic and hazard tape. The DNR boys fussed over them like grumpy midwives. The hole they'd left behind was already collecting water, a shallow, ugly pond.

"Get some temporary fencing around that," Eve told Harlan. "Last thing we need is a cow deciding to baptize herself in chemical soup."

"I'll run a line tonight," he said. "And maybe leave a few Pikes' names on salt blocks around the edge to keep 'em away."

Rowan watched the barrels being winched onto a flatbed. Each thunk as metal met wood felt like a punctuation mark.

"You okay?" CJ asked.

"No," she said. "But never before four p.m."

He huffed. "You get weird when we find physical proof."

"I'm used to ghosts," she said. "Ghosts don't need hazmat signs."

They packed up slow. The DNR trucks pulled out first, followed by the county rig, Patel's SUV, and finally the cruiser. Lucas's truck remained by the gate, tailgate down. He sat on it, boots dusty, watching the field like it might misbehave if he looked away.

Rowan and CJ wandered over.

"You look like you lost a bet," she said.

"I did," he said. "I bet myself this place would manage to have one secret that wasn't buried in something toxic. I owe me twenty bucks."

He nodded toward the churned-up patch. "I grew up being told not to fish behind Wexler's," he said. "Dad said it was too muddy, too snaggy. Guess he was just too polite to say 'because they poisoned it.'"

"You told him about the barrels?" CJ asked.

Lucas shook his head. "He's dead," he said. "But I'll tell him next time I'm talking to his headstone. He likes updates."

They leaned on the tailgate together in companionable misery.

"So now you've got drums, half-melted files, a trunk of fun from the river, and a town that just learned the ground they walk on is meaner than they thought," Lucas said. "What's justice look like for that?"

Rowan watched a crow hop along the fence line, eyeing something shiny in the churned dirt. "Messy," she said. "Partial. Slow."

He glanced sideways at her. "That what you're going to tell Emily's folks? Bledsoe's niece?"

"No," Rowan said. "I'm going to tell them we stopped pretending their dead got that way because of weather and God. Sometimes that's all you can do. Give responsibility a name."

Lucas considered that. "You sound more like your father every day," he said.

She flinched, then relaxed, surprised to find the words didn't stab like they used to.

"I hope not," she said. "I'd like to do at least a few things differently."

"Like what?" he asked.

"Not waiting thirty years to write 'truth comes due' at the bottom of something," she said.

They regrouped at the station as the sky went from blue to pewter again.

The county attorney's office had already sent over a revised plea framework. It sat open on Patel's desk, pages clipped, sticky notes bristling from the margins like angry flags.

Rowan skimmed the summary.

"If Pike pleads," she said slowly, "we get conspiracy, obstruction, felony dumping, falsification of public records, and accessory to environmental harm. He allocutes to knowledge of Sterling's chemicals and his father's role. We get a full record of the River Bend scheme, in his own words."

Patel nodded. "And?"

"And we drop the homicide-adjacent counts," Rowan finished. "The language acknowledges 'consequences including loss of life,' but doesn't charge him directly with those deaths."

CJ looked between them. "That enough?" he asked.

"For court?" Patel said. "Probably. For the Carters? The Bledsoes? Half the town?"

"No," Rowan said. "But it's closer than nothing."

The county attorney appeared in the doorway, tie loosened, hair surrendering to the humidity. "AG's office is game to push," he said. "Pike's lawyer is making noises about his age, his heart, the unfairness of revisiting his father's sins. We keep the environmental charges on the table, he'll fold. He does not want to die in a prison infirmary."

Rowan tapped the plea summary. "I want Emily's name in the allocution," she said. "Not just 'individuals harmed.' And Bledsoe's. And any reference to 'those who lost property or health' amended to 'including but not limited to the Carters, the Bledsoes, and the families at River Bend.'"

"That's a lot of names for one paragraph," the county attorney said.

"Then make it two," she said. "You want this on paper? Fine. Make the paper say what actually happened."

He considered. "We can push for name inclusion," he said. "Morgan will grumble about precedent. But we can frame it as historical clarity."

"And I want the drums and the river trunk entered as exhibits," she added. "Even if the lab can't pull every word, the fact that they existed matters."

"That's evidence, not plea language," he said. "But we can attach them to the record as part of the factual basis."

CJ leaned back in his chair. "So the story gets told," he said. "Even if the label on the shelf isn't the one we wanted."

Rowan let out a breath she hadn't realized she'd been holding.

"People will call it a slap on the wrist," she said. "They'll see a number of years and think it's too few. They'll see the charges we dropped and think we went soft."

Patel shrugged. "People want a clean ending," she said. "We're giving them a book of receipts instead. They won't know what to do with it at first."

"Then we teach them," Rowan said.

She picked up the plea framework again, mind already rewriting sentences, underlining phrases.

The river didn't do this. People did.

If she had to settle for a document instead of a thunderclap, she was going to make sure the document didn't lie.

It was full dark by the time she made it back to the levee.

Cedar Valley glowed behind her—porch lights, the hospital's lit cross, strings of bulbs over patios where people ate tacos from the food truck and pretended for an hour that the ground under them hadn't been rearranged.

The river moved, black and opaque, carrying the faint reflections of all that borrowed light.

Rowan stood with her hands in her pockets, the plea draft folded in her coat. Somewhere upstream, the newly exposed gap in Harlan's pasture waited for rain to fill it, a scar in the land that no one was going to pretend was just "bad luck" anymore.

She thought of Kayla, hands braced on her kitchen chair, learning that her uncle's death hadn't been an accident of weather. Of Ruth Anne, living her quiet life near some other water, about to get a call that would put old grief in a new shape. Of Emily's parents, who might not want to hear anything at all.

"Whose town is this?" Lydia had asked.

Tonight, it felt like the answer was simple and impossible: it belonged to the people who were finally willing to hold the ugliness right alongside the casseroles.

A shape moved at the edge of her vision. CJ joined her at the rail, shoulders slumped, jacket unbuttoned.

"Patel's on with Morgan," he said. "They're haggling over commas. Pretty sure that means we're taking the deal."

"Pretty sure," Rowan said, eyes on the water, "or hopeful?"

He considered. "Both."

They watched in silence as a log turned in the current, bumped a rock, and slipped past.

"You going to tell your mother?" he asked.

"About Bledsoe? The barrels? Pike maybe saying the right words for the wrong reasons?" She shrugged. "Yeah. She deserves to know why Dad drank too much coffee and stared at the river so often."

"You think this is what he wanted?" CJ asked. "Back then?"

She thought of the letter. *Filed under duress. Truth comes due. Do what you can live with, if you get the chance.*

"I think he wanted a version where nobody else had to bleed for it," she said. "We didn't get that. We got this."

CJ nodded. "Could be worse," he said. "Could be nothing."

A barge horned in the distance—low, insistent. The river answered in its own language, slapping gently against the banks.

Rowan unfolded the plea draft and smoothed it against the rail. The paper caught a bit of damp, edges curling. She didn't mind. The words would live in drier, more official places soon enough.

She read the line Morgan had penciled in as a concession, the one he'd muttered about while Patel watched him like a hawk.

The defendant acknowledges that decisions made for personal and financial gain contributed to the deaths, disappearances, and long-term harm of residents including, but not limited to, Emily Carter, Deputy John Bledsoe, and families residing in the River Bend development.

It wasn't everything. But it was on paper, in ink, in a court record that wouldn't wash away in the next flood.

"The river takes its own," she said quietly. "We don't have to help it lie about why."

CJ bumped her shoulder with his. "You know," he said, "for someone who hates speeches, you're getting pretty good at the epilogue parts."

"Shut up," she said without heat.

They stood there until the chill seeped into their shoes and the courthouse clock—four minutes slow, always—tolled nine. Each strike carried across the water, as if the town itself was counting, out loud, what it owed and what it was finally ready to pay.

Behind them, Cedar Valley pulsed with small, ordinary life.

In front of them, the river kept moving, carrying barrels and secrets and, now, the faint edge of something else: a story that no longer belonged only to it.

Rowan folded the plea draft again, slid it back into her pocket, and turned toward town.

There were calls to make. People to tell. Files to annotate. A future to write, in smaller, more honest lines.

The river would keep its own counsel.

She was finally keeping hers.

Chapter 22

Truth Comes Due

By the time the plea hearing rolled around, the river had almost convinced the town it was harmless again.

Morning light slid off the water in dull pewter sheets. The banks, newly combed and seeded, wore a fuzz of hopeful green. Sandbags still hunkered in odd places—at the corner of the library, behind the diner—like guests who hadn't realized the party was over. Cedar Valley moved around them the way you moved around a bruise: carefully, with a memory of pain but an eye on the grocery list.

Rowan parked two blocks from the courthouse instead of in the lot. Habit, mostly. It gave her a minute to walk off the feeling that her bones had turned to mismatched cutlery.

CJ fell into step beside her, tie skewed, coffee in hand. "You know, when I pictured taking down a corrupt mayor, I imagined… I don't know. Less paperwork. More theme music."

She eyed his cup. "Is that coffee or motor oil?"

"At this point?" He took a cautious sip and grimaced. "Both."

They rounded the corner. The courthouse steps had been scrubbed so many times they looked a shade paler than the stone above them, like a line on a wall measuring how high the water had gotten and how close the town had come. The clock overhead still lagged its four honest minutes.

There weren't TV vans this time. Just a row of local news cars, a scattering of folding chairs, and a knot of townspeople in clothes that tried to be their best and mostly succeeded. Two boys in basketball shorts leaned against the railing, pretending not to be there on purpose.

Lydia waited near the base of the steps with her notebook, pen already uncapped. The circles under her eyes said she'd been up too late again, trying to make cruelty fit in a column inch. "Well," she said. "Big day for men who thought they were unsinkable."

"Pike's people still threatening to move venue?" CJ asked.

"They can move venue all they want," Lydia said. "They can't move the river."

Inside, the corridors hummed with bureaucratic anxiety. Deputies moved in the brisk, careful way of people who'd been told the world was watching, even if it was only the county. The air smelled like lemon cleaner, paper dust, and nerves.

Patel met them near the courtroom doors, file under one arm. "AG's office is here," she said without preamble. "Judge Larson's on the bench. Pike's team blinked—he's ready to plead on the new counts."

Rowan's jaw ticked. "And the old ones?"

"Rolled in," Patel said. "Conspiracy, obstruction, evidence tampering, accessory to felony homicide, environmental crimes. They'll drop the top murder count if he allocutes clean and gives us everything on Gideon and Sterling."

CJ let out a low whistle. "That's a lot of everything."

"His lawyer's been earning his retainer." Patel's mouth twisted. "Victim families signed off. They want guarantees more than they want headlines."

Rowan nodded, even as something inside her bristled. She understood, in the way you understood gravity. It didn't mean you had to like the fall.

The courtroom was fuller than it had been for the earlier hearings. Not standing-room full. Not circus full. Just full enough that the air felt thick with breath and opinion. Emily Carter's parents sat in the second row, shoulder to shoulder, hands laced so tightly their knuckles had gone white. Bledsoe's niece, Kayla, sat two benches back, a ball cap in her hands, twisting the brim into something that didn't deserve it.

On the other side, a handful of Pike loyalists sat stiff-backed and offended, as if the very act of charging him was a personal insult. One woman wore a cedar-green blazer with a campaign pin from his first mayoral run. The pin looked out of place now, like a joke nobody could hear.

The bailiff called the room to order. Judge Larson took the bench, his robe hanging off him like a heavy opinion. "We are here on State of Iowa v. Daniel Gideon Pike," he said, voice rasped by years of smoke and sentencing. "I'm told there is a plea agreement to consider."

The county attorney rose first, flanked by the AG rep in his perfect suit. They took turns reciting the charges, the penalties, the terms. Words stacked up in careful, legal piles: knowingly and intentionally, in concert with, resulting in the death of. Environmental discharge. Fraud. Falsification. Conspiracy.

"Mr. Pike," the judge said at last. "You understand the charges against you?"

Pike stood at the defense table. He looked smaller than he had at the press conference—sleeves straight, hair neat, but a size too big for his own skin. "Yes, Your Honor," he said. His voice had lost its practiced warmth, the cadence he used at parades and ribbon cuttings. It sounded like it had been left in the rain.

"You understand that by entering a plea today, you waive your right to a jury trial, to confront witnesses, to make the state jump through all the hoops we keep around for their benefit?"

"Yes."

"And you're doing this voluntarily? No one promised you the river would forgive you if you confessed?" The judge's eyes flicked briefly toward Rowan, then away.

Pike's mouth tightened. "I'm doing it voluntarily, Your Honor."

"All right then." Judge Larson leaned back. "Let's hear the words. Count One: conspiracy to commit fraud and obstruction related to River Bend land acquisitions. How do you plead?"

"Guilty," Pike said.

The word landed like a small, hard stone in the room. It didn't echo. It just sat there, existing.

Count Two. Guilty. Count Three. Guilty. Count Four, accessory after the fact to felony homicide in the matter of Emily Carter. His lips almost tripped over that one. For a heartbeat, Rowan thought he might choke it back, swallow it like he'd swallowed everything else. But he said it.

"Guilty," he breathed.

Emily's mother's shoulders shook once, sharply, like someone had reached out and pulled a string between her shoulder blades. Her husband's hand tightened over hers. He stared straight ahead, eyes focused on a point above the judge's head, as if any lower would drown him.

The environmental counts came last—illegal dumping, falsified reports, endangerment. Those he wrapped his mouth around with something that almost looked like relief. Money and poison. Those were the sins he knew how to confess to.

When it was done, the judge steepled his fingers. "We'll accept the plea pending an allocution that satisfies me you're not just reading lines your lawyer wrote," he said. "Which means you're going to tell me, in your own words, what you did."

Pike's attorney leaned in, murmured something. Pike nodded once, then stepped up to the microphone.

"I..." He cleared his throat. His eyes flicked to the gallery, skated past faces he'd once sought out at fairs and fundraisers. "I participated in a plan to... to acquire land for the River Bend development using pressure. I knew about funds paid to certain families. I knew that reports on soil contamination were..." He inhaled, exhaled. "...altered."

"And the Carter girl?" Judge Larson said. Not unkindly. Just directly.

Pike's gaze went to the tabletop. "I knew my father had... spoken to the family. That he'd threatened consequences if they didn't sign. I didn't order what happened to her." His voice thinned on those words. "But I knew, after. I knew what he'd done. I helped... move paper. Hide accounts. Keep Sheriff Hayes from pushing too hard."

Rowan felt her throat tighten. He said her father's name like a tool, not a man.

"And you benefited," the judge said.

"Yes."

"With money?"

"Yes."

"With power?"

A pause. "Yes."

"And with silence," the judge said. "Which might be the worst currency we have in this county."

Pike flinched. For a moment, the mask slipped, and something almost like bewildered anger showed through. How had it come to this? How had a town he'd fed parades and pavements turned on him? Rowan recognized the expression. It was the look of a man who'd mistaken ownership for stewardship his whole life.

Judge Larson nodded once. "All right. I find the plea is knowing and voluntary. We'll proceed to sentencing."

Victim impact statements came next. The county attorney had warned Rowan. Hearing them wasn't required, but it felt like the only honest thing left.

Emily's mother walked to the podium like a person approaching a river crossing on a broken bridge. She held a single index card in her hand, not because she needed it, but because it gave her fingers somewhere to be.

"My daughter was seventeen," she said. Her voice was rough and low, like gravel under tires. "She was... sharp. Stubborn. She wanted to go to nursing school. Or write a book. Or both. She changed her mind a lot." A small, breathy laugh escaped her, surprised out of grief. "She liked the river. She thought it was pretty. I told her it was dangerous. She told me—" The woman swallowed. "She told me the river just did what rivers did. It was people you had to watch."

A murmur ran through the room. CJ's jaw set.

"After she disappeared," Emily's mother said, "we were told a lot of things. That she'd run off. That she'd fallen in. That she'd... made choices. None of those things was true. What was true is that men with names in this room decided our land was worth more than our girl." She lifted her eyes to Pike, and for the first time, he looked directly back at her. Her stare didn't waver. "You signed papers. You looked away. You let my daughter be the lesson you wanted to teach. I hope every night you have left, you see her realizing it wasn't supposed to be her."

She put the card down. The back was blank.

Bledsoe's niece spoke next. Kayla took the stand in a faded hoodie and clean jeans, as if she'd dressed up as herself and not known how to iron it.

"My uncle John was the kind of man who'd turn around to pick up a turtle if it was in the middle of the road," she said. "He died before I was born, so I only know him from stories and a picture in my grandma's hallway. Stories about the '69 flood and how 'the river took its own.'" She glanced at Rowan. "Turns out, the river had help."

The corner of Rowan's mouth twitched despite herself.

Kayla held up a copy of the photograph from his badge wallet—the young deputy and the girl with the ribboned ponytail. "We still don't know exactly what happened to him," she said. "But we know he tried. He tried to stand between the river and people who wanted to push others into it. He deserves a better story. So does that girl."

She folded the photo back against her chest. "Putting you in prison won't fix that," she said to Pike. "But it might make the next man think twice before he plays god with a flood."

Other voices followed. A farmer whose field had grown nothing but stunted corn since the dumping started. A woman who'd lost a brother to a cancer she would always half-blame on groundwater. Their pain was smaller, more diffuse than Emily's family's, but it came from the same source.

When it was done, the judge shuffled papers that didn't need shuffling. "Mr. Pike," he said, "I've known your family my whole life. Your father once told me the river was the best friend Cedar Valley ever had, if we just taught it who was boss." He tilted his head. "I disagreed then. For the record, I disagree now."

A faint ripple of rueful laughter moved through the benches.

"You took advantage of people's trust," the judge went on. "You hid behind your father's ghost, your office, and this town's bad habit of looking the other way. You helped bury evidence and truth where you thought no one would find it, except maybe the catfish." He lifted the sentencing sheet. "The state's recommendation is forty years with eligibility after twenty. Given your cooperation and age, I'll follow it. I'm also ordering restitution toward an environmental remediation fund and a trust for the Carter family."

He leaned forward. "Let me be clear. This is not forgiveness. The river doesn't forgive. It just keeps going. So will we. You'll be doing your going from a cell."

The gavel came down with a sound like a door closing somewhere deep under water.

Rowan felt something loosen in her chest. Not relief. Not victory. More like a knot that had finally stopped tightening.

As deputies led Pike away, he turned his head. Just slightly. His gaze landed on her. For the first time, there was no salesmanship in it. No performance.

"You could've left it buried," he said quietly, too low for the microphones, just loud enough for her.

Rowan held his eyes. "You could've, too," she said. "You're the one who dug the holes."

They took him through the side door. The lock thudded. Somebody in the gallery let out a breath they'd probably been holding since 1994.

Outside, the air felt oddly thin, as if the building had exhaled everything it had kept inside and forgotten to refill. Sunlight bounced off wet spots on the pavement where last night's brief storm had left its comments and moved on.

Lydia caught up with them on the steps, recorder in one hand, coffee in the other. "Well," she said. "That's one chapter titled and filed."

"Got your headline already?" CJ asked.

She flashed a mock front page she'd roughed in by hand. PLEA IN THE FLOOD CASE, in block letters. Underneath, in smaller script: The river's ledger, part two.

Rowan raised an eyebrow. "Subtle."

"I promised the copy desk I'd only go full biblical once a quarter," Lydia said. "This counts."

They moved toward the square together. The claim tables were still set up, but the lines were shorter now. A girl was coloring a sandbag with a purple marker, giving it eyelashes and a speech bubble that said I TRIED.

"Families okay?" Lydia asked quietly.

"As okay as they know how to be," Rowan said. "Emily's mom said she's tired of people asking if this gives her closure. She said there's no such thing. There's just... less open."

Lydia's mouth pressed into a line that wasn't quite a smile. "I'll steal that, if you don't mind."

"Credit the river," Rowan said.

CJ peeled off to return a call from Eve—something about preliminary results from samples pulled near the Wexler barrels. Lydia drifted toward a cluster of folks already arguing about which parts of Pike's deal were a travesty and which were a necessity.

Rowan found herself at the edge of the square, standing by the railing that overlooked the river path. From here, you could just see the bend where the old bridge had been, the water sliding past like it had somewhere to be that didn't involve human drama.

She didn't hear Lucas come up until he spoke. "Heard the news," he said. "Radio man made it sound like we just won state."

"Depends how you feel about trophies," she said.

He leaned on the rail, arms folded. "I feel like the river got some of its story back," he said. "That's enough for me."

They watched a pair of kids down on the path throw sticks into the current and time whose got carried away faster. One stick snagged on a root and spun there, trapped in its own little whirlpool.

"Dive team's going back out next week," Lucas said. "State wants more mapping up past Wexler land. Deep holes up there. Weird eddies."

"Looking for more barrels?" she asked.

"Looking for whatever else your mayor and his friends thought sank," he said. "Eve says she'll ride along if you do. She likes telling the sonar it's wrong."

Rowan huffed a laugh. "Tell her to bring Dramamine and bad jokes."

Lucas angled his head to study her. "You look... not lighter," he said slowly. "Just... less braced."

"I'm tired," she said.

"Everyone's tired," he said. "You're less... waiting for someone to push you in."

She didn't answer. He wasn't wrong. She just didn't have language for the difference yet.

Later, back at the station, the evidence board in the briefing room had been cleaned. Pike's photo had been moved from the center to the side, pinned under a fresh label: CONVICTED. The Carter case file had a new fold-er tab—CLOSED / HOMICIDE SUPPORTING DOCS PENDING. Someone had drawn a tiny wave in blue pen in the corner of the board with a speech bubble: TOLD YOU.

Rowan stood in front of it for a long moment. Then she reached up and pinned a new index card next to the cluster marked 1969.

JOHN BLEDSOE – FOLLOW-UP INTERVIEWS, she wrote. CORONER'S REPORT. BRIDGE FAILURE RE-PORTS. RIVER LEVEL DATA. She added: GIRL IN PHOTO – IDENTIFY.

CJ appeared in the doorway, Buckshot snuffling at his heels. "You know what normal detectives do the day after a plea hearing?" he asked.

"Sleep?" she guessed.

"Paperwork," he said. "Also sleep. Occasionally laundry."

She tapped the 1969 cluster. "We've got a window," she said. "Before Pike's cooperation notes drop and the AG starts calling every five minutes. I want to get a jump on Bledsoe."

He leaned against the doorframe. "You ever think about not chasing every ghost that points at the river?"

"Every day," she said.

"And?"

She shrugged. "Somebody has to."

He came farther into the room, studying the board. "Eve says the barrel samples match contaminants from those old Sterling manifests we found," he said. "We'll get charges on somebody for that, even if it's just the companies that inherited the mess. Whole other set of lawyers. Whole other set of headaches."

"Good," Rowan said. "Let them have some."

He shot her a sideways look. "You realize you just helped convict the sitting mayor and open up a forty-year-old dumping scheme," he said. "You don't have to solve '69 this week."

"I know," she said. "But the river's patient. People aren't. I'd rather get ahead of it for once."

He studied her face, then nodded. "All right. I'm in. But if a ghost from '69 tries to drag me into the mud, I'm blaming you in my victim statement."

"Noted," she said.

She spent the last hour of the day in her office, no lights on, just the glow from the window and the desk lamp. The Bledsoe file lay open, pages fanned like a hand of cards. Dive reports. Old newspaper clippings about the "hero deputy lost in the line of duty." The sonar printout from under the old bridge. Eve's memo about recovered remains, written in her precise, merciful hand.

On top of the stack, the photocopy of the badge wallet photo. John Bledsoe, upright and hopeful. The girl with the ribboned ponytail, half-laugh caught in her throat.

Keep her away from the water.

"Working on it," Rowan murmured.

When the light outside went from gold to that flat, tired gray that meant the night had decided to take itself seriously, she finally stood. On her way out, she paused by the evidence locker, touched the door with the back of her fingers like you might pat the shoulder of an old friend who'd held too much for too long.

The river path was busy in the way evenings got busy now. Joggers. Dog walkers. A couple sitting on a bench sharing a milkshake like it was a treaty. Lantern brackets still clung to the rail from the vigil, empty now, but ready.

She went to her usual spot where boardwalk met dirt. The water moved past in its unhurried, relentless way, carrying twigs, a plastic bottle, the reflection of the courthouse dome with its four-minute-late clock.

She thought about the plea, the ledger, the barrels, the car under the old bridge. About Emily and Bledsoe and Sarah and all the names she didn't have yet. About her father, signing his name and then arguing with himself in the margin.

"The river takes its own," she said softly. The phrase felt different in her mouth now—not as fatalism, not as excuse. More like a reminder. "But it doesn't get to pick alone."

Somewhere upstream, a fish broke the surface, a quick silver punctuation. Downstream, a towboat horn sounded, low and stubborn.

Rowan listened to it all. The water. The town. The scrape of her own breath in her chest.

Tomorrow there would be more work. There would be meetings with the AG about Pike's debriefs, scheduling for the next dive, interviews with old-timers about '69 and a deputy who'd gone into the river and never quite come back out. There would be casseroles and complaints and a hundred small, ordinary emergencies.

Tonight there was this: a river that had finally returned some of what it owed; a town that had stopped pretending not to hear; a detective who had traded a little of her anger for stubborn attention.

She turned back toward the square lights when the first porch lamps on the bluff blinked on, one by one, like a string of patient, domestic stars.

Behind her, the river kept moving, as it always had, carrying secrets, driftwood, and the thin, shining possibility that not everything would stay buried forever.

Chapter 23

The Ones the River Kept

Rowan, then Patel, "you dug him up properly. Not just his car. The kind of man he was. I can live with the hurt better now that I know it belonged to something that mattered."

Her voice thickened. She swallowed it back. "We don't know who she is." She lifted the photo—the one from the badge wallet, edges foxed and softened by fifty-six years of handling. "This girl. I've been talking to Grandma's old church ladies. Somebody remembers a cousin, a neighbor, a girl who vanished the same week as the '69 flood. We'll get there."

She laid the photo on the table gently, as if it might bruise.

"Until then," Kayla said, "I'm gonna call her 'the one he tried to keep away from the water.'" Her mouth quirked. "It's a long name. She deserves one."

Rowan's throat tightened. Lydia's pen hesitated for exactly one heartbeat before resuming its steady scratch.

The pastor came back, said a few words about service and memory and the uneasy truce between rivers and towns. Then he invited anyone who'd brought flowers to leave them by the water.

People rose, some shyly, some with the practiced economy of old grief. A woman in her seventies laid a single daisy at the edge and murmured something only the current could hear. A teenage boy in a baseball hoodie dropped a flat stone he'd painted: J.B. THANK YOU. It skipped once and sank.

Rowan didn't move until most of them had finished. Then she stepped to the table, beside Kayla.

"You sure you don't want the picture back?" she asked quietly.

Kayla shook her head. "Made three copies at the library," she said. "Even laminated one. Technology, baby."

Rowan almost smiled. She reached into her pocket and took out the cigar tin with three pennies inside. The metal was worn smooth; her father's superstition had rubbed it that way.

"For the ferryman," she said.

Kayla's brow furrowed. "What?"

"Old habit," Rowan said. "My dad's. You don't go near water without extra fare. Just in case someone gets greedy on the other side."

She flipped the lid and shook one penny into her palm. It glinted dull in the sunlight, all its useful shine spent years ago in vending machines and parking meters.

"Come on," she said.

Together, they walked to the edge where the bank fell away steeply. The river slid by, shoulders round and deceptively slow.

"For your uncle," Rowan said. "For the girl. For... the truth that took too long."

"Feels like we should have more pennies," Kayla said.

"We do," Rowan said. "They're just in different pockets."

She flicked the coin into the current. It flashed once, then vanished. For a moment, it left a tiny dimple on the surface, a small, circular refusal to accept the inevitable.

Then the river smoothed it away.

Kayla exhaled. "Okay," she said. "I can work with that."

Behind them, the cluster of chairs had become a knot of conversations—stories of the '69 flood, the '25 flood, Pike's fall, Emily's laughter, John's terrible singing voice. Cedar Valley's real language: overlapping anecdotes, interrupted by re-fills of lemonade.

Lydia drifted over, notebook closed now, recorder in her pocket. "So," she said to Kayla. "How do you feel about being the face of the 'We Don't Let the River Pick Alone' movement?"

Kayla rolled her eyes. "I feel like if you put my picture on the front page again, my aunt's going to start an intervention."

"I'll spell your name right," Lydia offered.

"You did last time," Kayla said. "That's what I'm worried about."

They moved away, Lydia already coaxing more quotes out of her, Kayla pretending to resent it.

CJ appeared at Rowan's elbow, Buckshot trotting at his heels. The dog had acquired a life jacket somehow, bright orange with a handle on top, like he was both emergency equipment and carry-on luggage.

"Eve brought it," CJ said when she raised an eyebrow. "Says if he's gonna keep charging the river, he needs PPE."

Rowan crouched to scratch behind Buckshot's ears. "You are not authorized to be braver than the professionals," she told him.

He licked her hand and leaned into her like a small, compact reassurance.

Lucas joined them, hands in his pockets, looking out over the water with the particular stillness of someone reading currents the rest of them couldn't see.

"You coming out tomorrow?" he asked Rowan. "We're running the sonar past the Wexler land again. State wants more mapping since the plea."

"Yeah," she said. "If you can stand my questions."

"No worse than the auditors," he said. "You just ask better ones."

Eve approached, sunglasses pushed up on her head, lab coat traded for a denim jacket that somehow still made her look like she belonged in a morgue more than in sunlight.

"I got the preliminary profile on our unknown girl," she said softly. "Sixteen to nineteen. Old fracture in the left wrist, healed. Probably a farm kid. Calcium lines in her bones match rural diets from that period."

Rowan's chest ached. "She ever break the riverside rule?"

Eve's mouth turned down. "Looks like she broke a lot of things," she said. "Healed them, mostly. Not this."

"Kayla's digging," CJ said. "Church records, school yearbooks, gossip. She'll flush her out."

"She already started," Lydia said, rejoining them. "Talked to three women who remember a girl who followed Bledsoe around like a shadow. Name might be Mary or Marcy or something that starts with M. One of them sent me a picture of a float from the '68 parade. You can see the back of a ribboned ponytail sitting next to him on the fire truck."

She tapped her temple. "River remembers. People do too, if you ask the right way."

Rowan thought of the late-night text she'd never answered—from an unknown M, after the dive. *Heard what you did with the river. About damn time. She never liked that bridge.*

We're still listening, Rowan had typed then deleted.

We are, she thought now. *That'll have to be enough for the moment.*

The crowd began to thin. People folded chairs and loaded them into pickup beds. Someone started a grill; the smell of charcoal and cheap hot dogs drifted down. A toddler, drunk on sun and attention, toddled toward the water, only to be scooped up by three different adults at once.

"River's popular today," CJ said.

"River's always popular," Lucas replied. "Folks just notice more when she's mad."

Rowan let her gaze follow the curve of the bank, up toward town, where the courthouse dome gleamed dull in the afternoon light. The dome's reflection wobbled in the water, distorted but persistent.

"Pike'll start talking next week," Patel said, coming up beside her, phone in one hand, sunglasses in the other. "Proffer sessions. Names, dates, bank accounts. All the mud he can sling upstream to save a little rock under his own feet."

"Think we'll get enough to go after Sterling's old partners?" Rowan asked.

"Maybe," Patel said. "Maybe just enough to make them sweat through their expensive suits and write some very large checks to environmental funds. Either way, it's more than we had when this started."

"Emily's parents okay with the plea?" CJ asked. "Still?"

"They're... resigned," Patel said. "They said something that'll stick with me. 'We don't get justice,' her mother said. 'We get evidence that says we're not crazy.' Sometimes that's all there is."

Rowan thought of her father's note at the bottom of the assignment agreement. *Filed under duress. Truth comes due.*

It had, in its crooked way. Not all of it. Not cleanly. But enough.

"State AG wants to make the most of this," Patel added. "New task force. Training. Rural corruption initiatives. We'll get more eyes on places like this."

"Places with rivers?" Lucas asked.

"Places with long memories and short paper trails," Patel said.

Lydia snorted. "I'll write them a slogan," she said. "'You can't bury a river.'"

"Trademark it," CJ said. "Put it on a T-shirt. I'll buy two."

They stood a while longer, not talking much, just watching as the last of the chairs disappeared and the impromptu gathering dissolved into smaller, familiar patterns. A man in a seed corn hat helped an older woman up the slope. Kids chased each other between cottonwoods. Somebody had brought a guitar. The first tentative chords of an old hymn floated over the water, warped but recognizable.

"Hey," Lydia said to Rowan, bumping her with an elbow. "You realize you've just wrapped your first official *Cedar Valley Files*?"

"Don't call it that," Rowan said.

"That's what my editor's calling it," Lydia replied. "Says it sounds like a podcast she'd actually listen to."

CJ raised his hand. "I'd listen," he said.

"You'd be in it," Lydia pointed out.

"I'd still listen," he said. "Mostly to correct you."

Rowan shook her head, but some small, reluctant warmth snuck in under her ribs. "There'll be others," she said. "Files."

"I'm counting on it," Lydia said. "My retirement fund depends on your inability to mind your own business."

"Speaking of," CJ said, "you know the chief's already got a list of cold cases he wants to throw at you now that you've proved you can bully the past?"

Rowan sighed. "Of course he does."

"You're allowed to say no," Eve added, oddly gentle.

"No," Rowan said. "I'm not."

Eve considered that, then nodded once. "Fair enough."

Kayla rejoined them, eyes red but steady. "They're going to put up a marker," she said. "For him and for her. 'In memory of those the river shouldn't have kept.' That's the line I gave them, anyway. Pastor tried to make it more poetic. I told him to save that for heaven."

Rowan smiled, small but real. "It's a good line."

Kayla looked at the water one last time, then shoved her cap onto her head. "I gotta go help my aunt herd casseroles," she said. "You coming?"

"In a bit," Rowan said. "I've got... another habit to feed."

Kayla didn't ask. She just nodded, squeezed Rowan's arm once, and headed upslope.

When the others drifted away—Lydia toward the parking lot, phone already out; CJ to return Buckshot's life jacket to Eve with a long argument about appropriate canine PPE; Lucas to check lines on the boat—Rowan walked along the bank, away from the makeshift gathering spot.

The boardwalk ended at its usual place. Dirt path took over, softer, less managed. She followed it to the curve where the water slowed, the spot she had claimed without meaning to weeks ago as her unofficial office annex.

The river was quieter here. Not silent—it was never silent—but its voice had dropped from accusation back to murmur.

She stepped to the edge and stood, listening.

Downstream, something metallic caught the moonlight for half a second before the current pulled it under—a glint too sharp to be driftwood. Rowan blinked, and it was gone.

The river, she knew, was never finished speaking.

"You've had a good run," she said under her breath. "Bodies, barrels, badges." She thought of the car still being processed in an evidence yard, the shoebox of records, the microcassette with Emily's trembling words. "You're not done with us. I know. But we're not done with you either."

A twig bobbed past, caught in a tiny side current, spun, and escaped back into the main flow. Somewhere upstream, a splash marked either a fish or a teenager with poor judgment. Farther down, the low moan of a towboat horn drifted up, stretched thin by distance.

Rowan reached into her pocket and pulled out a fresh, stiff manila folder. She didn't open it yet. Just weighed it in her hand.

CEDAR VALLEY – UNIDENTIFIED GIRL (CIRCA 1969), she would write across the top. Possible connection: Bledsoe. Flood myths. River stories.

Below that, smaller: *There's always a next part.*

For now, she just held it.

Behind her, voices floated down from the bluff—kids arguing about whose turn it was to hold Buckshot's leash, someone calling for more potato salad, Lydia laughing at some joke that hadn't asked permission to be funny on a day like this.

Life, messy and relentless, doing its job.

Rowan let the sounds wash over her, then nodded once—to the town, to the river, to the thin seam of ground between them where her work lived.

"The river takes its own," she said finally. The words felt different now—less like a sentence, more like a diagnosis. "But it doesn't get the last word."

She slid the empty folder under her arm and turned back toward the slope, the square, the courthouse dome and its four-minute-late clock. Toward paperwork and interviews and whatever the next file would bring.

Behind her, the water kept moving—steadfast, indifferent, carrying silt and secrets and the faint reflected shimmer of paper lanterns that had long since gone out but whose wax still clung in quiet, stubborn patches to the bank.

The river spoke in its old language: whisper and warning, memory and threat.

Rowan listened, as she always had.

The difference now was not that she finally understood it.

The difference was that she intended to answer.

Epilogue

Two months later, Cedar Valley settled into a late–summer stillness, the kind that made the courthouse dome look taller and the river look deceptively polite.

The water ran low now, slow enough to show sandbars, honest enough to show snags. The smell of flood mud had finally given way to sweet clover and grilling smoke. Tourists had started to come again—fishermen, antique hunters, a photographer trying to catch "that mythic Midwest light" and mostly catching mosquitoes.

Rowan stood on the narrow balcony outside her office, the old metal railing warm under her palms. Below her, Main Street breathed its familiar chorus: a screen door slapping shut, a truck shifting gears, Buckshot announcing to the entire county that a squirrel existed.

Her new case files sat on her desk inside, open like a half-finished sentence:

CEDAR VALLEY – UNIDENTIFIED GIRL (1969) JOHN BLEDSOE – FOLLOW-UP INQUEST RIVERBEND RESTITUTION – COMMUNITY REVIEW

She would get to them. She always did.

A soft chime from her phone broke the lull. A text. Unknown number.

You were right about the river.

It remembers.

Some of us do too.

— M

Rowan's pulse tapped once, lightly, like a pebble thrown against a window.

She typed back:

If you remember something worth sharing, my door's open.

She didn't hit send. Not yet. Instead, she deleted the draft and pocketed the phone.

Some truths needed more than an invitation—they needed timing.

A knock sounded behind her.

CJ stepped out, two coffees in hand, both cups sweating in the heat. "If you're brooding," he said, "I can schedule it. We're running out of brooding slots."

"I'm not brooding," Rowan said.

"You're on a balcony staring into middle distance," he pointed out. "That's textbook brooding."

She accepted the coffee. "Dive team found anything else today?"

"Not unless you count a rusted lawnmower and three tires the river apparently collected as a hobby," he said. "No new bones. No new barrels. No old secrets."

"Give it time," she said.

He glanced at her sideways. "You think this town will ever run out of them?"

"No," Rowan said. "I think it finally stopped pretending it didn't have any."

A towboat horn rumbled upriver, low and resonant, carrying over town like a throat clearing before someone spoke. Rowan turned toward it, feeling the vibration through the railing and into her bones.

CJ nudged her. "What's next, partner?"

Rowan lifted her coffee, inhaled the steam, and let the moment stretch just long enough to feel like a decision.

"Next?" she said. "We listen. And when the river starts talking again—"

CJ sighed. "We get our boots?"

"We get our boots," Rowan said.

They clinked coffee cups once, a quiet toast to whatever waited in the archives, the water, or the long, stubborn memory of Cedar Valley.

Below them, the river curved around town—steady, patient, carrying its old stories and the shape of new ones.

And Rowan, for the first time in a long time, felt ready.

Coming Soon

Beneath Blackbird Bridge

A Cedar Valley Files Novel

When the body of beloved local historian **Agnes Plum** is found beneath the infamous Blackbird Bridge, Detective **Rowan Hayes** is drawn into a chilling investigation steeped in the town's darkest legends.

As whispers of a long-lost fortune and a vanished heiress resurface, Rowan must unravel a century of deceit before Cedar Valley's buried sins claim another life. Haunted by her father's legacy and the ghosts of the past, she soon learns that some secrets are never meant to stay beneath the water.

Coming in 2026 — the haunting new mystery from *The Cedar Valley Files.*

About R. Davenport

R. Davenport writes atmospheric small-town mysteries that explore the darker undercurrents of the Midwest—where every river hides a secret, and every silence tells a story.

Her *Cedar Valley Files* series follows **Detective Rowan Hayes**, a seasoned investigator navigating the quiet, haunting beauty of Iowa's heartland while uncovering the truths that small towns try to bury.

R. Davenport's work blends character-driven suspense, emotional depth, and a strong sense of place. Each book stands alone but connects through the shared landscape of **Cedar Valley**, a world where memory, loyalty, and redemption collide.

When not writing, Davenport enjoys long walks along back roads, antique maps, and black coffee strong enough to hold a conversation.

Visit revadavenport.com to learn more about upcoming releases in *The Cedar Valley Files* and other mysteries set in the heart of the Midwest.

The Cedar Valley Files

Cedar Valley looks peaceful from a distance—church steeples, farmland, and the slow curve of the river. But beneath its still surface runs a current of guilt and silence that never stops moving.

In *The Cedar Valley Files*, Detective Rowan Hayes returns home to confront the unfinished cases—and unfinished business—her late father left behind. Each novel peels back another layer of the town's past, revealing how far good people will go to keep the peace, and what the river remembers long after everyone else has forgotten.

Also by R. Davenport

<u>The Cedar Valley Files Series</u>
Book One: *The River Takes Its Own*
Book Two: *Echoes in Cedar Valley — Coming Soon*
<u>The Marigold Lake Cozy Mystery Series</u>
Book One: *Secrets Buried in the Backyard*
Book Two: *Dead Air at the Morning Glory*
Book Three: *The Suitcase at the Morning Glory*
Book Four: *Flour Power at the Morning Glory*
Book Five: *The Missing Brooch at the Morning Glory*
Book Six: *My Sister at the Morning Glory*
Book Seven: *Christmas at the Morning Glory*
Book Eight: *Valentine Vendetta at the Morning Glory*

For updates on upcoming releases, exclusive extras, and reader team opportunities, visit **revadavenport.com** *or join the newsletter at* **revadavenport.com/newsletter**